Spilt Wine

by

Michael Walsh

Recent Fiction by Michael Walsh

Posted as Missing
Published 2017 - ISBN - 978-09940936-2-2

Missing
Published 2017 - ISBN - 978-0-9940936-3-9

Back In Action
Published 2017 - ISBN - 978-09940936-5-3

Unknown Diners
Published 2017 - ISBN - 978-0-9940936-4-6

Recent Non-Fiction by Michael Walsh

Sequitur - To Cape Horn in Comfort and Style
Published 2013 - ISBN - 978-09919556-0-2

Carefree on the European Canals
Published 2014 - ISBN - 978-09919556-4-0

Carefree Through 1001 French Locks
Published 2015 - ISBN - 978-09919556-7-1

Canal Cruising in France
Published 2015 - ISBN - 978-09919556-9-5

Spilt Wine

ISBN: 978-0-9940936-6-0

Published by Dark Ink Press, Canada

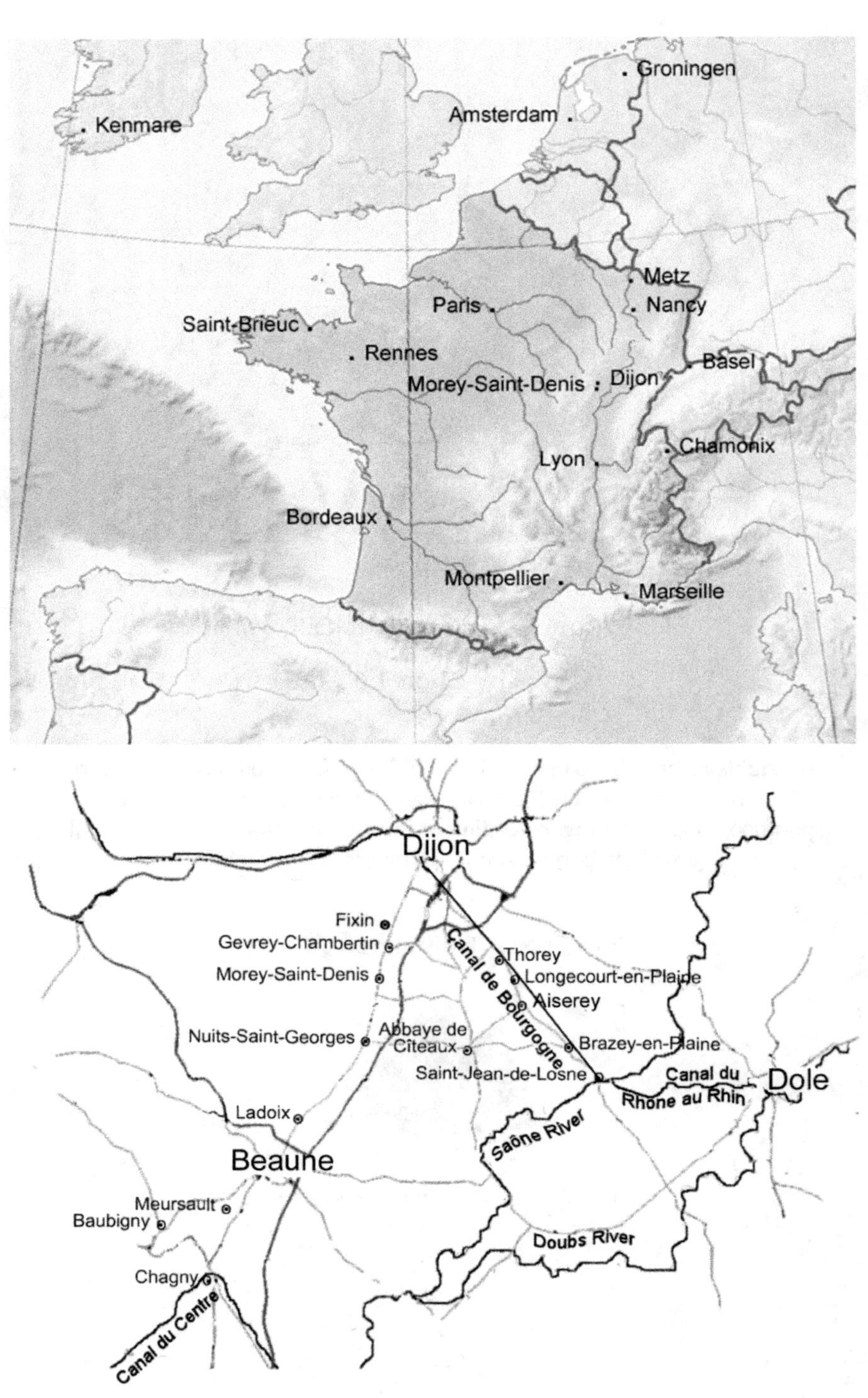

Kenmare
Groningen
Amsterdam
Metz
Paris
Nancy
Saint-Brieuc
Rennes
Basel
Morey-Saint-Denis
Dijon
Lyon
Chamonix
Bordeaux
Montpellier
Marseille
Dijon
Fixin
Thorey
Gevrey-Chambertin
Canal de Bourgogne
Longecourt-en-Plaine
Morey-Saint-Denis
Aiserey
Nuits-Saint-Georges
Abbaye de Cîteaux
Brazey-en-Plaine
Saint-Jean-de-Losne
Canal du Rhône au Rhin
Dole
Ladoix
Saône River
Beaune
Meursault
Baubigny
Doubs River
Chagny
Canal du Centre

Introduction

Although this is a piece of fiction, most of the locations, many of the adventures and some of the characters in it are real or are based in reality. Fortunately, the crimes and the criminals are fictional, and any resemblance to actual people or events is purely coincidental.

The story and timeline follow events from my own experiences, some of them slightly juggled to fit the crafting of the novel.

Michael Walsh
Friesland
July 2017

To Edith,
my reservations agent
at CP Air in Vancouver

Chapter One

Friday 28 March 1986

David stopped scanning and focused on the newspaper report:

Wine Theft *— The Gendarmerie nationale in Gevrey-Chambertin is investigating the disappearance this week of nearly four hundred barrels of wine from a cellar in Morey-Saint-Denis. The proprietor, who values the missing Burgundy at over three million Francs, discovered the theft Thursday evening when he returned from a business trip to Paris. No further information has been released.*

He abandoned his breakfast and rushed up to his room, taking the steps three at a time, rather than waiting for the elevator. *That has to be Louis... The quantity, the value, the Paris trip.* His phone call was answered before the beginning of the second ring.

"Oui. Allo?"

"Catherine, it's David. I've read the news. Is Louis there?"

"No, he rushed out in a rage last night after the Gendarmes left. He was cursing Grotkopf... Hasn't come back. They're now searching for him... David, I'm so worried."

"You okay? Is anyone there with you? Murielle?"

"Murielle's gone home for Easter; not back until Monday. I'm so afraid something bad has happened to Louis... I'm worried sick, David. What do I do?"

"Stay there, I'm in Chagny. I'll be there in less than an hour."

David phoned the front desk as he packed, asking to have his account ready. Four minutes later, he strode across the lobby, relieved to see the receptionist holding up his bill.

"Bonjour Monsieur Michaels, you have slept well?"

With a glance at the total, he pulled four notes from his wallet. "Yes, thank you. Keep the balance for my next visit."

He ran to his car, tossed his luggage onto the passenger seat and headed north, not having finished plotting his route. *My instincts will guide me.*

Forty-three minutes later, he crunched to a stop in the gravel courtyard and bounded from the car toward the open kitchen door as Catherine ran down the stone steps. "David! Thank God! Hug me. Hold me and give me strength, I've none left. I'm so worried, so afraid."

He wrapped her in his arms, she laid her cheek on his shoulder, and he gently stroked the back of her head as she shook with sobs. *Don't know what I should do here. Never handled a distraught woman — rarely handled any woman. Hope this helps.*

They held the hug as David quietly spoke, "Everything will be fine, you're safe, and Louis is also." He continued with other calming comments as they came to mind while he stroked the back of her head. She gradually relaxed as her sobbing abated. *This seems to be working. Probably best to keep holding...*

Then Catherine began sobbing more deeply again, blubbering out, "Murielle — a few minutes ago, just before you arrived. A phone call from Murielle's mother — asking for her."

"She's not there? Wasn't she was going home for Easter?"

"That was her plan. I checked her room, then called the Gendarmes. They'll be here shortly to expand the investigation."

Her sobbing subsided as she talked. *She seems to be regaining her strength.* They maintained their hug and David continued holding the back of her head with a gentle pulse of his hand. *This appears to help.*

Catherine continued to relax, and after a long quiet interlude, she said, "I must go compose myself before the Gendarmes come again." She led him inside and along to the second salon, where she pointed to the fireplace. "I'm cold, David. I'd appreciate it if you started building a fire. I'll be down shortly to help."

He had finished when she returned, and she motioned him to a wing-back chair. They sat silently for a long while, watching the flames turn from yellows and reds into greens and blues as the fire took hold and warmed.

She had just begun recounting the events when there was a knock on the door.

Chapter Two

"It sounds as though I'll have a larger audience for my story. That must be the Gendarmes," Catherine said as she got up and walked into the foyer toward the front doors.

Two uniformed men came in, and declining seats, they stood and asked Catherine questions about Murielle's routine and her habits. They then asked to see her room. It was obvious Murielle had not left for Louhans; her suitcase was on her bed, partly packed. While the younger investigator remained in Murielle's room, the older one returned to the salon with Catherine and took a seat. After a few more questions about Murielle, he began probing the events leading to the discovery of the missing wine.

Catherine recounted the highlights for him. *"Deux éditions...* Two editions of *Le Figaro* were in the box when my husband, and I returned from Paris yesterday afternoon. The kitchen door was unlocked when Louis tried to turn his key. We weren't concerned since there is almost no crime here and we often leave that door unlocked. We thought Murielle had simply followed habit when she left."

"Ce n'est pas une bonne idée," the gendarme said. "Not a good idea. People come to these villages more now, for opportunity."

"Vous avez raison... You're right, we've discussed this. We know we need to be more careful. So, anyway, after we had settled in, Louis said he must go top-up the *pièces* in the cellar, the barrels are still losing a little bit to absorption and evaporation, and he refills them now every two weeks. He looked for the key on the hook in its box. It wasn't there and he admonished himself to be more careful with details. I suggested he may have

put it on his desk again, but it wasn't there either. He remembered locking the door when he left the cellar with Monsieur Michaels, here." She pointed toward David. "Last week, Wednesday, I think it was when they tasted. He couldn't remember what he had done with the key."

"Oui, c'était mercredi... Yes, it was Wednesday," David said.

"How often does he misplace the key?" the gendarme asked.

"Not often, maybe two or three times a year." Catherine paused to think. "It's mainly when he's distracted by something."

"What would distract him last week?"

"He was excited to have David — Monsieur Michaels visiting, and I was in the clinic in Dijon to check on our new baby." She put a hand on her bulge as she looked down. "There might be other things, but I think these were the big ones for him."

"So, did he find the key?"

"No, he spent a long time searching. He finally gave up and told me he was going to the tool shed to get the spare key he hides there. A few minutes later I heard him bellowing. I didn't understand what he was saying, I was upstairs at the front. I ran down and out into the courtyard to see him dark red, holding his chest tightly, rocking back and forth..."

She stopped and looked up. "I need some water, please, David. I'll pause until you're back."

"Evian ou du robinet?" David asked as he got up and headed across the room.

"N'importe quel... Whatever, something wet."

"Thank you," Catherine said when he handed her the glass. After taking a long drink, she continued, "I couldn't understand what it was about. First, I thought he had hurt himself. I really thought he was injured." She paused and shuddered.

"I asked him what is wrong, and he told me the wine is gone. All the pièces are gone. The cellar is empty. I didn't believe him, I told him to stop joking, and he led me down the stone steps into the empty cellar, pointing to the key in the door. I still have trouble believing this has happened."

The inspector scribbled more notes in his book. "So the key was in the door. It could have been anyone who did this. Anyone roaming around and looking for possibilities."

"No," David said. "I remember watching Louis lock the door and hang the key on its rack when we came into the kitchen from our tasting last week."

"*Qui d'autre...* Who else knew the key was there?"

"*Presque personne...* Very few. Louis, me, David, Wychard — our friend and agent in Amsterdam," Catherine said. "And of course Murielle."

"Where were you this week, Monsieur Michaels?"

"I was in the Rhône and Midi all week until yesterday, when I drove back up to Chagny. I stayed the night in a hotel there."

"You have people we can check with?"

"I have hotel and restaurant receipts, I have wine producers…"

"You're not suggesting Monsieur Michaels would have done this," Catherine interrupted with an incredulous look on her face.

"He knows where the key is kept. We must examine all evidence, consider everything." Turning back to David, he continued, "You were saying…"

"*Oui, Catherine, il a raison...* Yes, Catherine, he's correct." He turned to face the inspector as he continued, "The wine producers I was with and the dining rooms I was in will account for most of my time. I'll give you a list."

"Now this agent in Amsterdam? How can we contact him?"

Catherine stood. "I'll get that for you, I keep a little book for Louis with numbers and addresses of all our agents and good clients."

"Later... Now, Murielle, she is the maid, yes?"

"The cook, the house manager, a friend," she said as she sat. "She's been with us, with the family, actually, since before I met Louis. Probably seven or eight years. David, how long?"

"She came just after Simone, Louis' mother died. When was that? Winter of '78…"

"A long time, okay. That's good. Why would she take the wine?"

"She wouldn't. Don't be crazy."

"I am sorry, Madame, we must look at every possibility. Nobody isn't suspect, not even you or your husband."

"But that is absurd... I'm shocked to hear you say this. Why would Louis or I steal our own wine?"

"Insurance. Insurance fraud is more and more common. I told you, we must look at every possibility and eliminate only the ones we can prove wrong."

With a forced grin, Catherine asked, "Okay, and where were you all week, Monsieur le Gendarme?"

"Exactement! Personne n'est suspect... "Exactly! Nobody isn't a suspect, not even me." He nodded, then smiled. "I have my logbook which will show my time. Now, tell me about when you last saw your husband."

The younger inspector came in and motioned their interviewer away. They stood near the other end of the salon in a quiet tête-à-tête.

"Ce n'est rien... It is nothing," he said, seeing her concern as he returned. "It is a normal procedure. Now, Madame, please continue, when did you last see your husband?"

"Il était à peu près... It was about fifteen or twenty minutes after the gendarmes left last evening. You can ask your colleagues when that was. He became angrier the more he thought about the situation. Louis was fuming and cursing when he left." She smiled and looked down as her hand followed the movement in her bulged belly. "Young Louis is kicking up a fuss as well."

The inspector's face warmed. "When is Young Louis due?"

"The doctor figures the first week of August."

The inspector smiled. "Did his father say where he was going?"

"No, but he was cursing Grotkopf as he left."

"Grotkopf?"

"Laurent Grotkopf of Maison Grotkopf in Nuits."

"Why was he angry with Monsieur Grotkopf?"

Catherine told the story of the family relationship, the wine dealings and the meeting Louis had with Laurent on Thursday last week. "That was the day before we left for Paris."

"Did Grotkopf know you would be away for a week?"

"How could he not? Louis' sister, Francine, is married to Grotkopf's son, and they live in Paris. We visited with them on Sunday."

"This begins to be very complex. Two missing people, millions of Francs in missing wine. Can we go look at the cellar?"

"Yes, of course. David can take you. You don't need me to be there for this, do you?"

"No, Madam. You remain here and try to relax."

They all stood, and David stepped across to Catherine to give her a hug, whispering in her ear, "You be strong, things will all turn out just fine. I'll be back shortly." She held the hug. *She seems calmed by this. This isn't as tough as I thought it would be.*

Chapter Three

"It would appear normal," David said. "Trucks regularly come to the producers' cellars to load barrels of wine. This is a common sight here, or in almost any other wine region."

"It must be difficult and awkward to move them up these steps."

"No, not up the steps, no, there's a big shaft up to the *cuverie* over here," he said, pulling the light along its wires as they walked through the empty cellar. "The door at the top opens, and there's a gantry up there."

"There is a broken barrique here, wine soaked into the gravel."

"Yes, under the bottom of the shaft. It appears to have slipped from the sling, or rolled off the truck up there." He tipped on another light and walked around to the end of the pièce. "No, the wrong end." He went to the other end.

Chalked in a round fluid script was *Bourgogne Rouge*. He breathed a sigh of relief. "Amazing, the broken pièce is a simple Bourgogne, a blend of the youngest new vines, worth under two thousand Francs. They probably dumped it back down. If it had been one of the best wines, we'd still be smelling the bouquet."

The younger gendarme bent to smell. "And how much would the more expensive barrels be?"

"For this vintage, more than fifteen thousand Francs."

After a low inhaled whistle, "How many pièces were here?"

"Between three hundred and seventy-five and four hundred, we can check the records — precise figures must be kept for the State, for tax revenue and for the FIVB and the INAO... Over there against that wall," he said raising his arm, "they left the *bidons* and *feuillettes*, probably too awkward to handle."

David turned and pointed at the shaft. "I can show you up top, in the back of the cuverie where the loading takes place."

"Yes, we need to see that too. It is locked?"

"For sure, the keys are kept in the same place as the cellar key," he said as they made their way back to the stone steps and up into the courtyard. "I'll go get them and..." He stopped himself. "Wait, check with your colleagues who were here last evening with Louis. Find out whether the cuverie and shaft keys were also missing. You look around, and I'll meet you over there." He pointed across the courtyard to the large sliding doors.

The keys were in their place on the rack, and as David picked them off, he thought, *Appears they powdered for fingerprints last night.* He walked to the doorway of the long salon. "This won't be much longer, Catherine, we're almost done... Are you okay?"

"I have some tea and some biscuits and I'm trying to get back into my book, though it's slow."

Back outside, he unlocked the door and slid it open on its rails. Across the floor, near the back was a low structure, a combing surrounding the shaft down into the cellar. On its top was a thick steel door, hinged along its far side. David motioned to the electrical cable winch on the I-beam above them. "Using the push-button control hanging from the winch, one man in the cellar and one up here, it would take fifteen, maybe twenty hours to load four hundred pièces."

"That long?"

"Yes, with more men in the cellar to move pièces, it would be a bit quicker, but not by much, the bottleneck is the hoist. We can see on its plaque that this one is rated at twelve hundred kilograms, so it could lift four pièces at a time. Louis père didn't like risking more than one at a time, so he never got a multiple slinging set-up, and young Louis continues this way."

"What if the thieves brought their own sling?"

"Much faster, likely less than five hours. You can check with the big *négociants* in Nuits or Beaune; they will give you a much closer idea of men and time."

"Who do you suggest?"

"Any of them. This was not a simple, impulsive theft. It would require a knowledge of the local wine business, a knowledge of this one, in particular, they would have to know they need to properly set the bungs in the pièces and how to do it. They would need four or five truck trips; they might have used four or five trucks. They would need a large place to cache the wine."

"How big?"

"Off the top of my head, let's say four hundred pièces a metre long and seventy-five centimetres in diameter, the dimensions are a bit less than that, but let's put it there to account for sloppy stowing. One barrel high would be fifteen by twenty metres. They can be stacked, but the pièces weigh a quarter of a tonne each and they're awkward to handle. Two high would need a space of ten by fifteen metres — they'd nestle, so a bit less than that. You can play with the figures."

"That is not a small space."

"No, and if they don't want to ruin the wine, to lose its value, it needs to be properly stored in a cool, stable and relatively moist place. In warm or fluctuating temperatures, it would quickly degrade."

"Could Grotkopf do all this?"

"He certainly meets all the requirements. He has the knowledge, the equipment, the resources, the…"

"The motive?"

"Yes, that is possible too. Every year for five years now, Grotkopf has sent his trucks here to load and haul away wine to his *chais* in Nuits. Louis told me he had been here in early March to take the 1984 vintage. You just heard that last week Louis had told him he could have none of the 1985 wines. You also heard that Grotkopf had been angry and had threatened him."

"Thank you, Monsieur Michaels, this has been very educational. You have opened many doors to things we need to look at, to follow-up. Here is my card, contact me at any time if you think of other things."

David looked at the card:

Jean-Marc Grattien, Lieutenant
chef de brigade
Gendarmerie nationale Gevrey-Chambertin

"Thank you, I will. My card has only my Canadian contact information, but I'll give it to you anyway. You can always reach me through Catherine — Madame Ducroix, we will be in close contact. I think I'll stay here for a few days and cancel next week's trip to the Alsace. I'd be too distracted. It would be wasted time."

"This is my new Adjudant, Yvon LeBlanc."

They shook hands, then David watched as they got into their car and drove out through the stone portal.

David's head was spinning with questions as he hung the keys on the hooks and walked from the kitchen toward the long salon. *Would she want me to stay? Would it be appropriate?* "Catherine, I'm sorry that took so long," he said as he approached the couch.

"So will you stay with me here for a while, David?" she asked wistfully, and seeing his nod, she continued, cutting him off as he began to open his mouth. "I have nobody close to me. I haven't been here long enough to be close to any of the other women in town. This is a much more closed community than I know from before. Murielle was my only close friend except Louis, now they are…"

She patted the cushion. "Rub my head again, it makes me forget." David sat next to her, and she laid her head on his chest.

Chapter Four

A week and a half earlier
Wednesday 19 March 1986

"Merde!" Louis cursed, after he had spat the wine to the gravel beside the row of barrels and a dribble rolled down his chin onto the front of his shirt.

"Merde?" David questioned, after he had swallowed his tasted sip. "Yes, just the slightest hint, but this adds to the complexity and character of great Burgundy." In tastings, David has always allowed small amounts of the greatest wines to slide down his throat, adding to the breadth and length of their aftertaste. He's never tired of joking about how he always spits when tasting wine, though, with the great wines, he spits backwards. *This wine is far too good to spit out.*

"No, no, not that." Louis laughed, smudging the dribble with the back of his hand. "I just dripped and made messy my shirt, but I agree the wee bit of barnyard makes the wine much more good."

"Your English has improved since my last visit, Louis, but we can speak in French so you're more comfortable."

"No, no, I must make practice. We keep in English."

"How much of this can you sell me this year?" David swirled and nosed his glass again. "It reminds me of the '64 and '69 I tasted here with your father. Amazing wines. I still have a few of those in the cellar."

"I have make fourteen pièces of the Clos de Bèze last year, so twelve must go to Grotkopf. He let me keep again only two, and you know one is between my brother and sister and me. That leaves only one for you, same as last year."

"Why are you still selling most of your best wines to Grotkopf? We've discussed this before, Louis. You know how they destroy your wine, blend it with the stuff from their own vineyards. What they turn-out is technically correct, but the quality, the finesse and the spirit of your wines are lost in their soup."

David curled his lip and continued. "If these were my wines, if I owned this domaine, I would stop selling to Grotkopf. You know, and everyone out there knows," he said with a big sweep of his wine glass toward the cellar steps. "They know your vines are the best sited on the slopes. Your wines are not soup ingredients, not bulk wine. They deserve so much more."

"I know this, I am many time tell Francine and Pierre. They all the time me told — no told me, I am backwards again. They told me they want the sure money every year, not the risk of not selling."

"Are they both still in Paris?"

"Oui, and both still all fact and figures. What do accountant or lawyer know or care about the art of creating fine wine?" With his usual Gallic shrug, Louis added, "They got their wine and their money every year, what do they care? You know it is not so easy since Francine married the son of Grotkopf."

"And the Clos-de-la-Roche and the Bonnes-Mares back there? Is it the same story with them again this year, mostly committed to Grotkopf?"

"Yes, the same, but with Clos-de-la-Roche, he gets only five pièces. I make only seven plus some bidons. The two rows we replanted, we make still as Morey-Saint-Denis. Maybe next year it will be good again to put in Clos-de-la-Roche," Louis added with another huge shrug.

And thus it had gone as David and Louis systematically roamed through the dank cellars with Louis removing bungs, thrusting the pipette through the hole and thumbing it to draw samples to their glasses. They had worked their way through the Village wines and the Premiers Crus, and now they were finishing the finest barrels of the tasting, the Grands Crus.

Louis and his siblings had inherited the estate from their father, and under French law, it had to be divided into equal shares among them. They had decided to do the modern thing, and instead of splintering the scattered vineyards into even smaller pieces, they formed an agricultural company and divided the shares. Louis was as passionate about wine as his father and grandfather had been before him, and he wanted to carry on with growing and making great wine. Francine and Pierre had no interest in wine other than in drinking it, so they had left the château, cuverie and cellars for Louis to run and to share with each of them a third of the annual profits. Part of their agreement was that each would get a third of a pièce, a third of a barrel, about a hundred bottles of each of the three Grands Crus: Bonnes-Mares, Clos de Bèze and Clos-de-la-Roche.

David shook himself out of reflections when Louis said, "We go now to lunch." Louis tapped the bung back into its place in the barrel, and they headed to the stone stairs, tilting the hanging electric lamps off a bare wire to darken the cellar as they went. They were silent as they emerged at ground level and waited for their eyes to adjust to the brightness of the midday sun. Louis rattled and twisted the huge key in the lock of the solid oak door, gave the door a heavy thump with his shoulder, and satisfied, they headed across the courtyard.

"You've finished your pruning, Louis?" David asked, raising an arm toward the rows of vines in Les Millandes at the edge of the courtyard. "How was the damage from the deep cold spell?"

"Yes, I finish the start of *mars* — I have to remember to say March. The start of March down here, and last week at the top of Genavrières and Monts Luisnats. I have a bit of cleaning to do, but not much. We have good chance with the *froid*, the cold. Only damage some young grafts at the bottom parts of the *vignoble* where there was no snow for protecting. Damage only on the Village wines and *un petit coin*, a little corner of the Premiers. None on the Grands Crus." Louis motioned toward the gentle slopes above the village. "We have bud break in two weeks or less, I think."

Louis fell silent as they walked across the courtyard, so David reflected. *Tense time, bud break. If it happens too early, a late frost can destroy much of the year's crop.* He ran his recent marketing write-up through his mind as they went.

Domaine Ducroix sits at the edge of Morey-Saint-Denis, a small village sandwiched between the great vineyards of Chambertin and those of Musigny in the heart of the best red vineyards of Burgundy's Côte d'Or. From it, the twenty-one hectares of vineyards are all easily accessible to work, though there are thirty-four plots scattered along three kilometres through three communes and across nine appellations. Splintered vineyards like these are common in the Burgundy, a legacy of the division of property under the family inheritance laws spurred by the Revolution and refined by Napoleon.

In a good year the estate can produce up to a hundred and ten thousand bottles, not many for the entire world. We are again privileged to offer you a wide selection of their production, from Village wines to Grands Crus.

David refocused as they reached the rear door, and he asked, "What have you changed, Louis? Your '85s are all so good, better than I remember from you, better than any since your father in the '60s and early '70s. What are you doing new?"

"It was nature, the year mostly, but we go with still more heavy pruning on the vines, less buds, more *concentrée*, and we also do more drop of some extra bunch in the summer. I have made this year only thirty-one hecto on the Grands Crus, thirty-six on the Premiers, much less than we are allowed. We do so many little things, tweaking as they say in *Californie*."

"The results are certainly worth it, but your production must be down even further because of this?"

"Oui, it is down a bit, between nine and ten percent less than we are allowed."

"You need to increase your prices, then?"

"*Bien sure, mais* not so much as I want. Monsieur Grotkopf say the market is still a little, how you say? Soft?"

"He says that because he wants you to keep your prices low."

Chapter Five

Louis walked across the kitchen and *fait la bise* with the woman at the stove, then said to her, *"Murielle, s'il te plâit, du persillé et une baguette au p'tit salon. Déjeuner dans une demi-heure, ou apres ça, quand Madame est arrivé."*

The aromas of braising boeuf bourguignon made David lose his thoughts for a while, but he quickly regained and continued. "The market may be soft for ordinary wines, even good wines, but yours are more than that, Louis. You have no problem selling everything you produce now. You should ask Grotkopf for a better price. I'm sure I can give you more for your wines than they pay you — I don't like to ask, it's not my way, but how much do they give you for the Grands Crus?"

"Last year it was eight thousand per pièce, this year, we not have yet the number. I see him this week." Louis turned to open a bottle of the '82 Genavrières as Murielle entered and placed a board in the middle of the table. On the board was a big slab of jambon persillé with two knives and an uncut baguette.

"Last year I gave you forty Francs per bottle — that's just over twelve thousand Francs per barrel. That's over fifty percent more than he gave you. Bottling expenses for three hundred and three or three hundred and four bottles don't come anywhere near four thousand Francs. He should have given you ten five, probably eleven thousand per pièce." David cut a piece from the slab of ham and popped it into his mouth.

He thought as he chewed, and when finished, he said, "I will gladly give you twenty-five percent more this year, fifty Francs per bottle for everything except your family share." He went to get glasses from the sideboard. "That's a little over fifteen thousand per pièce, almost double what they gave you last year."

"I wish I could do this for you, but my hands are in a rope, how do you say? *Mon beau-frère,* my brother-out-law will not let this happen."

David laughed, "I think you mean brother-*in*-law. You know I don't like seeing your wines sold in bulk, Louis, but for their quality this year, they need to give you fourteen thousand per pièce. Seventy-five percent more than last year... Thinking on it, maybe brother-*out*-law *was* the correct term — do you know what outlaw means?"

Seeing the shrug, David explained the meaning, and they both had a good laugh as the tension of the moment eased. Not that David was uneasy around Louis; he had known him for twenty years, from his early visits to the estate in the 1960s to deal with Louis *père*. The son was not yet a teen on his first visit, but he was already passionately into learning all he could about viticulture and viniculture and eagerly assisting his father with even the most mundane chores.

It was now four years since the death of Louis père and since Louis *l'aîné* had taken over. In that time, Louis had brought the quality of the wines back up from their slump in the '70s, when much of the family money had gone to educating the three children, and little was left for the vineyards or for the winemaking infrastructure. For young Louis, his schooling was in viticulture and oenology, studying at the University of Bordeaux under the guidance of the great Peynaud. Though education is not expensive in France, it was his later studies at UC Davis in California, which Louis père had insisted his son pursue, that had cost the family so much.

To make things tighter, in the mid-70s the whole French wine market had suffered from the fallout of the Cruse scandal, when a major négociant and Bordeaux château owner had been caught bottling simple wine and passing it off as Bordeaux. When this scandal hit in 1973, wine prices were at historic highs and climbing. The market stuttered, then slowed. Prices quickly declined. Although the scandal was in Bordeaux, the rapidly expanding French export market had painted all French wines with the same dirty brush. Louis saw his sales decrease, he lowered prices and watched the continuing slump in sales. No money was left over after expenses to add new equipment, little was available for needed repairs and very little if any for routine maintenance.

The market began slowly improving toward the end of the decade, and young Louis was back from his studies to help his father with long-needed maintenance. The family couldn't afford new *cuves*, but they replaced many bad oak staves in the old fermenting vats and bought a few new ageing barrels to replace the oldest. They grubbed-out most of the old and feeble vines in the vineyards and began a slow re-plantation routine as they worked toward a gradual elevation of the wine back toward its former quality.

Seated at the old mahogany table Louis used for meetings, for tastings and as an office desk, he and David shared the slab of jambon as they broke pieces off the fresh baguette and enjoyed the wine. They rambled through reminiscences from over the years, then Louis said, "This '82 is my first wine, made a few months after my father passed." He paused and stared blankly for a few moments, then shook his head and continued, "But, this is gone by, we are here now. What you think of this wine compare to the '85 in the barrels?"

David swirled and nosed the wine, paused a long while, then said, "Your '82 Genavrières in this glass is a fine Premier Cru, but your '85 Genavrières, even unfinished in barrel down there," he moved his glass in the direction of the cellar. "That is great wine. You can see the similarities to each other, but the differences are more obvious and amazing. You've done a superb job with the quality in such a short time. You can sell all your wines for much higher prices now — you need to raise your prices. You deserve much more — even for your Village wines."

Louis grinned and reddened. He got up and disappeared into the cellar, and came back with a bottle. "Voila, the '83, we taste this also," he said as he pulled the cork.

"You tasted the '84 in the caves. That year was **difficile**, bad weather, the grapes were so many green. I made only about half the normal amount, the rest went to Village wines and some to bidons for the pickers at the next harvest. A lot for *alcool industriel*."

He shrugged his shoulders. "Oui, the '84 is good, but I sacrifice a lot of quantity for the quality. I cannot ask too much for it, the market says

'84 is a bad year. I have lost two ways; low quantity and low price. But here, the '83."

David stood and crossed to the sideboard for two more glasses. "I can easily sell wines like your '84s. But they don't want to go to the normal market. They need to be placed in restaurants which have sommeliers and in wine shops with knowledgeable staff. They need to go to wine purchasing clubs, to wine lovers, and to the people who trust their own palate. It's not mass marketing, it's specific. This market is slowly growing and I have more than enough demand for wines like this, and at a price that is good for everyone, especially for you."

Louis poured slugs into each glass, they picked them up and resumed their silent mode, silent but for the sniffing and gurgling. Louis was the first to speak, "It was so hot that summer. The grapes almost cooked on the vines, many were rotted. We had to cut so many rots from the bunches for harvest. Sometimes the bins of rejects were more full than the ones for the cuve — I like this wine."

"You should be immensely proud of this — it's a great wine from a difficult vintage. Many of the '83s now coming to market show overtones of rot. Few took the sacrifices you did to sort the rotten grapes. It must have taken a lot of time?"

"We set-up tables in the court, hired many young people and old ones from the villages, ones too small or too weak to pick the vines. They come to cut the rot — you say rotten? The rotten grapes we put for the alcool industriel."

"Your wines have steadily improved through very difficult years. Your first vintage, the '82 was an easy one, but many made light and simple wines that year. Yours are deliciously concentrated and complex. Your '83s are the best I have tasted, and I am amazed by the quality you've achieved with the '84s. Now, your '85s, from a wonderful year stand on the shoulders of all others."

David swirled his glass again, nosed the wine and looked up into Louis' eyes. "Is there a written contract to sell your wines to Grotkopf?"

"Non, it is just a family agreement."

Chapter Six

David and Louis continued to swirl and sip, alternating between the wines as they nibbled away at the remains of the persillé and baguette. After a long interlude, David asked, "How much of your other wine do they take each year?"

"All the Grands Crus except for two pièces of each, and any small ones and bidons that I keep. For the Premiers Crus, they take eighty percent of the pièces and for the Village wines, they take half. It is like this since the time of my father. I do not know, but maybe it is a marriage agreement by words for my sister, but there is no paper that I know."

"Louis, I'm practically family here, too. I've been a friend with and have done business with your father since 1966. I've supported him and your family for twenty years, buying wine in every vintage, the better, the lesser, Grands Crus, Village wines, it didn't matter, I always took a good quantity of everything. These last five years, with Grotkopf skimming away most of the top end wines, my own market has been hurting. My clients wonder why my supplies of your finest wines are now limited. I've had to put them all on quotas and to search for other Burgundy producers. It's difficult."

"I will talk with my sister and brother. I am go to Paris this weekend for the conference next week. I see them then."

"Tell them they can get much more money, fifty percent more for the wine by selling it at market value. Point out that you are all throwing money away by selling so cheaply to Grotkopf. Maybe they will like the idea of more money..."

A deep-toned gong sounded, and Murielle popped her head through the kitchen doorway, *"C'est prêt."*

Standing at the entrance to the dining room as they approached was Catherine, a tall, slender redhead who was as stunningly beautiful as David had remembered her. She smiled broadly and began to fait le bise, then continued it into a big warm hug. "It's a long time, almost six months since you were here. I'm sorry I didn't greet you when you arrived; I was in Dijon at the clinic all morning and just got back. You're looking as handsome as ever. Still single?"

"Of course I am; no one will have me. Besides, I'm away travelling so much, I never have a chance to get to know anyone. And you, I need to congratulate you. Louis told me you are — how did he say it? With child. I'm so happy for you. For you both."

The three sat around the end of the long dining table, Louis at the head behind three cradles of wine. The table was set with three glasses each, and it looked like a long, slow afternoon.

"So boys, how are the English lessons coming?" Catherine asked looking in turn at each of them.

"His vocabulary has improved appreciably since I was last here. You've been teaching more it seems."

"The last two months we've been alternating days, one French, the next one English."

"I now think much more in English," Louis added as Murielle came in with three plates of escargots and set them in front of each in turn, David the guest, first, and then she placed a basket of thinly sliced baguette on the table in front of them.

Louis poured from the first cradle. "This is '69 Clos-de-la-Roche, the wine my father called his last really great one."

David has always loved these casual lunches and dinners with the wine producers he represents around the world. As enjoyable as they are, they are often serious working sessions, being the glue that bonds the friendships and fosters the business relationships. They're a vital part of David's business. As an importer and marketer, he gains titbits of information, background, foibles, family history, a broader awareness of the wine, all contributing to making his writing, promoting and talking about it so much easier and more personal.

To David, these occasions are sublime. He had long ago realised he needs to be fully present, focused and moving as events unfold. He is not the director, he needs to follow, maybe dig a little if a vein emerges, but to follow and learn, to absorb, to enjoy and to express enjoyment, which are most often the easiest parts.

The wine first, David thought as he picked up and swirled the glass, turning up the volume of the wine. He noted the brick colour around its edges, the deep garnet of its core, and the nose — the nose which grew in complexity and depth as he swirled. He was pulled into the wine by his nose — by its nose.

The seemingly insistent, "What do you think, David?" coming from Louis broke the spell of the wine, and David re-entered the room.

"Such depth and complexity, this is truly sublime. I've always loved the '69s, but the ones in my cellar lack that little *je ne sais quoi*, the *vif* of this one. I'm convinced great wines lose a little something in shipping. They always seem a bit better from the cellars of the producer. This is still youthful and bright at what? Sixteen, going on seventeen years."

He took a sip, sloshed it around and slowly swallowed, then he popped an escargot in behind it. *This is lunch, after all,* he thought as the wine, the garlic, the butter and the parsley sang a chant on his palate.

"It's a boy, Louis," Catherine said suddenly, squeezing and patting her husband's arm. "The doctor said we have a son. I'm so excited. He said he is healthy, everything is normal."

Her soft voice blended with the rapture David was enjoying with his alternating bites of escargot and sips of wine.

"Ils le connaît déjà? They know this already? How?" Louis asked with wide eyes and a beaming smile that deeply furrowed his cheeks and forehead. He took her hands in his and gently massaged them.

Catherine explained the new equipment which uses sound waves to show the shape of the baby in the womb. "The doctor showed me the image on a glass screen. I could see him moving inside me. When he turned the right way, I could see his little penis." She blushed.

"I will have a little helper now for the vineyards and the cuverie," Louis said excitedly. "Maybe he will be wine crazy like me and my father and grandfather. David, I will have a son! — we will have a son, Katy and me."

"Congratulations, I am so happy for you both," David said, raising his glass in a toast. "To your new son!" It was a mechanical moment, David knew, but he didn't know how else to express his emotions.

They chatted about little things as they slowly finished their escargots and sipped at the '69. Murielle returned and cleared the plates and tools, then came back to set a hot cauldron of bourguignon on a trivet in front of the trio, and beside it, she placed a large basket of frites. Louis poured the second wine, then looked at David. "This is the wine my father won you with, this is the '64 Clos de Bèze."

The bourguignon can wait, David thought as he raised his glass. *"À ton père,* to your father." After they had saluted, they all settled their noses into their glasses. It was captivating, intoxicating. They swirled and nosed and were transported. They all ventured a sip, then David blurted, "My God, this is great wine! It was great then, it is great now, it will continue…"

"So, David, you tell Katy what we talk about on Grotkopf." Louis' voice broke the spell that had enraptured David.

Between sips of wine and bites of the rich beef stew, David carefully outlined the main points of the discussion, then began to slowly fill in details. He added marketing information, pricing data, sales figures and so much more than he had shared with Louis. This wasn't because he had slighted Louis, but that he knew Louis gets bored with facts and figures. *He's an artist, he creates great wine. Numbers don't stir him.*

Catherine, though, uses both sides of her brain equally. She loves artistry, finesse, nuance, but she also seems to know where Francs come from and where they go and, importantly, how quickly. After David had finished, Catherine didn't comment. *She seems to be digesting and analysing all the details. That was a lot of heavy information. Maybe it was too much. Probably far too much. I can never tell.*

The trio continued with small talk as they finished their bourguignon and they were silent as Murielle came in and cleared the plates and cutlery, the empty cauldron and near empty frites basket. As she brought in a board of cheese and set it on the table, Louis poured from the third cradle. "This is the '61 Bonnes-Mares, the favourite wine of my father."

"He shared this one with me many times over the years," David said, picking up his glass by its stem and peering into the wine. "I've always been amazed by this wine, enthralled by its power and its depth." He swirled the glass and added, "The colour is still so dark. For a wine of more than two dozen years age, it appears so young. Louis, your '85 will be like this."

"You think so? You think it has the depth?"

"It certainly has the concentration of fruit, the complexity, the firm structure and the superb balance I remember in this wine when I first had it, what? — Nineteen years ago. It was my second visit in 1967, and your father was so proud of this wine that he had to show it to me. Yes, your '85 should evolve like this. You should be very proud of it."

David cut a wedge out of the Époisse and offered it to Catherine, "And what else?"

Catherine extended her plate to accept the cheese, then put up a hand, "I'm eating for two, not three." She giggled, then looked at the wine still in her glasses and added, "I'm drinking for only one, though, and the doctor said I should not have too much, it might not be good for our baby."

David was midway through plating a runny wedge of Époisse for himself when Catherine began speaking. "So by selling our wines to Grotkopf, we are giving away close to a million Francs every year, is this right?" She immediately answered herself much more aggressively, emphasised by a fist thud on the table at each syllable, "No, this is not right, we are cheating ourselves. This must stop."

"Oui, oui, Katy. We must stop it. I go to tell Laurent Grotkopf tomorrow when I meet with him. I tell him we have no more wine at low price."

Michael Walsh

Chapter Seven

Thursday 20 March 1986

Laurent Grotkopf is a big man, grossly obese, more the image of a Florida tourist than a French winemaker. He runs his family business from an impressive group of old buildings in the centre of Nuits-Saint-Georges, about six kilometres to the south of Morey-Saint-Denis. The business is operated as a *vigneron-recoltant-négociant*, which is to say in addition to growing grapes, harvesting them and making wine, they also buy grapes and bulk wines from other growers and producers. The results are blended, bottled and marketed.

They own just over a hundred hectares of vineyards scattered all along the Côte de Nuits, with parcels, plots or a row or two in most of the famous Grands Crus and many of the better-known Premiers. Laurent began expanding the vineyard holdings in the mid-60s when he inherited the company from his father.

David and Louis père had often discussed the wisdom, or the lack of it, that Laurent showed with his purchases. Though he bought the great names, the plots he chose were the inexpensive ones in the lesser corners or at the edges of the appellation. He gravitated to inferior *terroir*. They had joked that Laurent had the finest *assemblage* of poorly sited vineyards in the entire Burgundy.

But what the Grotkopf operation did own were vineyards whose wines could all legally carry the famous vineyard names on their labels: Le Chambertin, Clos de Bèze, Clos-de-la-Roche, Clos-St-Denis, Bonnes-Mares, Le Musigny, Clos de Vougeot, Echézeaux, and so on.

Grotkopf's prime market was the label reader, not the informed wine lover.

The expansion of the supermarkets through France, gradually in the late '50s, then accelerating through the '60s and early '70s, had given Laurent a target audience. Without the informed advice and opinion of wine shop staff, the shoppers had begun choosing their own wines from the supermarket shelves. Laurent had devised racks of little handout booklets which detailed the most famous wines of the Burgundy.

Through this, he had won a large following of shoppers, then he had added a line of generic and regional wines, which all carried the familiar Grotkopf label. The new inexpensive Grotkopf wines had flown off the shelves.

Strengthened by this, he expanded into less expensive wines from the Rhône and the Languedoc and shipped bulk lots of them by road tanker to his expanding facilities in Nuits-Saint-Georges. He blended and, as David and Louis père had often suggested, he likely confused what was cheap Midi or Rhône wine, and what was Bourgogne.

He is prosperous, he is aggressive, and he has a reputation as being ruthless. His already ruddy face turned an even deeper red in anger when Louis told him he had no wine for him this year. *"Impossible! Ce n'est pas vrai...* Impossible! That is not true. You had a large harvest last year. Stop playing with me."

"I am not playing, it is all sold or committed. I wanted to tell you early so you can plan."

"But we have an agreement of many years, with your father."

"Yes, informal, but not with paper."

"So, you come to ask me for more money for your wine?"

"No, I already have that, almost double. I have no more wine to sell this year."

"Impossible! Nobody will give you that much for your wine. I will give you nine thousand per pièce for the Grands Crus, four thousand for the Premiers."

"I tell you, Laurent, I have no more wine, it is gone."

"Stop playing with me, you young fool; your university degrees are all going to your head." Laurent squirmed and fidgeted as he fumbled with his huge hands. "Okay, I will pay ninety-five for the Grands Crus."

"But I can't — I have no more wine," Louis said calmly.

The veins bulged larger on Laurent's forehead as he grimaced. "Ten then, I'll give ten thousand, but that's it. No more. We shake on it," he demanded loudly as he lumbered to his feet and thrust out his hand.

"I tell you, Laurent, I have no more wine this year, it is all gone. Gone at fifty percent more than that, gone at fifteen thousand for the Grands Crus, sixty-five hundred for the Premiers. I have no wine to sell you."

Laurent slammed his fist on the desk and shouted, "Get out of here, you impudent little bastard! You think you are superior to me because you have degrees. We will see who is superior!"

Chapter Eight

Louis was still shaking with a combination of pride, elation and a concern bordering on fear, as he described for Catherine and David the events of the meeting. "I have concern that Laurent do something bad for us."

David shrugged. "What can he do? I think he is all fluster and bluster. He's like a bully, accustomed to getting his own way, but I think he's all noise and no action. He's like a barking dog, that once it has your attention, doesn't know what to do next."

"I think you're right, David," Catherine said. "What can he do to us? We have no scandals to uncover, no dirty laundry to point out, we have no debts, we are respected in the community and in the business. What can he do? Let's move on... Louis and I are off to Paris tomorrow morning for a week. I finally convinced him to take a break. It's our first trip away from here in three years. And you, David, where are you going now? What are your plans?"

"I'm meeting a winemaker this afternoon and into the evening, but tomorrow my plans are a bit strange, even to me. I'm heading to Saint-Jean-de-Losne, over on the Saône toward Dole." David hesitated and gathered his thoughts, then continued. "I've been thinking of getting a place to live while I'm in France searching for wines and negotiating. My thoughts are to buy an old barge on the canals and convert it to a pied-à-terre — maybe *pied-dans-l'eau* might be a more appropriate term. Anyway, I'll be looking at four potential ones with a broker in the morning."

"A *péniche*?" Catherine asked, her eyes widening. "My uncle had a péniche on the Saône for many years from Chalon. When I was little, he told many stories of his travels in the Alsace, Champagne, Paris, the Loire; he went everywhere there were loads to carry. I loved his stories, and I wanted to go with him, so the summer I turned fourteen I travelled with my aunt and uncle in their péniche. We went up le Petit Saône through Franche-Comté and up the canals to Nancy and Metz and then across the Vosges to Strasbourg and continued up the Rhine to Basel, where they put me on a train back to Rennes."

"Basel? In Switzerland? You go to Switzerland in a barge?"

"Yes, Louis, Switzerland. It was such a wonderful summer for me. We had canals where I grew up in Brittany, but there was very little traffic, and they had closed many of them over there. From the time I was a little girl I knew from my uncle that in the rest of France, there was a big network of connected rivers and canals, but to experience it, that was so great..." She shook her head. "So you're looking at some péniches?"

"I'll be looking at two péniches of thirty-eight metres and two smaller *luxemotors*, twenty-two and twenty-five metres in length. I told the broker a péniche is too big for what I have in mind, but he suggested I look at them just in case I'm wrong."

"This sounds *intéressant*, but I know nothing about the péniches or the canals." Louis shrugged. "It is uncomfortable, no?"

"No, Louis, my aunt and uncle lived in a very comfortable suite at the back of the barge with all the modern conveniences. While I was aboard, I was more comfortable than being at home. The neighbourhood and scenery outside were always changing."

"A converted barge can be as spartan or as luxurious as you wish, just like a house," David added. "The beauty is that if you tire of your neighbourhood, or maybe your neighbours, you can haul in the mooring lines and head off to a new place."

"And where will you moor the barge?" Catherine asked.

"I'm thinking of the basin in Dijon. It's a short walk to the train station, and you know the centre of town is just along from there. And of course, it is only fifteen kilometres from here. What time is your train tomorrow? I could drive you to the station on my way to see the broker — I have the rental car."

"That would be nice, it would save Murielle the trip. She really doesn't like driving. Our train is at ten fifteen; what time is your first barge?"

"Not until ten thirty, but if I get you to the station by nine fifty, I have lots of time. It's only thirty kilometres from there." He glanced at his watch, then continued — "I have a meeting this afternoon, and I should leave shortly — I'm meeting with old man Esmonin to discuss buying more of his Chambertin, and he has invited me to stay for dinner. From previous sessions with him, I'll likely be late, but I have my key so I'll let myself in. Don't wait up for me. I'll see you at breakfast, then we can leave at nine twenty."

"This sounds perfect." Catherine smiled and nodded. "You're always so well organised."

"*Bonne chance* with Esmonin. He is a character."

"Yes, I know, Louis, a delightful old man... *À demain,*" David said as he walked toward the door.

Friday 21 March 1986

At breakfast, both Louis and Catherine were eager to hear about David's adventures the previous afternoon and evening so he ran it through from start to finish. The wines he described as all being fine examples of what's possible with care in a great year, remarkably compact, complex and alive. "Many superb wines, among the best I've tasted, but missing the ultimate finesse of the 85s you've made, Louis."

Louis beamed at this and blushed, "So mine are better this year? It is a long time since Domaine Ducroix is better than Domaine Esmonin. Did you tell him?"

"No, that wouldn't be kind. He's a proud man, and rightly so, and he wouldn't take kindly to being told he is being bettered by a young lad."

"I'm not so young anymore," countered Louis. "I have now thirty-two years."

"He is fifty years older than you, and he made more than thirty vintages before you were born, well over fifty before you made your first one."

"Ahh, perspective — it is so good."

"And his prices? David, you haven't mentioned his prices."

"Catherine, you know it's not my way to discuss my business dealings with others, but I will say the prices Esmonin is asking are very close to those I've offered you."

David looked at his watch. "We need to be going soon. Can I help you with your bags? I'm already loaded."

"We have only two bags, and they're at the kitchen door. We'll meet you in the courtyard in a little five minutes."

He dropped Louis and Catherine in front of the station, and after a hug and a handshake, he said, "I'll see you in a week or so. You can tell me all about the conference, about your presentation. I had seriously thought of attending myself."

"I will share only the good parts with you, save the all boring ones for others." Louis laughed.

"I like that — after my barge hunting, I'll be in Ampuis and Tain to taste Côte Rotie and Hermitage and then I'm off into the wilds of l'Hérault to chase down a maverick winemaker. Bon voyage!" Nodding toward Catherine's small bulge, he added, "Take care of your son."

Chapter Nine

As he always has, David marvelled at the dramatic change from the Burgundy vineyards to the broad floodplains of the Saône. From the corduroy patchworks of vines on the concave slopes of crumbled limestone and marl that line the bottom of Côtes, suddenly the land is flat, rich alluvial soil. The vineyards stop immediately at the appellation line; across the line are grain fields and sugar beet plantations. It's about twenty-five kilometres from the bottom of the vineyard slopes to the Saône, and the angle across from Dijon is a bit longer as it follows through little villages not far away from le canal de Bourgogne. Along the way, he saw the backs of grain elevators and silos that load crops into the péniches.

David arrived in Saint-Jean-de-Losne and drove across the humpbacked bridge to the basin at Saint-Usage, where he parked in front of Atelier Fluvial. He was his usual ten minutes early for the appointment, a trait he had followed since his early days in the Navy. Navigational training does something to the way people organise their lives, or at least David thought so. *Some tell me I'm annoyingly precise and regulated in my comings and goings. Others find me extremely dependable. I much prefer the latter point of view.*

A grey Citroën drove along the basin and pulled to a stop beside him. The driver rolled the window down and nodded in greeting, "You must be David. I'm Jean-Luc." He parked, got out of the car and thrust out his hand, saying, "Welcome to Saint-Usage. The first barge is just along here in the inner basin — we'll walk."

Jean-Luc filled in some background on the péniche as they walked past the dry dock and picked their way around pieces from works in progress. "I have only one péniche to show you, the other one was sold last night. It was still a working Freycinet, thirty-eight five by five. The deal should close next week." As they reached the edge of the inner basin, he lifted his arm and added, "There it is just along there. The one we're looking at is over here." He pointed in the opposite direction.

"This one was built in 1922, also to the Freycinet gauge as an *automoteur.* It worked mostly along the Saône and the Rhône until about four years ago when the owner retired. He sold it to two couples from Oregon who had dreams of setting it up as a communal home. Now with nothing but unfinished projects and no money to continue, they have finally given up and are selling. It is not complete inside, but the hull is sound."

"Thank you for warning me, Jean-Luc," David said as they climbed the gangplank. "It seems very high in the water, it looks like it has no ballast back here. How's the machinery, the engine, the generator, the electrical system, the plumbing?"

"The engine and generator were seized and removed a few months ago to partly cover unpaid yard expenses."

"So it's an unpowered empty shell, then?"

"No, no, a lot of construction has been done inside; it's just not finished. It is only 90,000 Francs." Jean-Luc keyed the padlock open, flipped back the hasp, slid the hatch forward on its rails and opened the low doors.

David followed him down the steep steps and into the cavernous hold. His nose quickly found the pungent smells of mould and wet rot, then they caught in the back of his throat. He scanned the skeletal stud walls, the water-stained insulation, the uneven plywood sub-floors and the light bulbs dangling from wires in the battened but unsheathed ceilings.

"Let's go look at another barge; this sucks my energy. Let's go!"

Jean-Luc knew when to turn off one sales pitch and switch to another. As they made their way back through the yard of the dry dock, he offered a précis on the twenty-two-metre luxemotor. "It was built in Groningen in 1928 as a compact little ship to trade through the small canals there and through those in Friesland and across the Zuiderzee to Noord Holland and Amsterdam. It was converted from cargo to *woonboot* in Harlingen in the late 60s or early '70s and brought down to the Burgundy three years ago." The pair arrived at their cars.

"The barge is by the old mill above the second lock in the canal to the Rhine at Saint-Symphorien. The other luxemotor is also there. Do you want to come with me or follow in your car?"

"I'll follow you." *This'll allow my quick escape if the next two barges are also duds.*

They crossed the bridge back into Saint-Jean-de-Losne and then across the Saône to Losne and followed upstream a short distance in from the left bank of the river. After about four kilometres they turned off and followed a lane across the fields toward the river and then along to the old mill by the lock. There was a small collection of converted barges moored in the wide pound between the locks. David noted some *A Vendre - For Sale* signs as they walked along the grass verge past the column of moored barges.

"Here she is, *Vrouwe Catharina.*"

"I like this one already. She has a grace, very pleasant lines. The wonderful sheer of her gunnels makes her appear to be flirting."

"She was built as a shorter version of a twenty-eight-metre design, and you can see the yard did a wonderful job adjusting the lines. The sheer is emphasised with the shortening, and this gives her a jaunty appearance. Here's her spec sheet."

David stepped aboard to her foredeck from the grassy bank and sat on the anchor winch cover to scan the page of specifications. He got to the bottom and asked, "Is there a recent survey?"

"There is an older one in the file, done for insurance. I have it in the car."

As Jean-Luc headed to retrieve the file, David explored the barge, along the port side deck to the wheelhouse and past it. He stepped up onto the broad roof of the aft cabin. *Great place for a patio.* Down off the aft cabin roof, and along the starboard side deck, he examined the structure of the wheelhouse and noted its fine joinery and the fold-down design. He was back on the foredeck as Jean-Luc returned with a sheaf of papers.

"Let's look below. I'll scan this as we go," David said.

Jean-Luc unlocked the wheelhouse and swung open the door. "*Après vous*, after you."

The wheelhouse had a bright, airy aspect and David imagined adding high-backed stools at a tall pub table along one side to take advantage of the great all-around visibility. The settee along the other side looked very tired. *But the upholstery's easy to replace.* Steps led down into the large aft cabin with a very spartan heads set-up. *Upgrading to modern fixtures appears easy. All the plumbing's already in place.*

Down the steps forward from the wheelhouse led into a large saloon with the galley at its far end. *The appliances are old, out-dated designs, but these too can easily be replaced.* David explored farther forward, past the heads and into the fore cabin. He mused, *Move a bulkhead, put in another door, and the cabin gains an en-suite.*

"I like her bones. There's a good feel to her. The layout is clean, simple and practical. Where's the engine room?"

"It is accessed through here," Jean-Luc said as he took a few steps and swung aside a hinged bookshelf on the aft bulkhead of the saloon. "There are also lifting floor panels in the wheelhouse for major work and if the engine or other big components need to be removed."

"Wonderful, a big old DAF," David said as he crouched and headed into the space along the port side of the old Dutch engine. He noted the shelf of spare parts, the workbench and the appearance of long-time good maintenance. "Let me sit for a while and run through the survey."

He fingered his way down the pages, looking up and around as he scanned the entries, but mostly his eyes stayed focused on the pages. "Damn, I don't like this. Bottom plating at the bow and aft around the propeller was measured three point seven to three point nine millimetres. In many places along the turn of the bilges the steel measured under four millimetres, in some places down to three seven. This will all need replacing."

"No, not in France, here three millimetres is the limit for navigation and for insurance. Three point seven is not a concern."

"Maybe not for you, but it is for me. I want a minimum of four and as far as I'm aware, so does every other country in Europe and all the insurers except in France. Was this boat brought down here to France because the owners would have difficulty insuring or selling it in the Netherlands? — I think so. Here, the date." He answered himself as he pointed to the top of the first page, "This survey was done in Lemuiden in April 1983. Looks like immediately before the barge came to France."

He ran his fingers through his hair. "Damn! I like this ship — where do we go from here? Show me the other luxemotor."

Jean-Luc locked-up and joined David on the canal bank. After a long pause, they turned and strolled away. David stopped and turned his head to look back at *Vrouwe Catharina*. He stiffened as he gazed and quietly mouthed, "Lovely lady, so sorry you're a bit thin-skinned."

A few barges farther along the bank they stopped. "This is *Twee Gebroeders* built in 1926 in Rotterdam, twenty-five metres with a four point four beam."

"She certainly looks old and tired. Her topsides are heavily dented, I see a deeply pitted side deck, there's a lot of over-plating and patches." He pointed to a line of rough welding. "She's had a very hard life. The wheelhouse is way out of proportion. Let me stop there and ask: What are her good points?"

"She has a low asking price."

"That's not a feature for me. I saw two other for sale signs as we came in, what do you know about them?"

"The tjalk has major mechanical problems. It has been on the market for two years at a very strong price, and the owners won't budge. I've stopped showing it."

"And the other luxemotor?"

"That's actually a *steilsteven*. It has an accepted offer and has passed its survey. We're just waiting for the financial details to complete."

"Have you anything else?"

"No, but…"

"So, what do we do about *Vrouwe Catharina*? Can I make an offer subject to survey and specify a minimum of four millimetres on her bottom?"

"They won't accept the offer, they know it won't pass. We've tried this several times before."

"How long have they been trying to sell?"

"Since late last summer. They brought it down three years ago, and they have been coming back from Haarlem in the late spring to cruise around the region until early autumn. He comes down on his own two or three times in the winter to clean and do maintenance; he is very meticulous. Negotiation has been difficult with the distance, but now they have access to a facsimile machine, so it should be easier."

"Let's go enjoy a glass of wine and talk. Have you the time, or are you committed to something else?"

"No, no, I am open. This is still my slow season, and I have nothing left today. Let's drive to my office first to check my answering machine. Make sure nobody's chasing me. We can walk to l'Amiral from there. They have a nice house wine."

"Done, you lead again."

Chapter Ten

L'Amiral is a bustling brasserie and bistro bordering the town square in Saint-Jean-de-Losne. It sits in a dank little north-facing corner under the perpetual shadows of its own façade and those of the church across the narrow lane, and it looks out on the base of a monument. The bar was crowded and smoky when they arrived, so David pointed to an empty table in the back corner of the bistro and Jean-Luc led the way.

"This year we have big celebrations here marking three hundred and fifty years since *la Belle Défense*, the 1636 brave defence of the small town by a handful of men against the army of the Austrian Empire. The monument in the square marks the event, and there is a huge festival every fifty years... It's past noon, we could eat."

"I could easily do with a bite; what's good here?"

"He specialises in regional cuisine, with all the standards for the tourists, coq-au-vin, boeuf bourguignon and the like, and he has a wonderful pôchouse most Fridays. Do you like pôchouse?"

"I love it. Let's see if he has it today. How's his wine list?"

"Here it comes now," Jean-Luc said, nodding toward the aproned man making his way across the floor with a broad smile.

"*Ça va*, Jean-Luc?" greeted the jovial man as he wiped his hands on his soiled apron and extended to shake. "It is a long time. The winter is over now and your season begins, yes?"

"Oui, Giles. This is David, looking to buy a barge. I warn you, though, he is a wine *negoce* from America, so be careful with your carte," Jean-Luc joked. "You have pôchouse today?"

"Bien sure, and a delicious one. The fish selection in the Dijon market was superb this morning. I got tanche and anguille, so big flavours that beg for a big wine." He placed *la carte des vins* on the table, decidedly toward David's side, then quickly looking around at the busy room, he said, "I'll be back shortly."

After half a minute of scanning the list, David said, "A short list, but carefully assembled. It looks as if he knows, or knows someone who knows a lot about wine. Here, *André Nudant Ladoix Premier Cru 1982*. This comes from a vineyard at the top of the slope bordering the Grand Cru Corton. It drinks like a Corton-Charlemagne at only half the price. Or here, *Nudant Corton-Charlemagne 1978* from vineyards around on the other end of the hill. A great wine that Giles lists at a very fair price. I need a big wine to loosen my mind for negotiating."

Glancing over at the price, Jean-Luc said, "That looks way too expensive for me. My business is still small, and it has been a slow winter."

"No, no, no — this is on me. I represent Domaine Nudant and have for many years. This is a marketing expense for me."

"We need to do more business together. I like this."

David grinned, closed the wine list and caught Giles' eye. "You are quick with the list," he said as he arrived. "You have found something?"

"We'll start with a bottle of the 1978 Corton-Charlemagne from my good friend André Nudant. Pôchouse?" He caught the nod from Jean-Luc. "And we'll each have the pôchouse."

Giles pulled himself to rigid attention, and with a formal salute, said, "The Admiral congratulates your wisdom." He turned smartly and marched off toward the cellar.

"Giles is a character; he is the owner, the chef, the sommelier, and for his friends and good clients, he is also the waiter."

After a longish pause, David asked, "So now, how do we frame an offer on *Vrouwe Catharina?*"

"It is difficult to know. Sometimes I think they do not want to sell the barge. I have suggested they haul it out in the dry dock and have the thin areas re-plated, but I think they have trouble finding money to do this. They are retired and live on a small pension."

"How much will it cost to re-plate the bottom?"

"Dry docking charges are fixed and time in the dock is charged by the day. Cutting out plates and re-plating is easy if there is nothing on the inside of the hull. It becomes complicated when the flooring and the interior, the cabinetry, insulation, vapour barrier all have to be torn up and removed to allow a fire watch to be maintained on the inside during the welding. The regulations and common sense dictate this. This is where the expensive part comes in. It is impossible to gain access to the interior of the hull without a lot of destruction of…"

Giles arrived with the wine and two oversized *ballons*, and he presented the label to David with a little flourish. David nodded, and Giles began opening the bottle. "You know Nudant?"

"I've dealt with André and now with his son, Jean-René since the mid-70s. Enjoyed many delightful family meals with him in their home above the cuverie and the cellars. Wonderful family, great wines. Do you know them?"

"I found them maybe five years past when I drove around the small villages on the Côte looking for wine for l'Amiral. We are now good friends."

David swirled the sample *le patron* had poured into the large Riedel. "I am surprised to see you're using Austrian stems here, not French."

"Only for the great wines, Monsieur, they are too expensive and delicate for anything less. I met Georg at the Hospices tastings a few years ago. He had some very unusual glasses, and I was shocked at the difference the glasses make to the taste of a wine. We don't use them often here." Then with a chuckle, he added, "But maybe if you come back more."

David did a quick nose and said, *"C'est correct."*

Giles poured the wine as a basket of sliced baguette arrived at the table. "To *Vrouwe Catharina*," David said, as he raised his glass toward

Jean-Luc. "May we find a life together."

"Mon Dieu! I have never had a taste like this before, but I do not know much about wine. What is it? Where is it from?"

"Hold the stem of the glass, not the bowl. Otherwise, your hand warms the wine and smudges the glass. Soon the wine is too warm, and the bowl is so smudged that you can't see the colour and the brightness. Wine tasting is eyes, nose, palate and soul. All four together."

David slowly swirled the wine in the bottom of the glass, put his nose to the rim and gently inhaled, breathing out through his mouth to run the aromas over his palate. "The grape is Chardonnay, picked from the upper vineyards on the hill of Corton to the north of the city of Beaune. You know Beaune?"

"Yes, yes, I know Beaune, but I do not know wine like this. I know Aligoté and Bourgogne blanc. I know Rully and Macon and once for a special occasion, I had Meursault. This is something like that Meursault, but so much more complicated, concentrated, buttery, rich. It is like papayas and ripe peaches... and vanilla and…"

"You're a very good taster. A few wine classes will quickly polish your talent. Maybe you can do something with this during the slow times with the boat brokerage. Anyway, let's get back to the barge. You were saying about the re-plating…"

"Yes, well, the big cost is ripping out the interior and reinstalling it after the welding. This also disrupts the electrical and plumbing systems, the insulation and vapour barrier, everything inside." He swirled and nosed the glass and took another sip, copying now David's manners. *"Mon Dieu, le vin, c'est merviellieux!* — But it's hard to estimate what it might cost. This is I am sure why the owners have done nothing. They likely fear the cost of the restoration afterwards. Many potential buyers have walked away also because of this. It's certainly a dilemma."

"I am thinking of something that might work. What if…"

"Pôchouse, Messieurs," Giles said as he watched the waiter place the tureen on the table and set the soup dishes. "The wine is good?"

"Bring a glass and you tell me."

Giles clicked his heels, spun and ran, nearly sprinted away, calling *"J'arrive"* over his shoulder.

The waiter ladled large chunks of fish and a creamy broth into the large shallow bowls that were set on plates rimmed with dark croutons.

David added a generous pour to the Riedel that Giles was holding, and with a broad grin, he said, "Voila! Now I ask you if the wine is good."

There was a long pause as Giles nosed and tasted, then he said, "No, I am sorry... it is not good." Then after another animated swirl-sniff-sip-gurgle ceremony, "I must call it magnificent." He stuck his nose back into the glass, raised his head and wished, "Bon appétit!" Then stuffing his nose back into the glass, he slowly walked away.

"This is delicious fish soup. I much prefer the Burgundian style to the bouillabaisse of the Midi," David said, dabbing a drip off his chin. "Now, where was I?"

"You were saying you had an idea that might work with the luxemotor."

"The first idea I had, to get a glass of wine, seems to have evolved superbly. The next idea is to make an offer that accepts the thin bottom, regardless of survey. We know it's thin, but the survey shows this to be at the bow, some places along the turn of the bilges and aft around the propeller. These are normal places to erode and wear. The remainder of the bottom shows mostly between four and a half and five and a half millimetres. It's unlikely this has changed much in the three years since the survey."

He paused for another sip of wine. "The interior is, what? Sixteen, eighteen years old, maybe more, and the systems are dated. Though nicely designed, I saw things which told me the interior was done to a budget. I'm thinking of gutting the entire interior, all the systems, everything and starting over, so re-plating will be straight-forward. Basically buying an empty hull. But my pôchouse is getting cold, and my Corton-Charlemagne is getting warm." They both went back to their chowder and wine.

They talked all around the luxemotor, intentionally avoiding it as being too heavy and complex to interrupt their wonderful lunch.

"What I'm looking to buy here is the graceful sheer," David said as he finished his last spoonful of pôchouse. "I like her comfortable size, the jaunty way she sits in the water. These things are not affected by the re-plating. The craftsmanship on the wheelhouse is far superior to the remainder of the conversion, and it too is unaffected by the bottom work. The engine and mechanical systems appear sound and well-maintained. They are easy to do plate work around. Otherwise, there is very little, if any of the interior finish that I want to keep, and the thin steel I don't want either." He raised a finger as he paused to think and then continued, "Do all her systems work?"

"Yes, I'm sure they do. As I told you, they live aboard and cruise here in the summer, and he is a maintenance fanatic. He is Dutch, which usually means everything works very well."

"So, you see no reason I couldn't go for a cruise in her as soon as I take possession and while waiting for a time in the yard to do a full refit?"

"I see no reason at all."

"How easy is it to book into the dry dock? How much wait?"

"It is getting much busier now with the new rental boat business. Blue Line has a big base on the other side of the inner basin, over beyond the island," he said, motioning toward the far wall. "They now are doing their pre-season haul-outs, so the dock is very busy."

"What about docking for survey?"

"Same wait, I'm afraid, though you could use the slipway down at the end of the Quai National." Jean-Luc motioned and looked to the other wall. "We can walk over there, it's just past my office."

"What's the highest offer that the owners have refused?"

"They initially listed it at 285,000, lowered it to 270,000 in the winter, then to 260,000 last month. The highest offer they've had was 230,000, but there were a lot of conditions attached."

"Let's draw up an offer of 225,000, accepting the condition of the hull. Make it subject only to all navigational, mechanical, electrical and plumbing systems being found operable by survey or made operable by the owner before possession. Title search, of course, what else?"

"Those are always required, unless noted in the listing. I have my standard form here, we can start with it and then see what else we need to say.

Shall we continue here, or in my office?"

"Looks like it will be here." David motioned across Jean-Luc's shoulder. "Le Patron is bringing us snifters of brandy."

"Messieurs, les Fine de Bourgogne Hors d'âge," Giles said as he placed two over-poured snifters on the table and raised his own shorter pour in a toast.

They toasted, tasted and chatted until Giles was called away, then they went straight back to barge buying. Jean-Luc pulled out a compartmented folder of stapled pages intersticed with carbon paper, and selected one set of each. "Have you your passport? I need it to start the paperwork."

"You're well-organised," David said as he reached into the inside pocket of his jacket. "Yes, here it is."

"Organised, maybe, but I do this with all the spare time I have between clients." He began filling in the blanks on the four sets of pages.

Meanwhile, David cradled his snifter in his hand and gently rolled the deep amber liquid around to warm it and release its aromas and bouquet. "This is wonderful Fine, you should pause to enjoy it."

"I'm almost finished the form, I need only another minute, and also your address in France, then I'll pick up my glass."

David placed Louis' card on the table in front of Jean-Luc, and in less than a minute, Jean-Luc passed the papers as he said, "Okay, my turn with the Marc and yours with the paper. Read it over to see if it is correct. Do we need to add anything? Take anything out?" Jean-Luc nosed his snifter and sipped. "I usually find Marc de Bourgogne too harsh. This is so much more mellow and refined."

David looked up from the bundle of papers and answered, "The difference is that this isn't Marc, it's Fine. Marc is made by distilling grape skins; Fine is made by distilling wine, like in the Cognac and the Armagnac regions, and like them, it must also be aged for years in oak barrels, the longer, the better. This is Hors d'âge, a minimum of ten years in small wood."

David went back to the papers. "Possession date? You've left this blank. Shouldn't we put in something about when I will take possession?"

"Yes, I left it blank because we need to figure out a workable date. I use the facsimile machine in my lawyer's office so we can send the offer this afternoon before they close. This is Friday so the owners may not get it until Monday. I'll phone Henc tonight after the rates go down, and I'll tell him about the offer and recommend he accept it. If he accepts, he probably cannot return the signed documents until Monday. But a facsimile signature is still not binding here, so we need also to do it by post. Easter is the following weekend so the returning post might not be here until Tuesday 1 April. Then we can legally do a haul out for survey. To make it safe, we can book the slipway for Thursday 3 April." He looked at his calendar.

"If there are problems from the survey requiring him to make good, we must give him time to do that. From my impression of the barge and his maintenance, we should find no major problems to delay us, so a week should be sufficient. Let's see, starting the day after the survey, that takes it to the 11th," he said looking again at his calendar. "That's a Friday, how does Friday 11 April sound to you?"

"Let's do that. It fits perfectly with my banking. Fill it in and I'll initial and sign the document. To whom do I make the deposit cheque payable? To Heusdens or to you? Is ten thousand sufficient?"

"Yes, make it to *Bourgogne Bateaux en dépôt*. I also need some alternate ways to get in touch with you during the next couple of weeks... And we need to confirm we can haul out on the slipway on the third."

Chapter Eleven

Saturday 22 March 1986

"You still haven't told me which you prefer, Monsieur Michaels, the brunette or the blonde," Etienne said.

"Please, call me David — Both are beautiful, sensuous and voluptuous. Maybe the brunette has a little more depth and complexity than the blonde, a slightly tighter bottom, trimmer and more elegant. But the blonde's fuller body, fleshier and rounder structure are captivating, a bit dumber at the moment, but that will change. They're both still so young. I'd like to watch them as they mature — I'll take both. How much do you want for them?"

"The '85 was a wonderful year for us and our demand is very strong. Both are thirty-eight Francs a bottle ex-cellars, but I can let you have only three hundred bottles of each."

"Only twenty-five cases of each, not more? I'd like double that."

"Aah, I'm sorry, I can't, we have too many commitments from long-time markets already and so many new clients ordering now. It seems as though every starred restaurant in France wants some. We have big new orders from Switzerland and Belgium, and the Germans are buying more strongly. I am selling to you to expand our market in America, but I cannot expand the vineyards on the Côtes. Every square centimetre has been fully terraced and planted for centuries. No vineyards are for sale; we can't expand here."

Côte Blonde and Côte Brune, which means brunette in English, are two sections of the Côte Rôtie, the roasted slopes above the town of Ampuis on the banks of the Rhône some thirty kilometres south of Lyon. The

Blonde is the southern portion of the slope, the Brune the northern, both are equally steeply terraced, and both are planted mostly to Syrah with a bit of Viognier to add a floral aspect.

David had spent the night in Hôtel la Marine in Losne after booking a haul-out on the slipway for 3 April and then trying to get an idea of when the dry dock could take him for the bottom re-plating. It looked like it would be well into May and all of its holidays before he could be slotted in. The discussion of specific dates jumped all over the place, with big run-around illogic. Trying to get a commitment was as hopeless as bailing water with a fishnet.

Though he prefers the smaller roads, this morning he had taken the Autoroute to Lyon to cut an hour off the drive before taking the National, the N-86 to Ampuis. The Rhône was in flood, and he had paused above Givors to watch a lock-filling down-bound *chargé* sweeping at what seemed the limit of control under the bridges around the sharp bend. The barge had fifteen more kilometres of this near free-fall before a respite at Écluse Vaugris, the next lock.

David has often watched the barges along the Rhône and other rivers, and along the canals during his wine buying travels. He will sometimes pause with a baguette and a piece of cheese on a roadside wall top or other vantage point and watch the river traffic. This morning he bought a croissant and a chocolat from a table in the street market and had his cup charged with a double espresso in the brasserie. With these, he sat on the top of the retaining wall above the quai to be entertained by the passing scene while he thought.

He had been disappointed Jean-Luc couldn't reach Henc by phone last night. The deal was still at loose ends. The fax had gone through and was receipted, so at least the process was underway, but there was no way of knowing whether Henc had received it nor when he would. David had arrived with an hour in hand before his appointment in Ampuis, so he relaxed and enjoyed the early spring sun.

Just above the forty-fifth parallel now, he thought. *The sun has just crossed the equator into the northern hemisphere on its march along its ecliptic. It's getting warmer, and this will quicken as I head south.* Since his days as a naval navigator, David has always thought in a broader view. The position of the sun, the stars and the moon, his place on the surface of the globe and the relationships among all these were never far from the top of his mind. He mused that celestial navigation and planning ocean passages must do that to some. *Maybe it had always been that way with me. The naval training simply gave me new techniques, labels and names to use.*

He finished his coffee and wiped out the cup with the cloth he kept with it in the small bag. The staff in the brasseries and cafés were always amused by the notion of pulling espresso into his own cup. There was almost always a little conversation around the idea, and they frequently added an extra pull in the process. He got up and headed back to the car, wanting to watch the laden barge enter Écluse Vaugris.

The lock at Vaugris is just a kilometre above Ampuis, so he had filled in the last bit of time before his meeting by watching the barge approach and enter the lock. Fully laden and deep in the water, there was very little clearance beneath it as it passed over the cill. It was full lock width, close to twelve metres, so it had to pump its way into the chamber, almost as a piston being drawn into a hydraulic cylinder.

It was a slow process, and through it, David had arranged his approach to an increasingly famous wine producer whom he hoped to bring into his stable. He had pulled into the courtyard his usual ten minutes early and after a rather stiff and formal beginning, he and Etienne had begun to relax as they wandered from barrel to barrel in the cellars.

"Of course, I'll also take the Côtes du Rhône and the Condrieu. Can I have eighty cases of each?"

"Eighty? What's that — nine hundred and sixty bottles of each? Yes, we can do that. That's the '85, right?" And seeing the nod, Etienne continued, "I can give you a good price on the '84s; some ignorant wine writers are saying it is a bad year, and our sales are now slow."

"Yes, I saw what Barker said about the vintage. I assume they are in bottle now. Can we taste them?"

"*Bien sure...* For sure. We're finished here now. We can go to my office."

They were well past the Côtes du Rhône and into Saint-Joseph, Cornas and Hermitage when the receptionist knocked and came into the office. *"Pardonnez moi, Messieurs,* but I have a Monsieur Delong on the telephone asking for Monsieur Michaels."

"Please transfer the call to my phone."

Etienne passed the handset. "David, do you want privacy?"

"No, no, it's my boat broker, it's nothing confidential."

David's face relaxed as he listened and a smile grew to fill it. After a bit of animated back-and-forth, he returned the handset to the cradle. "Looks like I've just bought a barge."

"A barge?"

"A graceful little luxemotor built in 1928 in the Netherlands."

"What will you do with it, ship wine?"

"No, no. It will be my home, my pied-à-terre while I'm in France. I can move it along the canals and rivers and base myself almost wherever I want. It's comfortable now, but I'm going to have the interior ripped out and completely rebuilt in a more luxurious fashion."

"We have sometimes private barges stop here, down on the quai. They are heading down to the Midi or back up to the Bourgogne. Some come up to taste and buy from us and from others in the town. I've never thought much beyond that, but it must be a very different lifestyle. You have some experience with barges?"

"Not barges, exactly, but I spent time in the Navy as a navigator and eventually the captain of a training ship. I know the pointy end from the blunt end, know it's necessary to keep the keel side down, keep the water out and things like that." David chuckled. "But, back to the wine."

"Yes, the wine, but we must talk later about your barge. Do you want some of the '84s?"

David had long ago learned that to skim only the best wines and the best vintages from the producers' lists is not the best idea. The top wines are symbols of prestige, but they are costly to produce, and margins are often thin. Profits come from the lesser wines for which comparative ease of production allows for larger margins. The greater volume and larger margin wines keep the businesses afloat and allow more effort to be put into increasing the quality of the finest wines. Top end wines get the attention and the reviews from the press, which drive the market to the company name. The bottom wines support the prestigious wines and allow reputation to build.

"Yes, I'll take the '84s, both the Condrieu and the Côtes du Rhône; I'm amazed by the quality you've achieved in a vintage that's being damned. Can you let me have nine hundred and sixty bottles of each, the same as the '85s?"

"We can do that, thank you. And our Saint-Joseph, Cornas and Hermitage?"

"I wish I could, but I have already committed to those from Chapolet, and my market can take only so much."

"Aah! Chapolet, he makes great wines. You choose well — lunch? Will you join me?" Etienne had warmed appreciably from the stiff business approach when they met just an hour or so earlier. "Have you eaten at la Pyramide?"

"A good number of times; it's one of my favourites. Is Madam Point still with us?"

"Yes, but increasingly feeble now. We'll go. I must do some business there anyway, you know." He winked, then pushed the button on his intercom and said, "Marie..."

"Oui Monsieur."

"Marie, tell la Pyramide that I am on my way over with a good client for lunch."

Restaurant de la Pyramide, a short distance upstream in Vienne, has enjoyed three Michelin stars since 1933, eight years after Fernand Point had taken over the restaurant at the death of his father. When Fernand himself died in 1955, his widow, Mado took over, and she has maintained the three stars ever since. During the reign of Fernand in the kitchen, the restaurant was widely regarded as the greatest in France. More than thirty years later it is still held among the top handful, and it is one of only twenty with three Michelin stars.

Michael Walsh

A great restaurant will normally keep a table or two aside for occasions like this, to accommodate the last-minute impulses of their frequent clients. David was running these things through his mind. *In wine regions, this is even more common, because of the nature of the wine trade. Great wine craves great food, and equally, great food craves great wine.* He was looking forward to lunch and to cementing another supplier relationship.

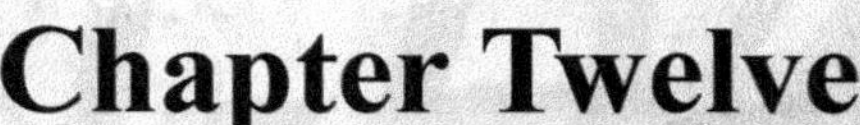

Chapter Twelve

After nearly three hours at la Pyramide, David and Etienne had gone back to Ampuis to formalise the wine order. In the process, Etienne *found* another fifteen cases of both the Blonde and the Brune to add to it.

It was late afternoon by the time David had driven south out of town. He didn't go far. Only six kilometres along, just beyond the old suspension bridge leading across the Rhône to Les-Roches-de-Condrieu, he pulled into the courtyard of Hôtel Beau Rivage. He had booked a room for two nights; his next appointment wasn't until Monday morning in Tain.

Beau Rivage sits on the banks of the river on a narrow strip of flats at the base of the steep vineyards of Condrieu. It's an upper-end four-star hotel with views out over the river from the terrace and the dining room, as well as from the windows and the veranda of David's favourite suite. He had stayed here many times before, and his preference was the top floor corner, where he could sit on his broad veranda and see up and down the river.

The hotel sits midway along the outside bank of a tight curve in the Rhône. The curve is the middle of a series of three bends in quick succession, which in the days before the river was tamed through here by dams and locks downstream, was one of the most treacherous stretches of navigation along its course. From his vantage point, he could see both upstream and down without turning his head. He did that for a long time and reminisced.

He thought about the events which had brought him here. Discovering wine in 1966 was the beginning of this trip. He had been on a

NATO posting in northern France, and he became curious about the wines in the bins at the base exchange. There was a wide range of prices, and his analytical mind needed to know why, and what a fair price might be. He had asked for help in making a selection, but the staff knew as little as he did.

One of them pointed to a book among the offerings on the shelf. "I use that one, *Frank Schoonmaker's Encyclopedia of Wine.*" Then pointing to another, slimmer book, she had added, "But this one is good too, *The Wines of France*, by Lichine."

David bought both books, and for the following few days, he devoured them, cover to cover, then repeatedly reread sections of greatest interest. He had gone back and forth between his room in the barracks and the bins in the exchange, comparing labels to what he was reading. Finally, he tired of theory and bought a bottle. He was intrigued by reading about the Burgundy, and there was a large selection of it from Louis Jadot. To make his tasting practice easier, he chose a wine highly praised in the books, a 1961 Chambertin Clos de Bèze. *I'm still amazed this was my first wine.*

My first real wine, David corrected his thought. *There was the sip I snuck as an altar boy one day when filling the cruets in the sanctuary before Mass.* He still remembered the rancid and oxidised taste of the sacramental wine, and how it had turned him away from trying wine again — until that day in the base exchange.

He had also selected some cheeses. David couldn't remember now, as he sat on the veranda, what cheeses they were, but they were likely recommendations from Schoonmaker or Lichine or both on what goes best with a red Burgundy. *Sitting in my room with a glass, a corkscrew and one of the greatest of all Burgundies, one of the world's greatest wines, I began my tasting adventures. This all seems so fresh and recent, but nearly twenty years have passed since then.*

The sun was sinking below the ridge, and he was feeling the chill of the late afternoon breeze. He moved inside and lay on the bed to continue reeling reminiscences through his mind.

The week after his first tasting he had driven south from the airbase in Marville to the Burgundy on a bleak November day. He was on a seven-three, seven-four shift on the flight line, which gave him three or four days off at a time. This first trip to the Burgundy started on one of his three-day breaks.

David grinned to himself as he thought of the drive. *It was before the expansion of the grid of Autoroutes when every National and Departmental road in France led into the centre of every town and village along the way. Every signpost showed the direction to Paris. There were no bypasses.* Not only was it necessary to crawl through the centres of every community, but in many of them, the merchants seem to have convinced the mairie to snake a one-way maze past every business on the way through. David's progress had been slow.

To make matters worse, the Lucas fuel pump in his ageing Healey didn't like prolonged slow speed. He knew the remedy of jiggling the external lever, which got things going again, but it was not a cure. *The three hundred kilometres took me nearly seven hours. That trip can easily be done in well under three hours these days.*

After an early start, he had arrived in Gevrey-Chambertin in the mid-afternoon. He drove through town and out its south side to where the book's map showed Clos de Bèze to be. *I remember thinking how bleak the vineyards looked. Rows of leafless skeletons leading up the shallow slopes to the tree line.* Then he had seen Clos de Bèze painted on the whitewashed side of a vineyard hut. *So this is it,* he thought, remembering his initial impression, *not as interesting as the wine. So, what now? I'm here, but why? For what?*

He had gotten out of the car and walked through a gap in the low stone wall and into the vineyard. The ground was wet from recent rain, and the mud stuck to his soles as he walked. It gathered and clumped, and when the clods became too thick, they sloughed off, and the building began again. He finally made his destination, a man who appeared to be binding a split vine stem with soft wire.

"Bonjour, Monsieur," David had said, rekindling his rusty French. He explained having enjoyed a wonderful bottle of Clos de Bèze the previous week and wanted more of it and wanted to learn more about it.

The old man said, *"J'en ai un peu...* I have some, these are my vines, but I am busy now..." He paused for a few moments, then continued, "Busy for a little half hour." Raising an arm, he turned and pointed, "You come later over there, the first house in Morey-Saint-Denis." *And thus I had met Louis...*

David drifted off to sleep. It was dark in the room when he awoke, and he was beginning to feel a bit hungry. It was still early, not quite twenty fifteen and the dining room would soon be busy. He quickly showered, pulled clean socks and a shirt out of his bag, and he was soon fresh and heading out the door.

He was led to his reserved table, his favourite corner by the window, from where he could survey the whole room if he wished or simply look out at the river.

"Does the chef have the coquilles de Saint-Brieuc this evening?" he asked the waiter when he arrived with the menu and the cartes.

"Yes, I served some earlier this evening, but let me check if any are left."

"If there are, have the sommelier bring me a bottle of Guigal's '83 Condrieu."

The Condrieu arrived, was opened and poured, and David sat back to enjoy the action in the room. It was off season, and there were several empty tables, but there were more than enough diners to make it a profitable evening for the hotel. He could spot two other wine buyers in the room, neither he knew, but he had learned how to spot them by little clues in their behaviour and manner. *I wonder if they can do the same with me.*

He instructed the waiter to have the chef prepare the scallops the way he likes them, seared very hot and very quickly, with thin-crusted ends and the centres like the way the Japanese serve seafood, raw or nearly so. They arrived at the table done perfectly.

Most French scallops are a far cry from the huge, tender and sweet Digby scallops he had grown up with, and much more difficult to sear properly; the corail doesn't take kindly to it. But the scallops from Saint-Brieuc on the north coast of Brittany are similar to the Digby ones, large and often sold without the corail. The Condrieu complemented perfectly, its rich oily texture and apricot-citrus fruit matching and harmonising with the rich, salty sweetness of the Saint-Jacques. He swelled with enjoyment.

Because of the lunch at La Pyramide, he wanted only a selection of cheese to finish. After the trolley had been rolled away, he sat nibbling from his small assortment of cheeses and breads and enjoying the remainder of the bottle. He continued reminiscing.

He had driven down the narrow road from Clos de Bèze toward the village of Morey-Saint-Denis past signs in the vineyards he knew from his books: Le Chambertin, Latricières-Chambertin, Clos-de-la-Roche. Then noting the place where he was to later meet, he continued into and through the village past Clos du Tart, Clos-Saint-Denis and Bonnes-Mares. He circled Clos de Vougeot. His fuel pump began acting up again, so he jiggled it into a more regular beat and headed back to his rendezvous, not wanting to be late.

The tractor had just pulled into the courtyard as he approached. "Come, but let me clean my hands, then we greet," said the stocky man, then added, "*Deux minutes,*" as he disappeared through a door in what he had earlier called *the house*. The house was an imposing three-storey château of beige and pale rose masonry with ornate façades in the Beaux-Arts style.

"I am Louis," he said as he emerged from the château with two wine stems and a long glass tube dangling from his left hand and his right hand extended to shake.

"I'm David, from Canada. Thank you for giving me your time."

"I thought back there at the vines, not many young people drink Clos de Bèze or want to know about it. This man is different I think, so I am curious." Motioning toward the big oak door, he said, "Come, come, it is cold out here. It is warmer in the cellar, always around 12°, winter, summer, it does not matter."

He led down the stone steps. "This is not a good time to taste the new wine, it is still in the cuves settling from fermentation. We can taste after the cellar maybe." Louis reached up, a light came on, and David was looking at a colour version of one of the photo plates in his wine books, rows of barrels fading away into the distant gloom.

"The 1965 vintage, it was a very difficult year for everybody in the Burgundy. Very wet and cold, not enough sun. Most of the grapes did not ripen. There was much rot. Then before harvest, a big storm that took away more than half my crop. We waited until October hoping for the rest to ripen. Some did. I made only thirty percent of normal." Louis walked along and swung a rod, placing the hooked crossbar at the other end onto a bare wire and making the electrical contact, turning on the light. *Nice simple set-up,* David thought as he looked up and analysed it, *an uninsulated crossbar on a pair of uninsulated wires.*

Louis slid the light along and said, "Here, we taste." He tapped the barrel bung back and forth until he could lift it out, then thrust the glass tube through the bunghole, put his thumb over the end of the tube and lifted out a column of wine. He flipped his other hand to upright the glasses, held them out, lifted his thumb and dropped tastes into each bowl.

"This is the '65 Clos de Bèze," he said extending the glasses toward David. "In normal years we taste this near the end, but the other wines this year are not very good. These I will not put in bottle. Sell them in bulk to not ruin my good name."

David took one of the glasses and tried to remember what he had read in Schoonmaker and Lichine. He watched Louis swirl his glass and put his nose deep inside. He copied. He watched Louis take a big sip and slosh it around in his mouth, and he copied again. He watched Louis spit a stream of wine to the gravel beside the barrels, and he did the same, then said, "Merde!"

"Oui, beaucoup de merde... much barnyard this vintage," said Louis, pouring the remainder of his wine back into the barrel through the bunghole.

David copied his movements, saying, "No, not that, I dribbled wine down my jacket."

"Come, let's go to the '64s," Louis said as he tapped the bung back into place and headed along between the rows of barrels, pulling the light as he went and tipping on new ones. "Here, les Millandes from beside the house," pointing to the white chalked script on the barrel end. He repeated the routine of pulling samples, this time, David holding his own glass.

"This will show you the quality I make; 1964 was a great year to grow wine. We had much snow in the winter, and the land was wet down deep. This is good because the summer was very dry and hot, only a sprinkle of rain in August. Before harvest in September, the grapes were very small and concentrated. Finally we have some light rain to fatten them just a bit and then we picked."

David had remarked how much he liked the wine and asked many questions. *Louis seemed delighted to have such an eager student, so I continued to enquire from my naïvety.* Though he had some vicarious knowledge from his recent readings, he was amazed to be immersed in the world his mind had tried to create the previous week from the books. He asked Louis why he called his barrels pièces, not tonneaux, or fûts, or barriques or other names he had read, but Louis said he didn't know. *Said it was probably just old tradition. That's still the best answer.*

Louis had explained the hierarchy of the vineyards; the finest are the Grands Crus along the upper parts of the slopes, the Premiers Crus border these, a few above next to the crags and trees, but mostly below the Grands Crus. Near the bottoms of the slopes, below the Premiers, are the Village wines. But there are exceptions; the quality depends on many factors, the angle of the slope, how it faces the sun, the soil composition, the drainage, so many things that Louis said they lump together and call *terroir*.

He had talked about how good wine cannot be made with poor grapes, and how if he is not careful, it is easy to make poor wine with good grapes. "My role as a winegrower is to coax from the vineyards the highest quality that nature allows each year. As a winemaker, I work to maintain as much of the quality of the grapes as is possible during the fermentation."

Louis had continued, "Fermentation is a natural process. I can only guide its progress, I cannot improve the quality. That possibility stops when I harvest the grapes. There are many things I can do to shape the character, the nuances, but I cannot make good wine from poor grapes."

Louis had illustrated his lessons with tastings from the various barrels, pièces he called them, as they worked their way through the cool, moist cellar. They enjoyed broad roaming discussions from pièce to pièce, talking of the qualities, the merits, the small flaws in the wines. Louis was bubbling with pleasure, delighted to have someone with whom to share his passion for wine. "This is my pride, this is my Clos de Bèze," he said, dropping generous slugs of the deep garnet wine into their glasses. "What do you think?"

"I have so little experience with wine, I started only last week. What is my opinion worth?"

"You have the passion, the curiosity, the understanding, the perception and you have a very good palate. You have the tools, maybe you do not know yet how to use them the best, but that will come easy for you. Already you know more than most. So, tell me about this wine."

David remembered now being embarrassed by the compliments. He remembered nosing and tasting the wine, then rattling off a long stream of what he had almost immediately thought was babbled nonsense, as he had tried to express his profound enjoyment of the wine. *Words which made little sense to me at the time. But they just poured out of my mouth. I was even more embarrassed.*

"Exactement!" Louis had exclaimed. "You have the way to say it... Where do you stay tonight?"

David remembered his confusion and his response, "I have no plans, nor for tomorrow. I only came down here to find Clos de Bèze. I don't know where I'm going."

"We have many spare rooms in the house, stay with us tonight, and tomorrow we can walk in the vineyards. The ground will be drier, and the mud won't stick so much. I need to go mark vines that want repair. My older son is off from school for the Armistice holiday, and he wants to come with me. We will wear our *bleuets* in the vineyards, and I can explain the terroir to the both of you."

"I'll wear my poppy, we can pause for the silence at eleven."

David sat now in his corner of the dining room staring into the last of his Condrieu and thinking, *God, that was so long ago, I was only twenty-two, but it seems so recent, it's still so fresh.*

He still remembered Louis' parting comments after his second breakfast in the house. "You come back in February, the '64s will be in bottle then, and the '66s will be in pièces in the cave. We can taste them. I think they are better than the '64s."

That had been the beginning of our friendship and of our delightful mentor-student relationship. So fresh, still... Seems like yesterday. Didn't know where I was going then, just experiencing and exploring. Seems still the case... I still don't know.

Michael Walsh

Chapter Thirteen

Monday 24 March 1986

David had been disappointed with the news he received at Chapolet in Tain. Georges, with whom he had dealt for several years was no longer there. Pierre, the man he met with this morning, was sub-titled *Directeur Commercial /Marketing Director* on the card he presented. Georges' card had read simply *Georges Chapolet, propriétaire*. There had been a corporate takeover and a re-structuring.

Pierre thanked David for his business over the years, and then he told him the company had signed with a national distributor. He was assured his orders for the '84 Hermitage and Saint-Joseph would be honoured, but there will be no new orders, and he will no longer represent the company. Formal severance notification had been sent to his office in Vancouver last week.

So Georges has sold. More likely he was forced to sell by his brothers. He had so often hinted they did nothing but take money at the end of each year, David thought as he drove southward on the N-7 toward Valence.

Ten kilometres downstream, he paused at Pont de l'Isere and watched the torrent of water in the river coming down from the early melt run-off from the western slopes of the Alps. A kilometre downstream, this churning volume dumped into the Rhône adding appreciably to the already strong current there. *This is not an easy time for river navigation.*

David sat for a while watching the tumult in the river and tried to gather his thoughts. He could likely buy the '85 Hermitage and Saint-Joseph from Etienne; he had been impressed with them, and they had been offered. *And add the Cornas; it too had been outstanding. I'll telex an addendum to the order from my next opportunity.*

Okay, but what do I do with the rest of the day now? He opened his satchel, pulled out his battered indexed notebook and thumbed to *R* for *Rhône*, but he couldn't find what he wanted. After flipping pages, he thought, *Of course, C for Châteauneuf. Here it is, Châteauneuf-du-Pape, Château de Beaucastel.* The entry was double underlined in red, meaning he must do something about it.

He had begun the notebook years before, adding contact information for properties and producers that interested him from his reading, from his tastings, and from recommendations. He had been a bit complacent with it the last while, and he knew some of the information was stale. It was also poorly organised. *I need to come up with a better way to index all of this. I've too often lost information in here.*

The listing read: *Château de Beaucastel - Jean-Pierre & François Perrin, SE Orange on N-7 to A-7 circle, 2nd right into Chemin de Beaucastel, right side 1200m past A-7.* The telex address and phone number were also listed. He glanced at his watch. *Twelve twenty, not a good time to phone. Lunch time in France — I haven't eaten, Georges' invitation hadn't survived the takeover.*

On his Michelin map, he saw the access to the A-7 was only two kilometres along from the bridge at the edge of Valence, and it was about an hour's drive down the Autoroute to the Orange exit. He decided to head down closer to Orange and pause for lunch at a rest stop where he could also find a telephone booth. He needed gas, so he filled at a station before the Autoroute, knowing prices were ten or fifteen percent higher beyond the toll gates.

I can never understand the mindset of the hypnotised captive audience who willingly overpay for fuel at the autoroute rest stops. Then he smiled to himself as he thought, *And here I am, about to willingly overpay for poor food at one of the same rest stops.* He changed his plan to continuing into Orange to find a proper lunch. *I'll be there by thirteen thirty, still too early to phone Beaucastel, but with plenty of time for a crêpe or a galette.*

David sat on the patio of Brasserie Romain, minutely examining the structure of the massive Théâtre antique d'Orange through the trees. In summer this is a well-shaded place, but now the leafless and heavily pruned branches of the plane trees blocked little of the sun nor much of the view of the imposing façade.

After he had finished his galette, he asked the waiter if he could use the telephone. The receptionist at the other end passed him on to Jean-Pierre, who after introductions and a few questions, said, "Yes, we can see you this afternoon. How is fifteen thirty?"

"That works well for me," David replied. Relieved, he returned to his sunny patio table to slowly finish the last of the pichet, studying the huge façade and running his recollection of it through his mind. The theatre had been built early in the first century when Orange was a strategic Roman settlement and capital of northern Provence. It's now one of the best-preserved theatres in ancient Gaul. *I'm amazed operas are still regularly presented here. I must arrange one of my trips to take in a performance.*

He easily found the estate from the directions in his battered book, and at fifteen twenty, he rolled up the pea gravel drive to the small courtyard at its end. He took a few moments to gather and organise his thoughts, then he tried to determine which door he should head toward. His quandary was answered when two men walked out through the largest doorway toward him.

After greetings and introductions and a brief summary by David of his background and his intentions, Jean-Pierre excused himself to head back to his office, while François led him into a tasting room and up to a table on which stood a line of bottles. "Some of these were drawn from barrel a short while before you arrived. We'll begin with the whites. First, the Côtes du Rhône Blanc."

David was accustomed to the formal pace thus far. It usually takes much of a visit, sometimes more than one, for the producer and the agent playing buyer and seller to relax as friends. He picked up the glass which François had poured and went through his look-swirl-sniff-sip routine. "This is big for a Côtes du Rhône, what's the blend?"

"Here's the information sheet. We have these for all our wines," François fanned-out the pages. "The vines for this are across the Autoroute, just outside the Châteauneuf-du-Pape appellation line, but the soil structure is the same, with similar big round stones and the climate is identical. It has equal parts Bourboulenc, Marsanne and Viognier and ten percent Clairette."

In this manner they worked their way through the tasting, progressing clinically from the smaller whites to the larger, then the lesser reds to the greater, from the younger to the older. David found the 1985 Châteauneuf-du-Pape a spectacular wine. "Deep colour, dark ruby, almost black — big herb, maybe rosemary, slight earthy overtones on dark berry aromas. Luscious fruit, raspberry, hints of chocolate... Tannins obvious, focused, controlled... Very long finish." David spoke his tasting notes as he wrote. "An impressive wine, with a long life ahead," he concluded.

"You have a good perception, you taste well. Look at the '84."

"Deep garnet with ruby core... Truffles, black cherries, spicy dried leaves... Plums, black cherry jam, old leather... Structured, but soft tannins, ready sooner." He finished jotting his notes and continued, "This one will be drinking beautifully for years while we wait for the '85."

"We've not prepared any of the older vintages for you. Do you wish to continue?"

"I would be delighted. Your wines are impressive. I can place whatever you can supply me," David said, having seen the prices on the spec sheets and gambling that supplies are short.

"We've had a heavy demand; three hundred, and sixty bottles is all we can allot to you of the '85 Château de Beaucastel Rouge, the same for the Blanc. We can sell you more of the '84s; there have been negative reports on the vintage and we are left with a stock."

"I saw what Barker wrote. Unfortunately, he's getting a huge flock of sheep who can't taste for themselves, so they trust and follow him instead. My market tastes. I can take six hundred of the '84 red and hope my clients continue to believe in themselves and to trust their own palates."

"It's a very strange development, isn't it?"

"Surely people aren't so gullible to continue much longer following his preference for high alcohol fruit bombs, for heavy tannin, for brett. His dismissal of finesse and nuance surely can't spread much further... But back to your wine, I can use twelve hundred of the Côtes du Rhône, both the red and the white. What older Châteauneuf-du-Pape have you?"

"What are your plans? Have you commitments tonight?"

"I have nothing planned before Aimé Guibert in l'Hérault on Wednesday."

"You know Aimé?"

"We've corresponded and talked by telephone, but this will be my first actual meeting with him."

"He is making amazing wine over there. He's a true pioneer, a maverick... We have some guest rooms in the house, you could stay and join us for dinner, then we can look at the older wines in their proper context."

"I would be delighted."

Chapter Fourteen

Wednesday 26 March 1986

Mas de Daumas Gassac is tucked up near the end of the broad valley of l'Hérault shortly before it narrows into the foothills of the Massif Central. Although it's only thirty kilometres northwest of Montpellier, this is a remote corner of France with only small Départemental roads interrupting its rolling hills. In 1970 Véronique and Aimé Guibert bought an abandoned estate there, along the narrow road from the village of Aniane.

David ran this research information through his mind as he bounced along the narrow, rough road which cut through the garrigue toward the blue hills. *I'm looking forward to finally meeting them.* He had been writing back and forth with Aimé for six months, since he had been captivated by a bottle of the '82 on a sommelier's recommendation at the end of his last trip to France. *The sommelier had called it the Château Lafite Rothschild of the Languedoc. An amazing wine; I can still taste it.*

Véronique and Aimé had been looking for a quiet place to settle and possibly do some farming. In the small creek valley of Gassac, they bought an abandoned farmhouse and the lands around it that had for generations been owned by the Daumas family. On the creek were the foundations of a Gallo-Roman water mill and there were cold artesian aquifers that fed the old mill pond. As they renovated the old *mas*, the local name for farmhouse, they were still trying to decide what to plant. Olive trees? Maize? Vines? They were neophytes to farming, so they sought advice.

Michael Walsh

A close friend was Professor Henri Enjalbert, at the University of Bordeaux, a geologist specialising in the relationship between land and grapes. He had published several works, including *L'Origine de la Qualité*, a book on the origin of wine quality. *What a wonderful book that is. I refer to it often.*

Enjalbert's visit to the property the following year led to events that would dramatically change the wine world's ideas on quality in the Languedoc. The Midi regions across the south of France had long been sources of cheap, coarse wines. Wines which are most often sold in bulk, and in the black and brown plastic bidons on the bottom shelves of the supermarkets. Its price was directly tied to its alcohol degree.

Certainly, there were a few wines of higher quality being produced in the region, mostly on small estates. *They're such a hard sell, though. What a long nose the snobbish wine world looks down.*

Professor Enjalbert saw a mix of terroir and micro-climate he was convinced could grow fine wine. He recommended planting the Bordeaux varieties: Cabernet Sauvignon, Merlot Malbec and Cabernet Franc, besides the local Carignan and Syrah. But he also suggested experimenting with the Tannat of Cahors, the Burgundian Pinot Noir and the Nebbiolo, Barbera and Dolcetto of Italy's Piedmont.

As David crested a small ridge, his eyes tripped over the silvery-green carpet of a lavender field. *Great place to pause, I'm a bit early.* He stepped out of the car and stretched. Then walking through the thyme and rosemary at the road's verge, he enjoyed the aromas released by his passing as he thought.

This'll all be violet in a couple of months. What a magnificent corner of the planet the Hérault is. So different from the Burgundy. Thinking of there, wonder how Louis managed with his brother and sister in Paris. Surely they'd be interested in an extra third of a million each per year. He checked his watch, then turned and headed back toward the car.

He continued reviewing his research on Mas de Daumas Gassac as he drove onward. The first vines were planted in 1972 and while waiting for the vineyards to grow, they began building a cellar and a winery on the foundations of the Roman mill. Beneath the cellar ran two cold aquifers that they utilised for natural air-conditioning to maintain the required temperature year round, even through the torrid Midi summers.

The first vintage was made in 1978 with the guidance and advice of Professor Émile Peynaud, the renowned oenologist from the University of Bordeaux. It was mostly Cabernet Sauvignon, with ten percent Tannat and a bit of Malbec. It sold slowly, mainly to family, friends and some sympathetic restaurateurs. *I wish I had learned of it back then.*

Aimé met him as if he were an old friend as he stepped out of the car. After greetings, Aimé led him up the slope to the office and tasting room above the cuverie. "There is a telex for you in the office. Let's get that first."

David opened the folded sheet and read, *Facsimile came from Henc. Initialled and signed but changed price to 250,000. What do you wish to do? Regards, Jean-Luc.* It was dated this morning. He looked up and tried to hide his disappointment, but he saw Aimé had noticed.

"You have a problem?"

"No, not a big thing. I'm trying to buy an old Dutch barge in the Burgundy, and the owner is being a bit difficult. I'll deal with it later." He folded the telex and put it in his breast pocket. "I continue to hear great things about your wine."

"A tjalk? A luxemotor?"

"A luxemotor. You know Dutch barges?"

"We have friends with a converted tjalk over in Frontignan. We cruise with them often on the Canal du Midi and through the Camargue." With a chuckle, he added, "They are always eager to have us come with our wines. Do you want to send a reply to the telex now?"

"I can do that later, after I run a response through my head. A bit of wine usually allows me to see things more clearly."

"Come, we'll go down and start with the '85 in barrel." He led through the cuverie, the fermenting room, explaining that the cold springs beneath the floors keep the temperature down to allow a long, slow fermentation and maceration to extract the maximum from the fruit.

"This has the austerity of a better classified Bordeaux, so remote to the style of Languedoc," said David as he continued to nose the glass. "Herbaceous, leathery, bright berry fruit, hint of spice," mumbled David as he scribbled his notes. "Dense, not overpowering, restrained like a Cos. Blackcurrant, firm structure, gentle tannins. Long. Very firm finish."

"It sounds as if you like my wine," Aimé chuckled.

"How much of this can you sell me?"

"We'll bottle about 60,000 of this at the end of the year, twenty percent more than last year, but I have so many orders. The first vintage, 1978, we made not quite 18,000 bottles, but we couldn't sell them all, so I put them aside to start a library. Our vineyards were only six years old then. The next three vintages gave between 40,000 and 42,000, then in the extremely hot 1982, production fell to 25,000. Even with that, I thought we would still have some left to put aside in the library. The big review publicity began in October 1982 with Gault-Millau. We moved prices up to try to slow the demand but had very little left.

"We raised prices strongly the next vintage to slow the demand. Nearly all 53,000 bottles were spoken for. Bad publicity on the '84 French vintage slowed sales a bit, so I still have bottles of it beyond what I want for the library. This is my long answer to your question."

"And the short answer?"

"Four hundred and eighty bottles in wooden cases of twelve. Forty cases only."

"Done!" David said, almost shouting, and a little surprised by his impulse, he paused and added, "I don't even know the price yet." He often caught himself committing to purchases emotionally, impulsively, but the results had so far all turned out superbly. He had learned that if he is passionate about a wine, his clients also will be.

"I like your style. Even I don't know the price yet, but it will be fair for us all. It will reflect demand."

"So how did you decide to move here?"

"My wife accepted a position at the University of Montpellier and we looked for a place close to the city, but out in the country. We had been in Paris and wanted more room. It's strange how events turn; I had no background in wine. For generations, my family were tanners and glove makers."

"You're now planning to make a white, I understand."

"Yes, this year we will make our first. We have vineyards of maturing Viognier from cuttings of Georges Vernay's vines in Condrieu. We also planted Muscat Petit Grain and Chardonnay, but the blend will be over half Viognier... Lunch?"

"I will be honoured to join you."

"Good, we can look at wines from the library."

Chapter Fifteen

Thursday 27 March 1986

Before David left Mas de Daumas Gassac, he telexed Jean-Luc, instructing him to counter with an extra 10,000 Francs, adjusting the offer to 235,000. He also told him to inform Henc this is his final offer, and to add that he is thinking of heading to the Netherlands where the selection is dramatically larger.

His intention had been to spend three days in the south, with little itinerary, mostly exploring and relaxing, but now contrary to plans, after his tastings and business at Château Vignelaure and only one night in Les Baux, he was well on his way back north. He had an appointment in Kayserberg on Tuesday in the Alsace, and a few leads to pursue in other wine villages nearby. Likely his anxiousness about the barge brought him back to the Burgundy. In the late afternoon, he parked in front of Hôtel Lameloise in Chagny at the southern edge of the Côte d'Or.

He had phoned from Les Baux to reserve a room. "Yes, we have a room for you, Monsieur Michaels, but for one night only, we are full all the weekend. It is Easter, you know. Do you wish just the room and breakfast or *demi-pension*?"

"Is Jacques in the kitchen tonight?"

"Let me check." Half a minute later she confirmed, "Yes, he is here tonight."

"Can I reserve a table for dinner?"

"No, Monsieur, I am sorry, we are full."

"Then I'll take demi-pension, please."

"Oui, Monsieur Michaels, we look forward to seeing you again."

David loved Lameloise. He had first dined here in 1975 on his way back through the Burgundy from climbing. Louis had brought him as a treat on a wine marketing visit, and he had been deeply impressed with the dinner. At the time the restaurant had two Michelin stars, which Jacques had taken over from his father in 1971. Jacques maintained the two stars, and then in 1979, he became the youngest chef in France with a third.

David preferred to dine free-style, à la carte. But by taking demi-pension, which is room with dinner and breakfast, he was limited to a simpler menu. At least it secured him a table, and if he wished, he could supplement, he could ramble off menu. He asked, "What time can I have a table?"

"You can come at eighteen thirty or at twenty-one thirty."

"Great! Put me down for twenty-one thirty." He much preferred dining late. *Don't have to rush from the table for later diners. It caps the day, is wonderfully open-ended and has no loose bits afterwards.*

He pulled back the drapes in his room, drew aside the sheers and slid the stuffed chair to the window to sit there, gazing out northward over the square. Basel, Vaud, Zurich and Glarus were the Swiss he could see. The Germans were Freiburg, Wiesbaden and K. *Can't remember what K is.* Most of the French licence plates in the parking lot were 21, Côte d'Or and 71, Saône-et-Loire. The dividing line between these two départements is the Canal du Centre, just up the street.

Thought of the canal reminded him he should phone Jean-Luc to find out what has evolved with the barge. But thinking, *If the answer is no, it may spoil my evening. If the answer is yes, it will still be yes tomorrow,* so he went back to his licence plate checking. Other French plates were 69 from the Rhône, two 75s from Paris and an 89 from the Yonne — *that's it, Cologne, the K is for Cologne, Köln in German. I must find a way to remember that more easily.*

For as long as he could remember, he had been interested in analysing licence plates, looking for both number combinations and origins. Here he was able to analyse the client base of the hotel and the restaurant. Though many plates were hidden from his view, those he saw told a story. There were more out of region and out of country plates than local. The cars were decidedly upscale, mostly Mercedes and BMW, and there was a Talbot and a Bentley, though the plates on them were hidden.

As he sat there, he had been listening to the creak, thud, rattle, click of the closing shutters draw closer. There was a gentle knock on the door, and he answered with, "Allo."

"Voulez-vous me fermer la fenêtre? Darf ich das Fenster zu schließen? May I close the window?" asked the voice on the other side of the door.

"Thank you, no. I'll close the shutters myself later. I'm enjoying the view outside."

"Oui Monsieur, bonne soirée, enjoy your evening."

David continued sitting in the window, with the receding creak, thud, rattle, click punctuating the calm evening. Occasionally, as if in echo, there was a similar set of sounds from up or down the streets as Chagny gradually closed itself for the night. He relaxed and read over his notes from the past few days of tasting. He was very pleased. New suppliers. New friends. Many great wines; a lot firmed up. He was looking forward to dinner.

At twenty-one thirty he was led to his favourite two-top in the back corner of the main floor of the restaurant. He could survey the whole room from his seat against the wall. Corners are by far his favoured position in a room. As he relaxed into the place, he smiled at the memory of a woman he had seen for a while. *She absolutely hated the corners, wanted to be out in the middle of the room where everyone would see her. She didn't understand why I thought the centre tables are the weakest seats in the house.*

When the sommelier approached, David asked, "Do you still have the '78 Clos-de-la-Roche from Domaine Ducroix?"

"I think we have a few bottles still. Allow me to check."

"If you don't, then bring me the carte des vins."

"Oui, Monsieur," he said as he nodded, turned and left.

He was quickly replaced by a waiter who asked about water and placed le menu on the table.

"A bottle of Pellegrino, please, and la carte."

"But you are pension, Monsieur," he said with a confirming look at his notepad.

"Yes, but often my pleasure is to order à la carte, to supplement, to explore."

"Right away, Monsieur."

David was amused by the strange way some French dining terms are twisted in English, particularly in the United States, and by cross-border contamination, in parts of Canada. *A menu in French is a set meal, usually comprising an appetiser, a main course and a dessert, called entrée, plat, dessert. In English, a menu is the list of food items which are available. In France, this list is called la carte. Dining à la carte is selecting individual items from la carte. In French, an entrée is the entry to a meal, the appetiser. Stupidly, in the United States, the main course is called an entrée...*

He was interrupted in mid-thought by the sommelier.

"Voila, Monsieur, this is a superb choice," he said, presenting the label to David. "How do you know it?"

"I represented the *vigneron* for many years, and now I continue with his son, Louis."

As the sommelier deftly worked the cork out of the bottle's neck, he said, "Their wines are back up to form again, this is so good to see. But we cannot buy their Grands Crus now. Every year they are sold out."

"I think this one, the '78 is the beginning of their return. It was such a great year, it was difficult to make poor wine, and young Louis was back from his studies for over a year by then. Two strong workers — but you know this..." He cut himself off as the sommelier poured a taste.

Still deeply coloured for an eight-year-old, with just the beginning hints of orange-amber at the edges. A perfumed mix of black cherry and dark chocolate and cake spices on the nose, he thought as he buried himself in the wine. He took a sip and nodded to the sommelier as he moved the wine through his mouth. He set the glass on the table and continued to enjoy the sip, pulling air over it to extract all its messages.

"Do you wish it decanted?"

"No, thank you, I'll play with it for a long while and watch it slowly evolve." He patted the side of the table nearest the wall.

The sommelier poured more wine into the bottom of the big ballon, placed the wicker cradle on the table where David had indicated, then nodded and left.

David knew sommeliers want to control the wine, to be always there to pour, but they also know when not to. He studied the menu and the carte side-by-side, accompanied by sips of wine. A basket of breads had arrived, and he started into it. *I haven't eaten since my late breakfast, well maybe I could call it brunch,* he thought as he set the menu aside and closed the carte.

A waiter saw the signal, and was quickly at the table. "Oui Monsieur, you have decided?"

"On the menu, I see the *noix de ris de veau* as a plat, but not an entrée. Can I have the sweetbreads done as an entrée? Then I would like as a second entrée, the *Foie gras de canard avec queue de boeuf confite* from the carte. For the main, I would like the *Poularde de Bresse et morilles.*"

"I will ask about the ris de veau, Monsieur."

"Tell the Chef Lameloise it's for David from Vancouver." He swelled in anticipation.

Chapter Sixteen

Friday 28 March 1986

After a wonderful dinner and a restful sleep at Lameloise, David had read the news about the wine theft and rushed north to Morey-Saint-Denis to comfort Catherine.

She had fallen asleep laying against his chest as he rubbed the back of her head. *She must be exhausted, probably up most of the night waiting for Louis to return. Emotionally drained.* He sat there for the longest time, watching random thoughts cross his mind. Incongruent things, non-sequiturs. *I like this, being with a woman. So peaceful. So different.* He looked down at her in his arms. *She's so beautiful. But she belongs to Louis.*

He sat there quietly and allowed the thoughts to come and go. *I've never been this close to a beautiful woman before. It's not as scary as I thought it would be.*

The ringing phone didn't register at first; it was a distance away, across the long salon and into the smaller one which Catherine and Louis use as an office. The ringing woke Catherine, though, and she was still trying to shake off her sleep as she rushed across the long room and disappeared through the doorway.

"David — David, it's for you, it's Jean-Luc Delong."

David's mind spun as he strode across the salon. *The barge, I hadn't thought about the barge since Chagny — only a few hours ago. God! That seems so long ago now.* Then taking the offered receiver from Catherine, he said to her, "It's the barge broker."

"Hello, Jean-Luc, you are well?" He listened, then, "Yes, yes it was a very successful trip south. I left Les Baux unexpectedly, thank you for tracking me." He paused with his ear to the phone. "That's great! Wonderful! So did he add anything else this time?" David's face relaxed as he listened. "I can come in and do that tomorrow..." Then he paused and looked at Catherine. "But there's a serious, complicated situation I'm in, and maybe..."

"David, please go ahead," Catherine cut in, rolling her forearms as a paddle-wheel. "Things must go on. We can't stop our lives."

David continued into the receiver, "What time tomorrow is good for you?" After another short pause, "Yes, eleven thirty would be fine. Can I go look at the barge again after?" He listened again. "Great! See you tomorrow, then."

He turned to Catherine. "The offer has been accepted. I need to visit Jean-Luc tomorrow to initial and sign revised papers."

"I want to come with you, is that alright? I'd love to see the barge, to see what you've selected."

"Are you sure? Shouldn't you stay here?"

"For what?"

"In case there's a phone call from the Gendarmes or from Louis or from Murielle. Besides, you need to relax."

"I can't relax here alone."

He slowly nodded his head. "No, I guess you're right."

"We can put a message on the answering machine tape, leave a note on the table for Louis and Murielle, and notify the Gendarmerie to tell them Jean-Luc's number if they need to contact us immediately. We need to keep living, David, not wither and die."

David liked the way Catherine had approached this. *She's looking at the broad picture and seems unafraid to venture beyond the familiar. I like the way she has quickly moved on, not getting mired in the muck of the situation. She rather reminds me of my own nature.* "Yes, let's do that. You must be hungry, have you eaten anything?"

"Cheese and fruit from the pantry last night. I couldn't cook. A croissant and coffee this morning. A tea and some biscuits a while ago when you were with the gendarmes." She glanced at her watch. "Quite a while ago. Seems I slept for a long time. Yes, I'm hungry, and I'm sure he is too." She patted her tummy. "You're hungry also, I'm sure." Then taking David by the arm, she lead him toward the kitchen.

She looked in the fridge and saw nothing fresh. "I suspected this. Murielle in her efficiency would have planned to leave nothing to spoil while she was away." Then she saw two large covered casseroles on the lowest rack. The note taped on one read, *Bresse au Vin, chauffer au four moderée 45 minutes.* A note on the other read, *Ragoût du Pintade et Cèpes, au four bas une heure.* On the next shelf up, was a large quiche wrapped in plastic film with a simple *Lorraine* taped on its top.

"Aah, Murielle, dear sweet Murielle." She stood staring into the fridge and trembling, her eyes welled, and she croaked a low, "David, come hold me."

After a long, gently swaying hug, Catherine had regained much of her composure, but her voice was still trembling a bit when she said, "We should close the fridge door." In a slightly more controlled voice, she asked, "What would you like for dinner?" Then, back in form she continued with, "This evening, Monsieur Michaels, we have *les spécialités de la maison, le Poulard de Bresse au Vin ou le Ragoût de Pintade et Cèpes...."* She trailed off, smiling to herself.

"The pintade sounds wonderful; I've not had guinea fowl for some time." Giving her a gentle squeeze, he unwrapped his arms from around her and closed the fridge door. "You're a very strong woman, and I admire the way you're handling this. We both know this is an awful situation, but we're not going to let it ruin the rest of our lives. We need to continue to be strong. Events can challenge us, but it's our choice on how to respond. We can be controlled by circumstances, or we can choose to remain in control... But you know this, Catherine, don't you? I needn't be lecturing."

Catherine, much more relaxed now, reopened the fridge and lifted the Pintade casserole from the shelf and turned on the oven. "Go down to the cellar and bring up some wine... Oh, my God, I hope they didn't take that too." She stood staring across at the door on the other side of the kitchen.

David already had the key off its hook from the pantry door and was turning toward the cellar door as she finished. Half a minute later he called up the stairs, "It's all here, it's safe. What would you like?"

"Thank God! Bring up something big — I need something big right now."

"A Grand Cru?"

"For sure — an old one."

David came back up, cradling a bottle in his arm and locked the cellar door behind him.

"And what has le sommelier chosen for us this evening?" she asked, straightening up from the oven and turning to watch him.

"I had this last night at Lameloise, the '78 Clos-de-la-Roche. It's a magnificent bottle. I'm sure it will be even more superb shared with you."

He placed the bottle in a cradle on the counter. "I'll go down the street to the boulangerie for a baguette to soak the sauce." After glancing at his watch, he continued, "They should still be open for quarter hour. I'll be right back."

"Told you I'd be right back," he laughed as he opened the door again half a minute later. "I just thought, you should phone Francine and Pierre again in Paris. They've not yet returned your calls."

Chapter Seventeen

Saturday 29 March 1986

David took the narrow D-109 from Vougeot and angled across to the D-116 at Villebichot, which he followed past l'Abbaye de Cîteaux. "Have you visited the abbey?" he asked Catherine.

They had been quiet since they crossed from vineyard to wheat stubble a few kilometres back. "No, I haven't, I'm sorry to say. We seem to always be too busy to do much else than wine. It looks interesting, tell me about it."

"It was founded in the eleventh century, and it's the birthplace of the Cistercian Order, and it's a wonderfully spiritual place to visit."

"I'm not religious. I stopped going to Mass when I left home; it had nothing for me. It had nothing for me long before that."

"Spirituality and religion aren't necessarily related, in fact, religion often subverts, even deadens true spirituality."

"You think that too?" She looked at him with a surprised expression. "I thought I was the only one who thinks that."

"There's a sentence inscribed in a stone in there in the abbey." He turned his head and nodded toward it. *"Listen carefully, my son, to the master's instructions, and attend to them with the ear of your heart.* I like that, listen with your heart, with your soul, as I like to say. Deep inside we know what's right, it's our minds which try to convince the other way."

"I've always known this, but the nun called me a blasphemer when I mentioned it and I questioned my need to memorise Catechism. She said I would burn in hell. I was still so young, and she scared me with evil thoughts and images."

"It's through our minds that religions trap us. Mohammed, Buddha, Christ, Krishna, none of them would like what so many of their professed followers have done, and still do with their messages."

"It took me a long time to realise I wasn't evil, not a sinner, not born with sin. What a mind fuck... Oops!" She giggled and reddened a bit. "But it's the truth, they've buggered our minds, buried our true spirit under layers of guilt and ritual and deceit."

"Guilt, ritual, deceit, exactly. When I was in Grade Two and being prepared for my first communion, I was taught to lie by the nun. Sister Mercedes, the school principal, we called her Mert, told us everybody sins. We are all guilty. When I told her I had no sins to confess, she took me aside and told me, '*You must confess your sins to the priest to receive forgiveness and penance.*' She told me to make-up some sins, told me I must confess, otherwise, I'll remain an unforgiven sinner and cannot receive communion."

"You too?" Catherine bounced in her seat with delight. "That sounds similar to my story. When I was innocently young, I would rattle off the same list of sins. I lied three times, I disobeyed Papa twice, and I touched myself once. What sins did you create for the priest?"

"The same ritual, but I didn't mention the touching. I didn't think it was a sin."

"I lied about mine. It was always more than just once," she giggled, then blushed lightly.

They arrived on the north side of Aiserey, and he looked at his watch. "We have about twenty minutes to spare. Canal de Bourgogne is just across there." He raised his arm to the windscreen. "About fifteen hundred metres. Do you want to go see it?"

"Oh, yes, I'd love to. I haven't looked at a canal for so long. I have such fond memories of my summer on the péniche…" She trailed off.

"It's not an exciting stretch from the Saône across the plain to Dijon, straight as an arrow for thirty kilometres, except for one slight bend that's barely five degrees. Then it leaves the plain shortly before Dijon, and after it curves through the city, it becomes increasingly beautiful as it winds its way up a narrow valley across the northern end of the Côte d'Or."

He stopped in the middle of the little bridge, and they looked left and right, up and down the canal. "See, I told you it was straight." Below them to their left was a lock. To the right, the canal tapered through the overhanging trees into the distance with a big brown shape in its centre, quite close.

"Look!" Catherine said with excitement, "a péniche is coming."

David moved off the bridge when he saw a car in his mirrors, and he pulled into the start of the towpath downstream. "Looks unladen, very high in the water."

"I preferred being unladen on my uncle's péniche. There was a much better view over the banks. Sometimes when we were heavily loaded, I couldn't see beyond the banks at all and I would climb up and stand on the hold covers." She pointed to the péniche alongside the quai. "Like that one. Deep in the water. This takes me back to that wonderful summer. I'm so glad we've come. We'll have to go exploring with…"

"We need to be going, we still have thirteen and a half kilometres to Jean-Luc's office."

"Thirteen and a half? Not thirteen? Not fourteen? Thirteen and a half?" she asked with a wide impish grin.

"Look, the *bourne* over there." David pointed to the squat stone marker beside the towpath, just ahead of the car. "It shows 232. This is two hundred and thirty-two kilometres from the start of the canal in Migennes, across the pass on the Yonne," he explained as he backed the car onto the road and started back across the bridge. "I'll zero the trip odometer, and we'll see how close I am."

"You still haven't explained the thirteen and a half."

"Then allow me to continue." He smiled at her. "At the end of the canal, just beyond the last lock is bourne 242, ten kilometres from here.

But we can't drive down the canal, and we are fifteen hundred metres off the road that goes through Aiserey and then the road winds through Brazey and around Saint-Usage before we reach Jean-Luc's office on the quai in Saint-Jean-de-Losne. I figured the winding and bending, and the distance through town to the office will add another two kilometres to the route, not much more, not much less, so I said thirteen and a half."

The odometer was trying hard to turn from thirteen point four as he parked in the empty slot a few cars short of the office. Catherine was grunting and rolling her hands in encouragement. "Come on, you can make it, just a bit more."

He pointed to the grey Citroën three cars ahead. "If there had been an empty space up there, my estimate would have been closer."

"You studied geometry, trigonometry in university?" she asked as he opened the door for her and offered his hand.

"I dropped out of school. I had trouble with math, but I'll explain this later. Right now we need to focus on buying a barge."

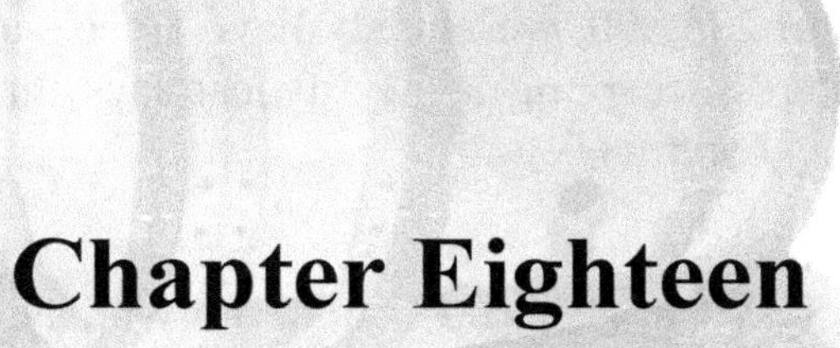

Chapter Eighteen

"Jean-Luc, this is Catherine," David introduced, as they were greeted in the doorway. "She's the wife of my dear friend and wine supplier, Louis Ducroix."

After the casual formalities, David continued, "You've probably read or heard of the wine theft and missing people this week on the Côtes." Seeing the nod, he added, "it's Catherine's husband and their maid who are missing."

"Christ! Merde! This is so terrible! Are you okay?"

David gave a brief outline of events, in a calm, regulated manner, skimming and filtering to the basic facts as he monitored Jean-Luc's response.

"But this is all so terrible. Are you sure you want to be here? Shouldn't you be doing something to find them?"

"I don't think that's safe. If Louis and Murielle are missing because of malfeasance, it's not safe for us to go poking around searching. The gendarmes have already done a thorough search of the property. Twice now. I think it best to leave this to them."

"Incroyable! We need to sit." He pointed to chairs.

"We need to do something to distract us from this," Catherine said. "Let's talk about barges or the weather, or, or…"

"She's right, Jean-Luc, let's set this aside for the moment. The Gevrey Gendarmes have your phone number so they can contact us, and the local Gendarmerie here can track us down through you if they need to. Let's carry on. The paperwork?"

"The ink on the facsimile paper is fading already, this is why we need original paper. I have photocopied the sheets, here," he said as he opened the folder on his desk and turned it toward David. "You need to initial the amendment to 235,000, we already have Henc's and Maddie's initials and signatures accepting it. My avocat says this will make it a complete, binding contract."

"Done, anywhere else?"

"No, that's it. My avocat also said I could draw-up a clean set of paper with the amended information and have it signed and witnessed by both parties if you wish, but he said the photocopied facsimile pages, bundled with the fading pages and the originals are sufficient. We can go ahead and confirm the haul-out for survey next Thursday."

"Can we now go see the barge?" Catherine asked, "I'd love to see it... Her — I should call her her, shouldn't I? I don't even know what her name is."

"Yes, boats, barges, ships are called her. She's *Vrouwe Catharina*, let's go introduce you to each other."

"What is Frowa?"

"That's the Dutch word for 'Lady'."

"And Catharina? That sounds like my name."

"Yes, she was christened the Dutch equivalent of Lady Catherine in 1928."

"No! This is incredible! I really must meet her."

"Two cars or one?"

"We'll go with you, Jean-Luc, I don't need an escape hatch this time."

Jean-Luc laughed, "That's a terrible péniche, isn't it? I'm glad it didn't scare you completely away."

They got into the grey Citroën and continued along the one-way street beside the quai, and as they approached the slipway, Jean-Luc said, "We can stop in now and confirm the haul-out."

"No, let's do that when we get back. Right now I want to introduce two beautiful ladies to each other."

"The river is quite high, and it looks like it's continuing to rise," Jean-Luc said after he had looped through town and was driving onto the bridge. "I didn't look at the gauge this morning, but last night it was still a good way below the PHEN mark."

"What's the fen mark?" Catherine asked.

"P-H-E-N, that's the abbreviation for *Plus Haut Eau Navigable*, the highest navigable water level. When the water reaches the PHEN line on the bridge abutment below us, the river is closed to navigation."

A while later, as they walked along the grassy bank after their short drive, Catherine exclaimed, "She's beautiful! She looks so proud sitting there. She's so much smaller than my uncle's péniche; a little sports car compared to a big dumper truck."

"The same difference in grace, too," David replied.

They spent nearly two hours aboard, much of the time with Catherine leading a redesign conference. David had taken her on a slow exploration from forepeak to aft cabin, pointing out his thoughts and ideas. Then she sat, pulled a pencil and sketch pad from her shoulder bag and began to draw plans, sending David and Jean-Luc off on measuring expeditions, turning pages and rendering plan views, elevations, obliques, sections and perspectives. When David complimented her work, she admitted studying mechanical drafting, and that she had started into architectural, before changing direction.

It was mid-afternoon by the time they stepped ashore, and she bade *Vrouwe Catharina*, "*À bientôt!*, until very soon!" After a brief stop at the slipway office to confirm the haul-out, they enjoyed a crêpe with Jean-Luc on the patio of le Navigation, a small café along the quai.

They drove back toward the Côte, and as they approached Cîteaux, Catherine suggested they stop for a visit. David had been unsure of the reception; it was Holy Saturday, and from his years as an altar boy, he knew it was a very full day for Catholic clergy. Surprisingly, they were welcomed in, shown around, and then they were asked if they would stay for Vespers.

Michael Walsh

David and Catherine had returned late in the evening and spent a quiet Easter, ignoring the long series of messages on the answering machine tape. The press had identified Domaine Ducroix as the scene of the theft, and there had been calls from many reporters, one particularly annoying one, who left repeated messages. Others were more polite, and many were simply the clicks of the hang-up. There were no calls from Louis, Murielle, Francine or Pierre, nor from the Gendarmerie.

"I still have the chants vibrating my whole being," Catherine said, as they sat Tuesday morning at the kitchen table with their coffee and croissants. "My soul is still gently pulsating."

"Other than sitting under the Chagall windows in Notre Dame de Reims a few years ago and listening to the Gregorian Choir practice, I cannot think of anything close. The choir was one of the few things that I found appealing about my days as an altar boy. We had a fine one at Saint Bernard's, but only for High Mass on Sundays and for Vespers on special days."

David took another sip of coffee. "The other masses Sunday, and those during the week had no choir. They were dead ceremonies. Most of the priests raced through their mandatory service so they could get back to other things. I much preferred serving the eleven fifteen on Sundays, the High Mass."

"But surely they weren't like Saturday night at Cîteaux. That was so special."

"No, nowhere near it. The Holy Saturday Vespers are the longest and most complex of the year. The monks at Cîteaux have spent most of their lives praying, meditating, and practising their chants. They live in peaceful harmony together, and their chants reflect this. Holy Saturday is all about death and resurrection, sandwiched between two big events in the Christian year. I have often thought of it as celebrating being knocked down and getting right back up again. That's likely the lesson the second- and third-century scribes wanted to pass along when they began creating myths around Jesus of Nazareth and writing them as fact. God, how all that's been distorted now."

David had phoned Lieutenant Grattien in Gevrey on Monday morning and asked if there was any development, any news on Louis and Murielle. He had also mentioned the many messages on the answering machine and asked if they would like to listen to or analyse the tape. It had been taken out of the machine and a fresh one inserted.

He also told Grattien that Catherine had not yet received replies from her repeated phone calls to Louis' sister and brother in Paris. She gave details on them, and Grattien said he would request that Paris follow-up.

The phone had rung frequently on Monday, and when Catherine tired of turning reporters away, David had taken over a little less politely. Similarly with knocks on the door. "What inconsiderate bothers these people are," Catherine said, "Don't they realise we have enough bothering our lives at the moment?"

As they sat at the kitchen table after breakfast on Tuesday morning, Catherine was running her finger around the rim of her cup and gazing out of focus across the room. "*Vrouwe Catharina*, my cousins used to call me Lady Catherine when we played."

"Dame Catherine?"

"No, Lady Catherine. They were Irish."

"So that's where the red hair comes from?"

"Oh, for sure. Mamère's family all had flaming heads like this," she said, patting her thick hair and smiling as she picked up a long tress that curled down the front of her right shoulder.

"They would come over to Brittany to visit with you?"

"No, I had gone to live with Mamère's sister and her family in Ireland after Mamère, Papa and my brother were killed in a car accident. That was just after I got back from the summer in the péniche, I was fourteen."

"How did it hap…" He caught himself.

"No, it's okay. No, it was a long time ago. I don't know how it happened, everyone said it was a miracle I'd survived. It looks like I was thrown out of the car when it crashed into the rocks, just before it went over the embankment. A driver had stopped later to look at the view and spotted me bloody and unconscious. We don't know how long after the crash this was."

She unwound the hair from her finger and gazed into David's eyes. "When I came to in the hospital, I was confused, and they said it took me a long while before I realised the doctor was asking me for my name and for my father's so they could let him know I was there."

"Oh, I'm so sorry," David whispered, taking her hand and gently pulsing it.

"The following morning the police found the wreckage."

"And you were only fourteen?"

"It seems everyone is leaving me — you won't leave me, will you?"

"Not until Louis comes back."

Chapter Nineteen

Wednesday 2 April 1986

"So what do we do about the survey tomorrow morning?" David asked into the telephone, then after pausing to listen. "How long do they think it will be up? One second, Jean-Luc," he said, seeing Catherine's concerned face. "I want to tell Catherine so she can follow along with us."

"The Saône's above PHEN, so we can't take the barge down to the slipway tomorrow for haul-out, l'éclusier won't allow us out of the canal onto the river."

"Sorry, Jean-Luc, I was asking you how long they think the flooding will last... That long?"

Catherine broke in. "There's a *conférencier* button here somewhere on the phone... Here!" She pushed it and said, "Hello, Jean-Luc. We can now all continue."

"Bonjour, Catherine — this is better. I will continue. A week, maybe more. The warm weather the last few days and now with the April rains coming early and heavy up in the Vosges, there is much melt in the snowpack and a lot of water coming downstream."

"You've talked with the lock keepers? Or do you just think they'll not let us out?" David asked.

"No, I've not talked with the lock, but when I saw the river above the mark, I called l'Office national de la navigation, and I was told that they have ordered the locks into the river closed."

"Can we head upstream, up canal de Rhône au Rhin? Is there a place to haul her in Dole?"

"There's no facility that can take her until closer to Besançon, and we can't get past Dole anyway, can't even get there actually, the canal enters the Doubs before town and that river is in flood too. We wouldn't be able to get beyond Écluse Prise d'eau."

"What's *Vrouwe Catharina's* weight?"

"I would say twenty-eight, maybe thirty tonnes, let me check the papers, what are you thinking?"

"Is there a mobile crane in the area that can come to the pound and lift, what? Around six or seven tonnes?"

"Why would you want that? — Here it is, she's twenty-nine point two tonnes."

"So a seven-tonne crane would be sufficient, we could probably get away with as little as six."

"I'm not following here."

"Brilliant idea, David," piped in Catherine. "I see where you are."

"Okay, so I'm the only slow one here, then," Jean-Luc said.

David explained, "Lift her stern enough so the surveyor can inspect the propeller, the stern bearing and the rudder bearings. There must be a work raft there he can use." He beamed as he watched Catherine delightedly nodding.

"My thinking, Jean-Luc, is that we already know about her bottom plating, and I've accepted it. The integrity of her hull structure, her ribs, frames and stringers will be checked from inside anyway, through the sole hatches and through the inspection panels in the backs of the lockers and so on. The systems are all inside except the stern gear. That's the only part of her we need to examine out of water. Everything else is above water or inside. With the crane, we can ease the stern up, we don't need the slipway, we don't need the haul-out."

"There are several small construction cranes in the area. I'm sure I can find one available. It will cost less than the slipway."

"Great, we can drink the change."

"I got a phone call from Henc last night telling me he and his wife are driving down today and will stay aboard. They want to be there for the survey and to do any needed work before title transfer. Also to start packing personal things to take off afterwards."

"We look forward to meeting them. Anything else? — Yes, I need to contact the surveyor to tell him the change of plans. He was coming to the barge at nine to begin the mechanical and then do sea trials on the way to the slipway. The timing on the crane can be anytime after that until about thirteen hundred, though preferably much earlier. We can sea trial up the canal."

"Sounds a good plan."

"Phone us if you can't find a crane."

"Don't worry, there are several to choose from. Probably closer than Dijon or Dole. See you at *Vrouwe Catharina* in the morning."

David and Catherine looked at each other with wide smiles; she took a slow step toward him, picked up his hand, and they continued to merge into a long hug. Quiet, comfortable, reassuring.

The gentle moment was shattered by the jangle of the phone.

"Oui! Allo?" Catherine said into the receiver.

"It is Lieutenant Grattien here," said the voice on the other end, and Catherine pushed the conférencier button.

"Your phone has been busy, I have been trying to reach you. Have you news?"

"No, nothing."

"I have some, but it is grave, Madam. Our office in Paris has not been able to trace either Pierre Ducroix or Francine Grotkopf. They have not been to their offices since last Wednesday. You have not heard from either of them?"

"No, no returned calls, nothing at all."

"We will continue, then with plans to enter their homes. This becomes much more complex. And I am sorry to bring you even more bad news

— Philippe Grotkopf has disappeared too. The pharmacy where he works hadn't seen him since 24 March."

"Him too? This is becoming bizarre. Speaking of Grotkopf, have you talked with Laurent Grotkopf in Nuits?" David asked.

"Non, Monsieur, but we are watching closely. We brought in a special team from Lyon to watch them without being seen. It is better now to be quiet and invisible. Do you want security at the domaine? We can place a man outside and one of our women inside in street clothes, looking like workers."

"Is that necessary?" Catherine asked. "Maybe too much…"

"I think it's wise for now," David interrupted her. "This thing has grown strange."

"I will arrange to post two there from this afternoon."

"We'll be away from early tomorrow, gone most of the day. We'll be in Saint-Jean-de-Losne and Saint-Symphorien, and you have our contacts there."

"But you are there at the château his afternoon?"

"Yes."

"Good, I will bring my people over to introduce you to them. You can show them around and familiarise them with the place, show them some common things to do to look normal there."

Mid-afternoon, Grattien brought two gendarmes to the château. The man was in the faded blue overalls of the common French worker. David set him to work picking up winter twigs fallen from the trees, raking the gravel in the courtyard and cleaning the lawns around the château. *The typical snail's pace progress of the French labourer will ensure several days of employment and should fit inconspicuously with the scene. That's if the gendarme can slow down that much.* David chuckled to himself.

Inside, Catherine showed the young female gendarme a variety of cleaning chores to play with if there were visitors or knocks at the door. "We need to donate to your brigade fund in Gevrey." She laughed. "We're getting our spring cleaning done by the State."

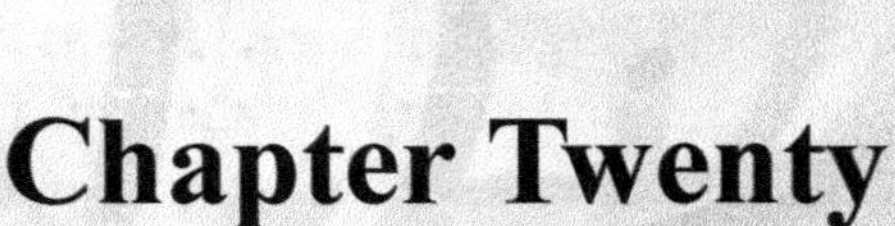

Chapter Twenty

Thursday 3 April 1986

David and Catherine arrived at the old mill at zero eight forty-eight and pulled next to Jean-Luc's Citroën. "Two minutes early," David said, looking at his watch.

"Twelve minutes by my watch," she countered.

"No, two minutes; I always plan to arrive ten minutes before an appointment. This gives me a little wiggle room in case there's a delay. I think it rude to keep people waiting. It shows I don't value their time."

"You surely don't do that with everything?" She looked up and smiled as he opened her door and offered his hand.

"No, on longer trips I begin with more spare time and adjust as I get closer. If I'm ahead of time, I'll pause a short distance away to relax and prepare myself."

"And if you're behind schedule? Maybe you never are," she jousted, as they walked toward Jean-Luc and an elderly couple on the grass verge of the canal. "But if you..."

"Bonjour, Jean-Luc. You have chosen nice weather for this," David greeted, spreading his arms toward the sky.

They were introduced to Henc and Maddie and were casually chatting when Jean-Luc motioned to a car slowly bouncing along the two mud tracks through the grass past the mill. "That's the surveyor."

After another round of introductions, David turned to the surveyor. "Jean-Luc tells me the crane is coming at ten thirty. Where would you like to start?"

"I'll start on deck, forward and work aft, then we can go below and look at the structure and systems. We'll let the crane interrupt us."

The lift went smoothly, Henc and the crane operator devising a set of safe slings with the advice of the surveyor. Maddie and Catherine had stowed everything below for the tilt forward, and Jean-Luc pulled a small painting raft into the space astern the barge. The surveyor was happy lying on it to turn and inspect the propeller and to lever its shaft against the hull to check the bearing clearance. He couldn't see the lower pintle of the rudder, but with a few forceful movements of the rudder and some prying with a lever, he was satisfied with its soundness. He had David turn the helm from lock to lock and back a few times and then shouted, "Good, that's enough."

The remainder of the survey had gone smoothly, and during the short cruise up through Écluse 73 and along the pound to the first winding hole, the surveyor gave a very positive verbal report. They wound around and headed back down through the lock. *Vrouwe Catharina's* old DAF ran smoothly and quietly, not missing a beat.

"I'll deliver my written report tomorrow to Monsieur Delong's office, probably before noon. I'll recommend you proceed with the sale. The only requirements are fresh fire extinguishers and a new bulb in the starboard running light." Then turning from David to Henc, he said, "I am very impressed with your maintenance."

Friday 4 April 1986

Catherine followed in her car as David drove the rental out of Morey-Saint-Denis, across to the N-74, then northward into Dijon and to the train station, to the Europecar office there. Catherine had asked, "Why do we need two cars?" He returned the rental car, cancelled the remainder of its contract, and they continued to Saint-Jean-de-Losne in hers.

"We could close early, you know," Jean-Luc said, as they sat in his office with the written report on the table in front of them. "I see no reason we can't complete now. Henc has put new fire extinguishers aboard and replaced the running light's bulb from his spares."

"There is one reason." David raised his forefinger. "I have a term deposit in Canada which will mature on 7 April, on Monday. I've given my bank instructions to have the proceeds exchanged to Francs and wired to my account over here as soon as it's available. It will arrive on Wednesday, Thursday at the latest, in time for our closing on Friday, our agreed date."

Tuesday 8 April 1986

There had been no trace of the now five missing people, no clues on the missing wine, but fortunately, there had been no fresh problems stacked onto Catherine's full plate. The courtyard and lawns of the château looked meticulously groomed, and Catherine was delighted so much of the interior had been cleaned. The three young female gendarmes who came in shifts hadn't been able to sit around doing nothing.

"I'll go to the box to get Le Figaro — it must have arrived by now." David rose from their breakfast at the kitchen table and headed toward the door.

A half a minute later he returned. "Look at this. Front page — *Franc Devalued. EMS Announces Revised Currencies. Monday morning the European Monetary System announced a 3% devaluation of the Franc. The German Marc and the Dutch Guilder were revalued upwards 3%.*" He read aloud the lead story as he walked across the kitchen.

"Is that good or bad?"

"Yes, it is."

"Which?"

"Both."

"Okay, you're doing that again, aren't you?" She giggled, realising that he had correctly answered. "Is it good?"

"Yes, for me, I got more Francs for my exchange yesterday in Canada. For Henc and Maddie, they get a three percent smaller Franc to exchange into a three percent stronger Guilder. They lose over fourteen thousand Francs, probably over five thousand Guilders with the new rates and the exchange fees, and they still have to pay Jean-Luc his brokerage fees."

"Why do they change the rates? Do they do it often?"

"The system was set up a few years ago, 1979 or '80 to try to keep the European economies in balance with each other. Yesterday, they also revalued the

Danish Krone and the Belgian and Luxembourg Francs up one percent, so the story here reads. This shows that the Dutch and German economies are much stronger, the Dane, Belge and Lux a bit stronger and the French much weaker than those in the other European countries. So, yesterday they balanced."

"How often do they do this?"

"Yes, I forgot that." He smiled at her. "As often as they see the need. This drop in the Franc is probably related to the fall in foreign revenue from decreasing tourism resulting from all the news stories reporting the series of department store bombings in Paris last fall and again this spring. The last rate change I remember was July last year. With that one, the Franc and several of the other currencies went up 2%, so your wines cost me more, and so did the Rheingau and the Mosel wines I had contracted for. The same day, they dropped the Italian Lire a whopping 6%. I saved enough on my Piedmont and Tuscan orders to more than cover the German and French shortfall."

"You like this stuff, playing with money, don't you?"

"Long ago, I realised money is a marvellous tool, but it's not meant to be gathered and amassed for itself. That's a mistake, unless you collect and study it as a hobby, as a numismatist..."

"As a new what?"

"A numismatist. That's the formal word for a coin geek, someone who collects and studies coins."

"You do that too, I'm sure."

"Of course I do." He put up a hand. "But let me continue with my thought. Amassing huge amounts of money has no merit of its own. Its value is in what is done with it. You could use it to stuff your mattress, but that's not its purpose. It's meant to be used as a tool, as a medium of exchange. It makes trade easier."

"This is interesting, I've never looked at money in this way." She looked into her empty cup, then across at his. "I'll pull more coffee if you'll tell me more."

"That's bartering." He chuckled. "Let's imagine in the old days, before money. A man goes to the town to get a bag of wheat to make bread, taking a calf with him to trade. The calf is worth many bags of wheat, but he doesn't want many, only one. With no medium of exchange, he is faced with either paying too much for the wheat or taking much more wheat than he can use or even carry."

David watched Catherine at the espresso machine. *My God, she's so gorgeous.* He shook his head and continued with the story. "The man could take the extra wheat and sit at the side of the road to trade it, but what does he want in exchange, he needs nothing but a single bag of wheat. But none of the grain traders in the town want his calf. Money is the tool that eases trade, that allows commerce to flourish. It was devised and developed as a portable measure and store of value."

"When did money begin? Where?" She spoke over her shoulder as she tamped the coffee in the portafilter.

"Historians disagree on this, as they often do with so many other things. The earliest evidence of grain and cattle being used as items of barter date to about fifteen thousand years ago. But as we have seen, trading with them was difficult. Archaeologists have dated pieces of obsidian related to exchange to about ten thousand years ago in Anatolia, eastern Turkey. The obsidian was the raw material used for making stone-age tools. It was relatively scarce, so it had value. It is strongly believed these bulk pieces were the first money."

"And metal money? When was that?" She pushed the button to start the machine. "This really fascinates me... More, though, I'm intrigued by the sparkle it brings to your eyes."

"I've always been fascinated with it — well not always, only since my grandfather introduced me to coins and collecting with gifts on my eleventh birthday."

"So continue your story — metal money. When? Where?" Catherine brought the coffees to the table.

David moved the cup under his nose, inhaled lightly then took a sip. "You pull a great espresso." He peered into her eyes. "You really are interested in this, aren't you?"

"I'm interested in what drives you, in what drives your intense and diverse interests. You are certainly not a simple person."

"Okay... We know the Egyptians had gold in fixed weights over five thousand years ago as a medium of exchange. There is earlier evidence of silver bars being used in Mesopotamia for exchange. A three-thousand-year-old tomb in China held what is believed to be the earliest coin, a piece of cast copper with designs."

He stopped to take another sip of his coffee, then continued with the story. "Among the first monetary systems was the shekel of Mesopotamia around five thousand years ago. The shekel stood for the value of a measure of barley and also for the equivalent values of silver, bronze and copper."

He paused and thought. *She really is interested; her eyes haven't wandered, they haven't glazed-over.* "Anyway, to cut the story short, much later, the British used this concept of a single unit to stand for both weight and currency. Their original pound was a piece of silver weighing one pound. Dividing this, twelve ounces to the pound…"

"Twelve? No there were sixteen ounces to the pound when I lived in Ireland." She smiled, then with a giggle, she added, "Your math isn't infallible after all."

"Yes, sixteen, you're right, but that's in the avoirdupois system. Money uses the troy ounce; twelve to the pound. You're sure I'm not boring you with this. Women have always been bored with it."

"Not at all, I'm actually fascinated with it. I'm fascinated by your passion for it."

"Okay, but please stop me when you need to breathe." He grinned. "So, with twenty shillings to the pound, twelve pence to the shilling, the first British penny was a piece of silver, weighing one-two-hundred-and-fortieth of a pound."

"When was that?"

"The first are those in the seventh century struck by the Anglo-Saxons. They're the people who invaded Britain in the fifth century at the fall of the Roman Empire. Many of the people they displaced there fled, many of them crossed the Irish Sea, others crossed the Channel to Brittany." He looked at Catherine's rich red hair. "Probably your early ancestors."

"So, what about…"

"Enough about me." He gazed into her eyes. "Your eyes are green like mine, but your hair is much redder. Tell me more about you."

"But my life is so uninteresting compared to yours." She looked down at her finger doing circles around the rim of her cup.

"Let me be the judge about that. Come, tell me about you."

Chapter Twenty-One

Thursday 10 April 1986

David and Catherine were sitting in one of the private banking offices in the Banque Nationale de Paris branch in Place Darcy in Dijon. The accountant had confirmed the wire had come in on Wednesday and had added 265,237.34 Francs to the balance in his account. They were waiting for the drafts to be completed.

When David was giving the accountant instructions, Catherine had asked, "Shouldn't that be for two thirty-five?"

"No," he had replied, "I gave a deposit cheque for ten thousand when I signed the offer. This is the balance, and from the total, Jean-Luc will take his selling commission and give the remainder to Henc and Maddie. This will happen tomorrow with the lawyer when the ship's title is signed over to me. I still have to pay the lawyer's fees and the invoice for the crane that Jean-Luc should have. I paid the surveyor yesterday when he delivered the report."

They sat comfortably as David outlined the process which would be happening the following day, and he was starting into plans for *Vrouwe Catharina* once the deal was completed, when the accountant interrupted.

"Voila! Monsieur Michaels." The accountant looked up as the documents arrived. "It looks as if they are ready. Let us review to make sure they are correct. One for 225,000 to Bourgogne Bateaux en depôt and the other a blank one for 15,000... Yes, they look good."

After the usual, "Anything-else-we-can-do-for-you, Monsieur Michaels?" and other learned sales phrases, as they got up to leave, the accountant added a non-standard, "You have a very beautiful lady, Monsieur Michaels." His eyes were very obviously enjoying Catherine.

"Thank you, I think so too," David replied with a smile as they left and started across the marble floor of the lobby. Halfway across he looked into Catherine's eyes. "Would the very beautiful lady care to join Monsieur Michaels for lunch?"

"Let me check her calendar." Catherine giggled, and after a long pause, she said, "Yes, she would be delighted to fit him in."

Directly across Place Darcy from the bank is Hotel de la Cloche, an elegant grand old building in the architecture of Restoration France. It is wedged into a corner of two streets radiating from the circle that is Place Darcy.

As they walked toward the hotel, David asked Catherine, "Have you ever wondered why they call a circle a square here?"

"What do you mean? Is this another of your geometry quizzes?"

"No, the British — the English language calls this place a square. Place Darcy in the English guides is Darcy Square, but its shape is circular."

"You see such strange things, Monsieur Michaels." She laughed, then added, "But slowly I'm beginning to see them too."

"Please call me David, Madame Ducroix, Lady Catherine."

They laughed as they passed through the doors which had been swung open for them as they approached arm-in-arm. Inside, through the lobby, they headed out the other side and into a garden framed in by the splayed wings of the hotel. The restaurant was sparsely populated; it was still a few minutes before noon. "It has a Michelin star and will soon be crowded. Where would you like to sit?" David asked as they surveyed the room.

"That looks like a lovely place, over there in that corner, under the tree." She nodded across the restaurant.

It was the exact place David had chosen, and he swelled with relief. "You prefer the corners too?"

"Everything can be easily seen from them... So you made three percent with exchange on the deal," Catherine said as they settled into their side-by-side chairs across the corner of the table, facing out into the room.

"A little more than that."

"How's that?"

"The Canadian dollar had risen strongly all last week against Franc, and I gained almost seven percent more than what I had calculated a week ago. But it's much more complex than that."

"You're not going to stop there, are you?"

"It's another long story, are you tired yet of my long stories?"

"Not anywhere near tired of them." She gazed into his eyes as if trying to draw out more.

"It's a complex one, I warn you."

"Spill it out, I'll tell you if I want you to stop."

"Okay, let's see... Aah, let's begin five years ago this week. On 7 April 1981, the official Canadian bank rate was 18.25%. For good clients, the chartered banks were charging 19.5% for loans and considerably higher than that for regular customers. The rates had started up sharply in the winter, and I thought the banks would be looking for money to lend. I started selling spare coins from my collection, assembling money and making term deposits. Lending the banks money, in effect, at the best rates and for longest periods I could find.

"The note which matured this week was my second five year one, $22,000 at just under sixteen percent, compounded monthly. The yield calculation is nearly $48,500, and the wire arrived here in my bank in Dijon after exchange and wire fees as a little over 265,000 Francs."

"So for $22,000 Canadian, you're buying a beautiful barge."

"It's much better than that, actually, there is significant change left over. But the coins I sold for that 1981 deposit had cost me nothing more than many hours of pleasurable searching through rolls in the banks when I was a kid, picking out scarce dates and varieties... Well, that and the face value of the coins and the lost use of that money for the twenty or twenty-five years I had held them."

"How much? I need to know how much. What was the cost of the coins you sold?" Her eyes strained wide in excitement as she shifted and bounced in her chair.

"In a moment — here comes the garçon. Would you care for a glass of wine?"

"The son doesn't want any, but I'll start a glass. You can finish it for me if need be."

David ordered a demi pichet of Aligoté and the two warm goat cheese and walnut salads they had decided on.

"So how much will *Vrouwe Catharina* cost you?"

"I sold a lot of my nickel spares — Canadian five cents pieces are called nickels because of the metal they've been made from since 1922. They were silver before that, but that's another story. I had a small hoard of the scarce dates, 1925 and 26 Far, and a lot of the popular varieties, 46 Bugtail, 47 Dot and the like.

"I also sold most of my spare Victoria and Edward twenty-five and fifty cents pieces but kept the ones in higher grade. It was the result of many hundreds of hours of focused spare time, searching, selecting and setting aside the coins."

"You *are* weird." She laughed. "But I like weird because it reminds me of me... Please continue, I need to know how much."

"There were thirty-five rolls of nickels, twenty rolls of twenty-five cents pieces and twelve rolls fifty cents pieces. So what's that? At two dollars a roll, the nickels come to seventy dollars. The twenty-five and fifty cents pieces are ten dollars the roll. That adds another three twenty, so a total of three hundred and ninety dollars."

"That's a very inexpensive boat." She smiled as she studied his face.

"Essentially, yes, but actually no. I had added significantly to that amount, added my knowledge from focused research, added coins I learned were scarce, added my skill. I had added my intense interest, my heart, my soul and I had added many hundreds of hours of my time. What are those things worth? What is enjoyable time worth?"

"How did you find so many valuable coins?"

David caught the motion of the garçon approaching with the pichet and looked up. "Here's the wine."

When her glass was a quarter filled, Catherine signalled with a small wave, and the pour was stopped. "*Rien pour la bébé,*" she said to the waiter, who then poured David's glass.

"To *Vrouwe Catharina*." Catherine raised her glass.

"To both of them," he added with a broad smile. "I enjoy you..." He paused and blushed. "You're very pleasant to be with."

"As are you. Very enjoyable... Very... So finding the coins..."

"Yes, back to that... At noon, from school. I'd take my peanut butter sandwiches to the banks just down the street. The school was only a block off Main Street, and all the banks were ranged along there, concentrated in four blocks. I'd buy bundles of rolls from the tellers; they all got to know me, and many went out of their way to help me. I'd spend my lunch break at the marble-top tables going through rolls pulling out the keepers and putting them into my right pocket and replacing them with change from my left. When I started, my chin barely made it above the slabs of marble."

He saw her eyes hadn't lost their interest, so he continued. "I'd count and re-roll the coins and initial the ends to indicate which rolls I'd searched. At noon I could do five bundles of fifty cents pieces, there are only twenty in a roll, two hundred in a bundle. I could get through three bundles of the other denominations..."

"Our salads are here." Catherine nodded toward the approaching waiter. "But please continue. Don't worry about talking with your mouth full. I love watching your little boy eyes sparkle."

He enjoyed a bite of warm chèvre and a sip of Aligoté, before he continued. "During the summer and on other holidays I would spend much longer times in the banks. I would go until my eyes turned funny, then walk home with my stash and get more change, before attacking another bank. Most of the bank tellers got to know me, and they soon learned not to give me any of the rolls I had initialled."

"That's a hundred dollars a bundle. Where did you get that much money as a kid? Where did the money come from to put away all the selected coins? Young kids don't have money like that."

"I had a paper route, actually two paper routes, later three. I delivered the *Times* on the way to school in the mornings and the *Transcript* on my way home. My commission was a cent a paper for the afternoon paper, two cents for the big edition on Friday and a cent and a half for the morning *Times*."

"That's not much money — how can you get to a hundred dollars that way? And the money for the coins to put away?"

"If you add it up, it was. My routes grew to eighty in the morning and more than a hundred and twenty in the afternoon. That's seven twenty a week for the morning papers and eight forty for the afternoon, fifteen sixty a week. In those days, from the mid-'50s to the early '60s, my father made sixty dollars a week working very hard. When I was thirteen, I earned half as much as he did by simply enjoying myself and getting lots of exercise."

"But fifteen sixty isn't half of sixty, it's barely over a quarter."

"Yes, but then there were the tips. My grandfather told me about tips, said the word came from *To Insure Promptness*, though I later found out it really didn't mean that. But I learned early that satisfying customers is very important. I never missed a delivery, I would always put the paper where it was wanted, not simply tossed toward the house. If it was raining, I made sure the papers stayed dry and..." He paused for a sip of wine.

"I was rewarded for all this with tips. Many would give me an extra five or ten cents each week. The extra often added up to more than my commission, so I continued to improve my service. Making over thirty dollars a week became normal."

"My God, barely a teenager and already making half your father's wage, and from working only part-time." She stared at him with wide eyes.

"I asked my customers to pay me with the oldest coins they could find each week. I ended up with a lot of Victorian, Edwardian and George the Fifth pieces. One old woman gave me a five cents silver from her hoard every week as a tip. Others dug out old large cents from their stash. I added a lot of pieces to my collection and expanding hoard."

He enjoyed another bite, then resumed. "Later, I began delivering the *Star Weekly* on Saturdays when I went around to collect from my customers. I bought my first car when I was sixteen."

"I'm exhausted just listening to this."

"I told you I'd bore you with it." David turned back to his salad.

"No, not that." She patted his arm to assure him. "Not at all that. I'm exhausted just thinking about how hard you worked, how tired you must have been from delivering all those papers."

His eyes lit up again. "It was on my way to and from school. I made the mile's walk into about four. I had the *Times* drop a bundle on our front porch every morning, and I'd start my zigzag route to school about seven thirty. Carrying all the weight and doing the daily walks allowed me to develop strength and endurance. I became very strong and very fit." He flexed his shoulders and chest.

"The *Transcript*, the afternoon paper, I'd pick up at the newspaper office just four blocks from school. The presses were often just beginning to roll, so I had to wait until the bundles of papers started up the conveyor. I began trading customers with some of the other paper boys to refine and shorten my route."

"I see the image of a young budding entrepreneur."

"He's still here... Still young and still excited inside."

Chapter Twenty-Two

Friday 11 April 1986

David had trouble accepting it had been two weeks since he read those brief two paragraphs in the paper reporting the wine theft. Two weeks since Catherine told him that Louis and Murielle were missing. He quickly realised Catherine needed a focus to keep her mind off the terrible incidents, and he had spent many hours with her recounting things from his past, things he had thought little about until now, and he hadn't hesitated in responding to her questions.

As they drove toward Saint-Jean-de-Losne for their appointment to formally close the purchase, she asked, "So, for your investment, for the five-year deposits — where did you learn how to do it? You must have studied finance or economics."

"I didn't. Don't you remember I told you I had dropped out of school?"

"So where did the knowledge come from?"

"From inside, I suppose. While most people were in panic over rising interest rates, I saw it as an opportunity, a wonderful opportunity. I had learned to listen to myself, to trust my instincts. Some call it risky and seat-of-the-pants, I simply call it living." David smiled to see her nodding in agreement.

"As the bank rate continued to climb, I sensed I needed to do something. In June, I resigned my naval commission, took severance pay and return of pension contributions. In July, I sold my house and put everything I could scrape together into term deposits. Some for two years at 19.5%, some for three years at 18.75% and one huge ten year one at just over

17%. In August the bank rate peaked a little short of 23%. Then it steadily declined."

"Throwing away your naval career, your house, your stability. Those are rash moves aren't they?" She seemed shocked.

"I had peaked in the Navy. In each of my previous three postings, I had replaced a Lieutenant-Commander, and when I was posted onward, I was replaced by a Lieutenant-Commander. I was a Lieutenant with an after-the-fact high school diploma. Actually, a Captain for a while as dumb-thinkers in Ottawa integrated the system too far, forcing Army ranks on the Air Force and Navy. During that mess, Admirals resigned, not wanting to be called Generals." He shook his head.

"Anyway, I got the clear message; I could go no further in the hierarchical system that demanded university diplomas and gave little value to innate intelligence or ability."

As David slowed for the stop sign at the D-996, Catherine pointed to l'Abbaye de Cîteaux. "That was such a splendid experience," she said with a sublime look on her face. "My whole being vibrates when I think of it... But back to your story."

"Yes, it *was* sublime, wasn't it? — Where was I? — Resigning my commission. I was being very well paid, but I made much more as a coin geek and a wine importer on the side. I realised I would likely go no further in the Navy, and it became increasingly obvious my commission was holding me back, restricting my free movement." He looked at her and shrugged.

"They offered to put me through university, but the prospect of surrendering my being to the system again — I had endured many months of high school make-up in 1967 and early '68. Not as bad as the first go through, but the thought of four more years of being crammed with others' ideas, my creativity being dismissed, my mind muddled with information and mired in concepts..." David let out a deep sigh.

"My being, my soul demands that I know — not simply know about. The idea of being crammed with unknown thoughts, filled with foreign stuff, repulsed me. I couldn't do it."

Looking intensely into Catherine's eyes, as they paused for cross-traffic in Brazey-en-Plaine, he asked, "Do you know the source of the word education?"

"No, I've never thought of it."

"Think of educe, to draw out and educo, to lead forth. I have long considered education as being the process of inspiring people to draw from within. Certainly, there is a need to add a layer of fundamentals and facts as a base to examine against, to dissect and to compare what comes from within. But the focus on the continual cramming-in of information hinders the process. It blocks the creative flow of free-thinking minds. It turns the creative among us away from the modern educational system. That's the main thing I learned in school."

David shook his head again. "For the vast majority, the malleable, the non-creative people, the mass education system works well. For a few, it fails, and we are left to educate ourselves…"

Catherine broke in. "Now I'm starting to realise why I didn't want to go back to school when I moved to my aunt's in Kenmare. I had never stopped to ask myself why. I had simply accepted it as being from the shock of the death of my parents — and my brother."

They remained silent for a long while until they arrived in Saint-Jean-de-Losne. David could almost hear the cogs turning in her head, the creak of doors opening, the memories flooding out, the stream of realisations.

"I've never examined those experiences. So much is buried in bad feelings I didn't understand — still don't understand. I need to look at those things. Can you help me? Will you listen?"

"I was hoping you would ask. Do you want to start now?" He pulled to a stop on Quai National. "We can sit here for as long as you wish, for as long as you need."

"We'll be late for our rendezvous if I start now. Let's go in and finish the deal, then we can go sit in *Vrouwe Catharina*, and you can listen to Lady Catherine spill her guts." She looked at him with a slightly crooked smile.

Henc and Maddie were in Jean-Luc's office as they entered, and they were still greeting as the lawyer arrived with a folder of papers. David pulled the envelope from his breast pocket and gave the larger of the drafts to Jean-Luc. After Henc and Maddie had signed the transfer, and the lawyer had witnessed and stamped it, David handed Henc the other draft.

"What's this?"

"You lost a lot of money with the EMS adjustments on Monday. I made a lot. I hope this helps."

"Fifteen thousand Francs! This is too kind of you."

"It simply takes the price back up to what you were asking in the counter-offer. The bad exchange takes it back down to where we settled. This costs me no more than I had bargained for, so why should I gain and you lose? I cannot do business that way."

"But this is so unusual, I don't know what to say."

"You need say nothing. Just know that it's right."

After their lunch in Dijon on Thursday, David and Catherine had walked along to Nicolas to select a bottle of Champagne to rechristen *Vrouwe Catharina*. He had been delighted to find a bottle from Bruno Paillard, the young maverick producer from Reims whom he represents in Canada.

Instead of the old tradition of smashing the bottle over the prow of the ship to wet her bows, David prefers wetting throats. So he was into his second flute of Champagne, and Catherine was still nursing her first, remembering what the doctor had said about the baby, as they lounged back into the deep cushions of *Vrouwe Catharina's* saloon settee.

"You're a strange businessman, David. You gave Henc and Maddie fifteen thousand more than the contract. A few weeks ago you offered us much more for our wine than we are asking. I don't understand this."

"To me, it's fundamental business, Catherine. There are three people, three parties in my wine dealings. The producers at one end, my customers at the other and me in the middle. A proper deal needs all three to be satisfied. I need to sell at a price that pleases my customers and makes them want to continue buying from me. I need to give the producers enough to allow them to continue producing top quality wine and wanting to sell more of it to me. In the middle, I need to make enough to cover my expenses and have a little left over. Good business has all parties satisfied."

"Yes, but Henc and Maddie didn't appear unhappy with the transaction, and you won't have to deal with them again."

"Maybe *they* weren't unhappy, but *I* was. I needed to adjust the balance so I can feel comfortable about the deal."

"You *are* a strange man, but I like this kind of strangeness."

"And you're a lovely lady with so many things turning in your head. Let some out, share it with me. Talking about it helps."

She stared at the bubbles streaming up from the bottom of the Champagne. "I had never fit in," she began slowly. "I was always thinking in another direction, wanting to go a different way, not be a part of the crowd. My teacher, the nun in my seventh school year told me I was too proud. She took me aside to lecture me, telling me pride is a sin. I didn't understand her and asked for an explanation. She slapped me, told me to stop being so proud." Catherine closed her eyes and grimaced.

"I pretended to be sick so often that spring so I didn't have to go to school. I played weak and headaches and nausea. That's the year I started bleeding, so I had to say it wasn't from that. The doctor could find nothing wrong, and he told my mother it was only my adjustment to my cycle."

She shook her head and stared again at the bubbles rising in her Champagne. "Fortunately, the school year soon finished, and Mamère had finally let in to my pleas and allowed me to go spend the summer on the péniche. That was such a wonderful summer..." She paused for a long while.

"Some nuns have rather evil streaks," David said to continue the flow. "My sixth grade teacher, Sister Leonora was an angel, a truly delightful woman, but my seventh grade teacher, Sister Mercedes was the devil incarnate. She was into physical and emotional abuse... Were you slapped and abused often?"

"Just that once, but after that, I went out of my way to avoid her — I can't even remember her name. When it looked like I wouldn't be able to avoid being alone with her, I played sick. Maybe I actually was sick from the fear of her. She wrote a horrid report on my character at the end of the school year. I've often wondered why such people are allowed to influence young and impressionable souls and minds."

Catherine stopped her reminiscing there, and they talked of other more pleasant things. David tried a few times to gently turn her back toward her school days, but she veered away from the area, and he didn't push.

Before they left to head back to Morey, they walked along to the lock house at Écluse 75, the first lock of the canal, or the last, depending on the direction of travel. This is the seventy-fifth lock down from the summit in the Vosges at the border with the Alsace. The flooding on the Saône had crested on Monday, and the level had slowly subsided, revealing the PHEN line on the bridge abutment Wednesday evening.

David informed l'éclusier that they wished to descend at 1030 on Saturday and head down to the canal de Bourgogne. He was told that locks 74 and 75 would be ready for him unless there was a commercial at that time.

As they drove back toward Morey, Catherine asked, "What did the lock keeper mean with the commercial? I thought only television was interrupted by them."

David laughed, "Commercial is the term used for a commercial barge. They have priority over pleasure traffic on inland waters. If one approaches or is scheduled when we want to pass through a lock, we have to wait. You must have seen some of this that summer on the péniche."

"No, I don't remember it — I don't remember any pleasure boats, either — or maybe I just didn't recognise them. My mind was filled with dreams, I was celebrating my freedom from school, from that evil nun..." She stopped again.

Chapter Twenty-Three

Saturday 12 April 1986

Dressed in Louis' blue work trousers and a bulky maroon wool sweater, Catherine looked like a seasoned deckhand as they motored *Vrouwe Catharina* past the upstream gates and into Écluse 74. She looked at her watch, and from the foredeck, she called back to David in the wheelhouse, "You're twelve seconds late for the ten thirty rendezvous."

He chuckled. "I'll try to improve. This is only our first lock."

Vrouwe Catharina handled easily, responding to his measured helm and engine movements and she slowly came to rest against her fenders alongside the starboard rim of the full chamber. Catherine pointed at a bollard as she looked back to David, and seeing his exaggerated nod, she dropped the eye of the mooring line over her indicated target.

David stepped ashore to close one gate while the lock keeper closed the other, and he was back aboard and looping a bollard with the stern line before the lock keeper started opening the downstream sluices to drain the chamber.

Locks are easier to transit downbound, since the water level slowly recedes with none of the churning, turbulence and back eddies of a filling chamber in an upbound lock. The mooring lines need to be tended only to ensure they run out smoothly without snags or riding turns. David had discussed the safety elements of the process with Catherine, and she had said she remembered them from her péniche experiences.

"It's a very good refresher for me also," he had replied, adding, "we need to remember to review the locking and mooring procedures frequently and not become complacent."

"My uncle had a big plaque in the wheelhouse with red letters. *Complacency and Inattention are the Major Causes of Accidents.*"

They quickly worked their way down through the two locks, and shortly before eleven, they were out on the broader Saône and turning to head downstream in its still rather strong current. "There's still a lot of water coming down," David said as Catherine rejoined him in the wheelhouse.

"I remember the Saône here and upstream as a much more peaceful stretch of water in 1967."

"So you're thirty-two. You don't at all look your age."

"Your memory for numbers... Your math is so quick!"

"That's why I failed math in school."

"How do you mean? That doesn't make sense."

"I always had numbers in my head, saw answers to problems immediately in my mind, but I couldn't figure out the complex way the teachers wanted me to solve the obvious. I didn't understand what they meant by showing my work, so I accepted being stupid and inept at math, as they told me I was."

As he steadied from the turn, he increased the engine speed to 1800 rpm. "To pass time when I was stumped by trying to figure out one teacher's methods, I taught myself to do squares and square roots in my head. I had seen an obvious progression, a sequential relationship. The teacher had no interest in what I was explaining to her, and she told me it wasn't the sort of math I needed to concentrate on in Grade Five."

"What do you mean with this progression, this sequence?"

"The square of the next number in sequence is the sum of the current number squared plus itself and the next number in sequence."

"Okay, you've really lost me this time."

"A simple example, the square of two is four, the square of three, the next number in sequence is two squared plus two plus three, which is nine. The square of five is twenty-five, so the square of six is twenty-five plus five plus six, which totals thirty-six. The square of twenty is four hundred, so the square of twenty-one is four hundred plus twenty plus twenty-one, which totals four-forty-one. Very obvious and very simple."

"And none of the teachers realised your ability?"

"None."

"And besides math, what else did they miss?"

"Starting with Grade One, Miss Grannan…"

"You remember your first-grade teacher's name?" Catherine interrupted.

"Yes, of course I do. Anyway, Miss Grannan asked the class the first day of school *Who knows the alphabet?* A few of us put up our hands, and I was the second one chosen to get up and recite it. I asked her, *frontwards, backwards or Underwood?* She said, *No more playing. You're in school now, you must learn to be serious.* She told me to sit down."

"Underwood?"

"My grandfather had an Underwood typewriter in his store, and I memorised the qwerty keyboard sequence."

"I'm sure you still know it, and the backwards one too."

"Of course I do. I knew them at the age of four, and I still do — but back to you. I had guessed you were still in your mid-twenties when I was first introduced to you after you had married Louis four years ago, shortly after his father's de…"

David suddenly pointed forward through the wheelhouse window. "Look! There's Saint-Jean-de-Losne." He was relieved to have a diversion from mentioning Louis and death in one breath. "It's such a short leg on the river between the canals," he continued to keep up the conversation shift. "Only four and a half kilometres to the entrance of canal de Bourgogne. It's little more than a hundred metres beyond the bridge between Saint-Jean-de-Losne and Losne, then to starboard. Jean-Luc asked me to blow our horn as we near his office. He wants to help with our lines at the first lock up into the basin."

His well of words was about to run dry when Catherine pointed. "Look, isn't that Jean-Luc, waving from the quai?"

"Mind your ears, I'm going to toot him a greeting."

Catherine purred an echo. "Baaawoooom — such a wonderful voice she has, so deep and mellow."

"We'll have to turn to starboard now." David chuckled. "That's what one short horn blast means."

"Well do that, then. Head in closer and let's cruise by slowly. This is such a pretty setting. Can we moor here?"

"Yes, it's quite lovely, isn't it? We could moor here if the river weren't still a bit high. The edge of the quai is still flooded. You remember the broad sloping steps down from the street? We'd be high-and-dry on a step if the river dropped quickly."

David was relieved that Catherine was here in the present and not dwelling on the tragedies, the ones so very recent and the ones buried deep in her past. He watched Jean-Luc jog along the quai, moving ahead of *Vrouwe Catharina*, pausing to raise his camera for some shots, then running to catch-up again and pass them to repeat the cycle.

"He's getting many wonderful photos, I'm sure," Catherine said excitedly as she watched him and waved at the people who had stopped on the quai and roadway at the sound of her horn, and had remained admiring her passing. "I want copies."

Jean-Luc stood at the rim of the chamber, nearly three metres above them, as they motored in under the little bridge and into the first lock of canal de Bourgogne. Catherine's first attempt at a line toss hit him squarely in the chest. Perfectly aimed, but a bit too strongly thrown. "Seems I'm much stronger than that fourteen-year-old kid on the péniche," she apologised.

David mused that her strength was far more than physical, but he wondered how deep her emotional strength was. *Is it a frail shell ready to crumble? A façade held up with props like a Hollywood cowboy town?* He was sensing there was a depth to her strength, there certainly had been signs of it, but he still was not sure.

They had decided to head up the canal to the quai in Aiserey, where they had paused earlier on their way to Catherine's introduction to *Vrouwe Catharina*.

"Less than ten kilometres to go," she said as they motored out of the lock and into the basin of Saint-Usage. "We've just passed PK 242, and PK 232 is across from the quai."

David smiled and complimented his budding navigator, then said, "We learned early on in our naval training not to steer a course of 232°, to avoid the number if possible. Among the many forms we had to carry aboard ship was *DNS-232 - Report of Collision or Grounding*. Any use of 232 was to be avoided."

"Let's carry on above the lock, then. Moor along the bank. Or stop on the bank short of the bourne. We don't need to tempt fate."

"We'll make only two more locks before lunch, anyway, so we'll have lots of time to decide as we pause."

"Yes, I'm sure the locks still close midday for lunch as they did in 1967 and the same as everything else does in France. What time do they close here?"

"The break on the Bourgogne is twelve thirty to thirteen thirty. We can easily be through the Brazey lock before they close, but making the Port Hémery will be tight. Besides, there's one more lock above it before Aiserey, so it makes no sense to even try."

"What is Brazey like as a stop?"

"I have no idea, but we'll know when we get there. Let's plan on stopping there for lunch and see if we want to continue or stay for the night."

There was no traffic on the canal to delay them, and they were above the Brazey lock shortly past twelve ten. David pulled to the right bank a short distance out of the lock, and they moored to a pair of old stone bollards there.

"This is a delightful spot," Catherine said as she turned the end of the bow line into a coil. "It must be lovely in the summer with leaves on the trees, a cool, shady tunnel through the overhanging branches. Can we stay here tonight?"

"I don't see why not. I can walk into town, there must be a phone booth close, where I can call the Gendarmerie in Gevrey and update our location. There may even be a Gendarmerie here in town."

"*We* can, David — *we* can go take a look. We can have lunch when we get back. I'm not hungry yet from that huge breakfast you prepared." She swayed her back and glanced down. "Not all of this is the baby, I'll have you know."

"I keep forgetting you're pregnant."

Following a casual mid-afternoon lunch, they settled back into the settee cushions to relax. After a quiet interlude, Catherine asked, "Do you still search for coins?"

"I've never stopped, but I don't search through rolls anymore, though. Stopped that when the last of the silver disappeared from circulation in the late '60s. I had gathered all the silver as its value quickly rose to face value and above and hoarded it. At the end of December 1979 when I sensed the price of silver bullion had risen too far, I sold my hoard at close to thirty times face value Now I focus on finding abandoned Canadian coins in foreign countries."

"Abandoned Canadian coins? I think you've lost me again."

"What do you do with your Swiss Francs, your Italian Lire, your pocket change when you come back from a trip?"

"I travelled a lot before I met Louis. I love travelling, exploring." She blew out a deep sigh. "I had little bags to keep leftover coins in when I crossed the borders. Saved them for the next time I visited. I still have a lot of... Aha! Abandoned coins, now I see."

"I began searching for Canadian coins that had come back to Europe from travels many decades before. Old Canadian coins are among the scarcest in the world. We had a small population, and the mintages were low. We used the coins heavily, wearing them down to smooth discs until they were culled by the banks and sent to Ottawa for melting and re-striking. Uncirculated Canadian coins of Queen Victoria are rare, some dates are unknown in any of the higher grades." He smiled at her apparent continuing interest.

"Abandoned pocket change has stopped circulating, it has stopped being abused and worn smooth, so I started to ferret it out when I first arrived in France in 1966. I ended up with a large accumulation of high-grade coins, some of them now still among the finest known to collectors.

They're mostly common dates, but they're what a few serious collectors now refer to as condition-rare."

"And where did you look?"

"I started with the coin shops in Metz and Nancy, then in Luxembourg, which was quite near. Then in the *puces, brocantes* and in the street markets. Many of my better finds were from small town street markets, affairs that were like a whole-community garage sale. Of course, not everyone had coins, and the few who did rarely had any Canadian, but it was entertaining and well worth the time and effort." *She's still interested in this.*

"But there wasn't much travel back-and-forth between France and Canada in the 1800s. I tried to imagine from where the most travel would be. I went to coastal Portugal and struck it rich..."

"Portugal? Okay, this is another of your stumpers, isn't it?"

"Fishing the Grand Banks off Newfoundland and Nova Scotia. The Portuguese are fanatics for cod, and there was a steady stream of their boats crossing the North Atlantic for the great cod fishing there. I figured they surely put into Saint John's or Halifax or other east coast ports for water and crew break, or even to hide from a storm. Fishing the Grand Banks wasn't easy. The crew would bring unspent change aboard, then tuck it away when they got back to Portugal."

"Like I always did, tuck it away." She laughed. "I'd often misplace or forget my little stashes before I travelled again. I still have most of it." She nodded "All tucked away, God knows where."

"Many of those little stashes eventually make their way to the flea markets, knick-knack shops and so on."

"Who else would relate coins to cod fishing?" She looked at him and shook her head. "You're really weird. I like weird. Reminds me so much of me."

"That weirdness allowed me to fish up many high-grade coins, both Newfoundland and Canadian. Some of them are still the finest known survivors of their date. I'll probably have to set-up as a coin dealer sometime and start selling them."

Chapter Twenty-Four

Sunday 13 April 1986

David and Catherine both slept in. The gentle lapping of ripples on the hull from the breeze had been a comforting, almost hypnotic sound. David in the aft cabin was the first up, and he was probing quietly through the galley cupboards searching for utensils, a fry-pan and things to prepare breakfast. He must have made too much noise.

"You're awake!" Catherine called from the fore cabin.

"I've been up for a long time, maybe four or five minutes. Come on, lazy bones! Feet on the deck. We have a ship to run here. Do you remember seeing a coffee press or a Melita in the cupboards? We brought some nice grind, and I'd hate to boil it."

"I saw a press there when Maddie and I moved things around during the survey. She had told me they were leaving all the galley things and tableware aboard, along with the linens and towels. It's probably right under your nose. Give me a couple of minutes to put myself together, this broodmare is growing and needs a bigger harness." She grunted. "The girls are getting too big."

"That's a pretty fine broodmare," he said as she came into the galley. "Looks much closer to a thoroughbred filly to me."

"You don't need flattery to get me to search," she said with a laughing smile. "I'd find the press anyway, I want coffee myself."

It was 1045 by the time they had finished breakfast and slipped their moorings to continue up canal. They watched Écluse Pont Hémery being prepared for them as they approached. "It appears l'éclusier saw us coming, there's the churn of the water at the bottom of the gates," David had said nodding forward.

They passed up through Hémery and then La Biètre and continued along the pound. "There isn't much traffic, not like I remember it that summer," Catherine said, dreamily.

"There's been a big decline in barge use on these smaller canals. It's difficult to compete with trucks now with the better roads. Bulk loads are the most common now, mostly sand and gravel and the grains and sugar beets in the silos and elevators, like the ones we can see now through the trees at Aiserey."

"Trains too. My uncle told me the coming of the railroads a century and more ago started the slow decline of the canal system."

"Yes, and between the two wars, there was additional decline as trucks took more loads. Fewer tolls for the canals caused maintenance to suffer, sections of canals and river navigations were closed. The growing rental boat business might save some."

"There were large closed sections in Brittany. Papa showed us one when we went..."

There was a dull thud aft, and the engine stalled.

"Damn!"

"What happened?"

"Don't know. May have picked up something in the prop. Good thing we've slowed to enter the lock."

They had been drifting in neutral slowly losing way as they approached Écluse Aiserey, waiting for the lock to ready. The chamber drained more slowly than he had anticipated and he had just shifted to astern to slow further when the thud came.

"I need to ease into the bank and scrub off the last bit of way. Go look over the stern counter to see if anything looks unusual. Careful you don't fall overboard."

David gently eased *Vrouwe Catharina's* starboard side to the grassy bank and felt her gradually slowing.

"There's some rope and a piece of rag streaming out back here," Catherine called forward.

"As I suspected." After a short pause, he added, "Too much risk of damage to turn the shaft again." He looked along the bank. "Come here and take the helm." He stepped aside.

"Just hold her cheek along the bank," he instructed as she looked questioningly at him from the wheel.

"Are we going to be okay?"

"I feel we have it under control. I'm going forward."

David walked briskly to the foredeck, sensing no need for greater speed, picked up the coiled back spring and hopped onto the top of the grassy bank they were scraping along. He strode forward and across the tow path, dropping winds from the coil of line as he went, then once around the bourne, he headed back across the towpath and jumped aboard *Vrouwe Catharina* as she slowly passed. He took two turns around the staghorns and prepared to warp the spring as the load of the barge came on it. The initial juddering eased as the barge was gently snubbed to a stop.

David then walked aft and stepped off with the fore spring, walked it around the bourne and back aboard, where he turned it down on a cleat. "Good! We're here." He looked up and smiled. "PK 232 isn't so bad after all."

He continued aft past the wheelhouse, grabbed a boathook off its rack, and smiling at Catherine, said, "Isn't barging full of fun and adventure? I'll go untangle the screw."

A dark stain grew on the water as he prodded and pulled at the rags with the hook. "This is very heavy... No! — Oh, my God! Oh, fuuuu...."

"What is it, David? Are you okay? Do you need some help?" Catherine said as she started aft along the side deck.

"Stay there, Catherine, you don't want to see this — I don't want to see this."

"What is it? What's wrong?"

He dropped the boat hook on the bank and got up from his crouch, pale, weak-kneed and nauseous. He slowly walked forward and sat on the grass, "I need some water, Catherine — something much stiffer later, but now a glass of water."

"David, what is it. Are you okay?"

"Yes, I am, I just need to sit a bit — need to quell my gag."

He lifted his face from his hands. "I think you should sit also."

She sat beside him, and he peered into her eyes, then he turned his head to look aft. "There's a body wrapped in those rags."

Chapter Twenty-Five

"We need to call the Gendarmerie. There's a phone at the lock. Let's go!"

David and Catherine moved silently, both deep in thought, as they walked the hundred or so metres to the lock keeper, who was looking at them with concern.

"Problèmes avec l'hélice?... Problems with the propeller," he asked as they neared.

"Nous venons d'attrapé des chiffons... We've caught some rags in it. We need to call the Gendarmerie."

"They can't help with that, you need a…"

"There's a body wrapped in them; a man's, maybe a woman's."

The first Gendarme car had arrived from Saint-Jean-de-Losne quickly, then two more soon followed. Within half an hour Grattien and LeBlanc arrived from Gevrey and with them came three more cars. *Médecin légiste* and Gendarme photographers recorded the slow extraction of the corpse from its tangles. David was surprised to see so many people out so quickly on a Sunday. Grattien and his adjudant weren't in uniform, but all the others were.

"We were just about to leave for lunch at my mother's when the call came, so my mother and wife eat without me again this week." Grattien shrugged and sighed. "My adjudant was at home when I phoned, so I picked him up on the way here."

It had been difficult to release the bundle from its winds around the prop. What eventually emerged was a large, tattered piece of burlap with a long piece of rope, one end still around the ankles of the mangled, bloated body.

Soon after the corpse had been transported toward the morgue for autopsy, the team of divers began searching along the canal bottom for additional evidence. Catherine and David accepted Grattien's offer of a ride back to the château. They locked up *Vrouwe Catharina* and left.

During his training in the Air Force and Navy, David had been through the psychology of handling death in battle. He had been closely involved in the aftermath of crashes while working with Search and Rescue, and he had convened boards of inquiry into the results of training exercises which had disastrously turned too realistic. He had twice experienced the death of a climbing companion in the mountains. *This is more difficult. Much more.*

"We will let them identify the remains," Grattien said as they drove across the plain toward Morey-Saint-Denis. "There was no sense to start there on the canal bank, the lab is a better place."

"It was a small bundle — not a big person," Catherine said a bit haltingly.

"I know what you're thinking. A lot smaller than Louis." David pressed her hand gently.

"But it could be Murielle."

"That's possible, but it could be so many others, too." He tried to ease her concern. "I'm sure there are several other missing people in the area it might be."

"Not so, it is not violent like America here," Adjudant LeBlanc said from the front seat. "There are only two missing here."

David winced and watched Grattien clench his jaw. *The young adjudant seems to have missed a few of his psychology classes at the academy, or forgot their message,* he thought, but decided not to say it. *Grattien will surely counsel him later.*

He had thought also of countering with, *By Americans, I hope you are not including Canadians; we are Americans also, North Americans. Canada has less violent crime than France.* But he remained silent as he continued to hold and pulse Catherine's hand.

Monday 14 April 1986

"Oui, allo!" Catherine answered the phone, automatically pushing the speaker button to include David as she did.

"It's Grattien here, The médecin légiste has now confirmed it is Murielle Dupuis — I am so sorry to bring you this news."

"We already knew that, didn't we?" Catherine replied.

"Yes, we knew... The report shows her death was very quick, she would not have suffered. She was dead long before she was put in the canal."

"That's a mercy." Catherine sighed.

"Did the divers find anything else?" David asked.

"Several interesting things, I was going to tell you right now. They found three rusty pieces of scrap iron. The lab is analysing the rust traces on the rope and on the cloth. It appears the person who made the bundle had no experience tying knots. They also found two more pieces of rope farther down the canal. There is a possibility they are not related. Those and other things picked up along the bank are also at the lab."

"Have you informed Murielle's family?"

"No, I wanted to see if you might wish to let them know."

"Thank you, that's very kind," Catherine said. "When will her remains be released for services?"

"They are finished gathering all the evidence they need. It can be arranged easily in your own time, in her family's time."

David wrote down the morgue's phone number as Grattien gave it, and after confirming the undercover guards would remain at the château, they clicked off.

Catherine phoned Murielle's mother and broke the news. She was trembling as she hung up, her cheeks streaked with tears. She stood quietly staring at the phone and then began to convulse. Deep sobs, body shaking sobs. She turned and blubbered, "Hold me, David... Rub my head."

Chapter Twenty-Six

David sat on the couch, and Catherine lay against his chest. Two hours later, when she awoke, he said, "Your car is still by the old mill at Saint-Symphorien. I should go get it."

"*We* should go," Catherine corrected, "You're not going to leave me here alone."

"Let me rephrase. *We* should go get your car and *we* can stop at *Vrouwe Catharina* on the way back, she's still sitting there to the bourne on her two springs. We need to improve her moorings. I was too distracted to arrange more secure moorings before we left. How do we get there?"

"Louis has an old motorcycle in the shed. He uses it sometimes to go to the vines, it's easier and quicker than the tractor."

"I don't have a motorcycle licence."

"Why would you need one? You'll be sitting on the pillion. I'm driving."

She took the canvas cover off the old Triumph and hung it on the hook. After checking the fuel tank, she shook the bike, pumped the kick-start a few times with her foot, turned the key and kicked the engine into action. With a few twists of the throttle, she coaxed the second cylinder to fire more regularly, and soon the machine was running smoothly.

David nodded and pursed his lips. "You've obviously done this before."

"Not for a while — a few years. This was my bike when I met Louis."

"But didn't you say this is Louis' bike."

"It is, I gave it to him when he bought me the car after we married." She smiled. "I thought it was a good deal."

The roar of the engine was too much for easy conversation, so as they headed across the plain toward the Saône, David thought. He was pleased to see her able to talk about Louis without much obvious emotion. *I wonder, though, what is she like inside? Is she putting up a brave front and hiding a crumbling interior? I don't think so, and I hope I'm right.*

"I'm only the helmswoman here, you're the navigator. Which way do I go up ahead?" she shouted over the noise.

"Take a right." It was easier to talk now in the lessening noise as she slowed for the intersection. He guided her to the old mill, and she pulled in beside her Peugeot.

"This won't fit in the car," he said. "You'll have to follow me back. I'll go slowly, I don't want to lose you."

"Don't worry, the last thing I want is to lose you."

They arrived at the lock in Aiserey and parked on the towpath beside *Vrouwe Catharina*. "My idea had been to move across to the bollards on the quai, but that péniche is still there," he said as he unlocked the wheelhouse door.

"Except for the quai, there are no other bollards along here, let's go see what mooring arrangements are like above the lock."

They walked to the lock house and saw a line of old stone bollards on the right bank across from and a short distance beyond it. David told l'éclusier they wanted to move up through the lock to leave the barge in a safer place for a few days. He answered the lock keeper's questions about the outcome of the investigation and asked him to keep an eye on their barge.

Back aboard, as David was preparing to motor toward the now opened lock gates, he said, "I smell wine; there must be a broken bottle down below in one of the lockers. I smelt it yesterday when we were here talking with Grattien."

"Yes, I smelt it then as well. I thought a bottle must have fallen out of the wine rack and broken as we thumped along the bank, but there were other things in my head at the time than looking for spilt wine in cupboards."

"We'll look for it after we've moored up there, but right now you need to head to the foredeck to do the line."

"Aye, aye, Captain Michaels." After a fluttering little salute, she turned, popped through the side door and headed forward.

They passed up through the lock and moored to the bollards, setting bow and stern lines and doubling-up two long springs. Satisfied, David said, "There's very little disturbance here from the downbound traffic. They're going dead slow heading into the lock, so there's barely any effect from their passing.

"Upbound barges, though, will move us around a fair bit. We'll be dropped down and sucked away from the bank as their propeller draws water from ahead of them when they exit the lock. Then there'll be the churn and turbulence of their prop wash as their stern passes. Most commercial skippers move slowly past moored barges to lessen the effect. But even if they don't, we're secure."

He finished adjusting the lines. "Let's go nose out that wine."

They searched and sniffed around without success for a few minutes, then Catherine said, "The smell is gone now, the open wheelhouse doors must have aired-out the boat."

"Probably right. Let's secure here and head home — head to your place, I mean."

"*Home*, David, it's *home*."

"There's a stiff breeze picking up from the north, we should get going quickly." He pointed up at the darkening clouds. "That thunderhead looks like it wants to dump on us quite soon."

David quickly locked the barge, and after doing another fast look at the lines, they headed to the lock and crossed on its gate walkway. Then after bidding "à bien tôt" to l'éclusier, they hurried back to the car and bike.

"You know the route from here, right at the stop above Aiserey, and after half a kilometre, left into D-116. Straight ahead following signs to

Cîteaux and Vougeot. Go as fast as you want, I'll keep up. Let's beat that thunderstorm home."

Catherine smiled at the challenge, looked up at the advancing dark mass, kicked the bike into action and roared off. David tried to keep up with her, then watched her recede into the distance, make the turns and speed west. He finally caught up as she waited for him at the stop sign for the D-996 at Cîteaux. She turned and smiled at him, just before she squirted through a small gap in the steady cross traffic, and she pulled away more quickly this time.

She stood in the kitchen doorway, leaning against its frame and looking at her watch as he dashed through the cloudburst on his way from the car. "What kept you?" she asked with an impudent grin. "You're sopping wet. You should have come before the rain as I did."

Chapter Twenty-Seven

Wednesday 16 April 1986

David and Catherine arrived in Louhans a quarter hour before the service was scheduled to begin, and they walked down the centre of the church to a pew half a dozen rows from the front and sat next to the aisle. There were few others there yet, but soon by ones, twos and small groups, the number increased.

"That must be them, the family," she whispered, squeezing his arm and nodding lightly toward the small group; five silver-haired women in black, being ushered to seats in the front row. "I've not met her, but you can see the resemblance in her mother — that has to be her mother." She continued to whisper, "Those look like aunts, at least two of them do, the other two, I don't know."

"I don't see any young people in the group," David whispered back. "Sitting somewhere else? Maybe not here yet."

"She told me she had only two brothers, both killed when they were barely out of their teens with the army at Dien Bien Phu. She had no sisters. Shhh, it's starting."

David sat back and watched the familiar ceremony. One of his frequent duties as an altar boy had been to serve at funerals. *It was voluntary, but Grandmother had expected I always volunteer — I was the second son, destined for the priesthood.*

He mused. *The dreadfully mournful Catholic funeral is in such contrast with the Irish wake. One is a long drawn-out and structured downbeat ceremony, full of symbolism and often accented by a voice or two that could be recruited at short notice midweek to sing some dirges off key with a few trills and warbles in an attempt to disguise the lack of talent. The other is a celebration of life. What the Hell have religions done?* His thoughts were interrupted by movement in the aisle.

As he watched the censer being swung back and forth on a slow circuit of the casket, he wondered if this priest would crash it into a corner and spill a glowing piece of charcoal onto the lacquered finish and start melting into it, like Father Lafitte had done so many years before. *Nope, this censer has completed its circumnavigation unscathed.*

As the priest droned on, David thought of later funerals he had attended. Those of retired Air Force and Navy friends or colleagues. So often he had gone to their retirement parties just a year or two or three before. *They had made no plans for after retirement. Retirement was their plan, and they worked toward it, counting down the years, then the months, then the days to the big moment. They died of apparent boredom in their mid-fifties, early sixties.*

David mused that musing like this was how he survived the church ceremonies he had been forced to attend. *The Masses, the Vespers, the funerals, the weddings, oh, yes the weddings, they were the only ones I liked.* He had volunteered for as many as he could. They were normally on Saturday mornings, and he could fit them in after delivering the Times and before heading out with the Star Weekly. *There was always a tip for the altar boy at the wedding, usually a silver dollar or two. Even without the silver dollars, I liked the weddings. They were happy, joyous events, celebrations of new beginnings. There were as many wet eyes as there were at the funerals, but the tears were for very different emotions.*

Then David thought of his grandmother. *A pious woman, rigid and severe. My father was her first son, thank God! His duty was to procreate, and so I exist. Poor Uncle David, born the second son. He was packed off to the seminary to become a priest. What a silly tradition, second son, second daughter. Aunt Mary-Louise forced to become a nun just because she was the second daughter.*

David focused to see where the service was, then went back to his musings. *Grandmother was a powerful person, always so severe, so strict, so angry.* He smiled to himself. *I always thought she died of anger. After her funeral, my uncle left the priesthood. Took off his collar and carried on with life. He got married and had a family.*

He looked up at the mournful drone of the priest's incantation, then returned to his thoughts. *Poor Mary-Louise. Twenty-three years in a cloistered convent. It took her a long time after the funeral to gather the strength to release herself to real life, to finally kick the habit. We all celebrated with her when she finally...*

His musings were broken by the low rumble of the draped casket being wheeled along the aisle. He squeezed Catherine's hand gently as they stood to watch it roll by. When the family joined in procession behind the bier, Catherine tugged on David's hand and headed into the aisle beside the woman whom she knew was Murielle's mother. "Hello, I'm Catherine, Murielle lived with us."

"It is so kind of you to have come." The old woman raised her elbow. "Come take my arm, we both need some support."

Catherine linked arms and walked along with her, saying, "This is our old family friend, David. He is my solid support since this started. He'll take your other arm."

After the graveside service, with its droning mumbo-jumbo and symbolism, after the sobs and wails as the symbolic spade of earth was tossed on the lowered coffin, and after a sharing of emotions with Murielle's mother and aunts, Catherine and David headed back to the car.

"That is so sad, what she said just now; the only things that came back from the Front the first few weeks of the war were announcement telegrams. She lost her husband, her sisters lost theirs, she lost her brothers, and all that was left were five widows and three children... Now only five widows."

They sat in the car in the parking lot quietly for a long while, then David said, "That was such a morose ceremony. We need to go celebrate Murielle's life. What did she like? What were her interests? What were her dreams? You knew her closely for four years, let's go celebrate her spirit."

"She often talked of playing along the river and having conversations with the swans. There was a ridge she loved to climb and sit on its top on clear days to look across at the Alps. She loved looking at the mountains and dreaming. When she was in her late teens, she had started climbing. Her favourites were her ascents above — above Shammy — something like that, I didn't recognise it, but she told me she loved Mont Blanc."

"Could it be Chamonix?"

"Yes, that's it." Catherine smiled and nodded. "Do you know it?"

"Intimately." David glanced at his watch. "It's still early. Would you like to drive to Chamonix, to Mont Blanc and take Murielle's spirit with us."

"Silly question... Yes, of course, I would. Is it far?"

"Less than two hundred fifty kilometres by road. We can take the Autoroutes most of the way, less than two and a half hours. I used to make it from the exit in Macon in well under two and a half. Not much more than that from here, through Bourg-en-Bresse."

"Why are we still sitting here, then? Flash up the engine; let's get going."

As they headed southward out of Louhans, David said, "It's not quite eleven, we can be there by thirteen thirty. Can you wait until fourteen hundred or so for lunch?"

"After that huge breakfast, you made for us? You're not feeding a horse, you know."

"Good, there's a place with a view where we can share lunch with Murielle."

It was a beautifully clear day as they drove, and David pointed up at the sky. "Behind that line of thunderstorms on Monday afternoon and evening, a large high moved in, and it appears to be quite stable over us now, there's no wind and no clouds."

"I don't understand weather, I've just listened to the radio forecasts or read them in the papers. It seems to me the radio and papers don't understand weather either." She snickered.

"It was necessary for me. My safety while climbing depended on being able to read the skies, sense the wind directions, the changes, the patterns. I needed to know when to head down, when to seek shelter, when to carry-on up. Later in the Air Force and then the Navy, I had formal training. Weather is very important for flying and for voyaging at sea."

"But before your formal training — for your climbing before that, how did you learn?"

"Experience. It rains frequently on the west coast from mid-autumn to mid-spring. I got wet a lot at first, so I began asking myself why, and I looked for clues to…"

"West coast? I thought you lived on the east coast."

"I grew up there, but I left when I quit school to begin my education."

"You think so strangely — so refreshingly, I love it!"

They continued a steady conversation as they wound their way toward and into the Alps, David interrupting from time to time to point out a peak or tell her what was up this valley or up over that ridge. Just before thirteen thirty, he parked in a crowded lot.

"This doesn't look very inspiring," Catherine said as David opened her door and reached out his hand to assist.

"Not yet."

The valley floor sank quickly below them, the steep rooftops of Chamonix grew smaller, their chimneys fading from view. "This is amazing I've been up the elevators in the Eiffel Tower, but I've never been in a cable car. How far up does it go?"

"We'll stop shortly up there." He pointed up through the windows in the top of the car. "We're going almost vertically now as we approach the midway station. The cable's catenary has us climbing nearly straight up this final bit."

"The cat in what?"

"Catenary, the sag in the cable from its own weight. It's a very graceful curve, the same force that gives such a beautiful shape to a woman's breast."

She squeezed his arm, and they remained silent in their thoughts for the remainder of the lift.

"It's cold up here," she said as they walked with the crowd toward the next car. They were among the few without skis and gaudy-coloured clothes.

"We're rather high up, I forget the exact elevation here for the moment — it's about 2300 metres, but at our next stop, we'll be at 3842 metres. It'll be much colder there, below zero. We'll have to move slowly also not to get dizzy. The air is much thinner."

"Not 3840 or 3845?" She laughed. "Your head is so full of numbers. We should have brought warmer clothing, I feel out of place in my funeral clothes. Won't we freeze up there?"

"We can stay mostly inside. There's a tunnel, a corridor that leads from the car station through to a bar and then a cafeteria and a restaurant. The lunch crowd should be thinning when we get there, and we might get a window table."

A couple was rising from a window table as they arrived in the cafeteria and David quickly led Catherine across the room to stake a claim. "In the summer, there's a rather fine restaurant just along there," David said, with a sideways tilt of his head, not wanting to take his eyes off the panorama through the window. "But this view will do very well for now."

"This is spectacular! I've never imagined anything as wonderful as this." She looked at his beaming face. "Now, I'm sure you know the names of all those peaks out there."

"Of course, I do, and I've met many of them intimately." Not taking his eyes from the scene through the window as he reacquainted himself with old friends, he continued, "Now, let's have lunch with Murielle. What would she like?"

Chapter Twenty-Eight

David and Catherine watched the sun settle below the line of the Côtes as they left the Autoroute at the Nuits exit and started their dogleg through the town. Along the way, they passed under walls prominently painted with names of the producers, the négociants, the wine houses: Gelin, Moillard, Grotkopf...

David pointed to the tall wall emblazoned with *Grotkopf* and subtitled *tous les Grand Vins de Bourgogne*, and began speaking, "Grotkopf..."

"Grotkopf," Catherine interrupted. "We know he's connected to this whole thing; I wonder if he thinks we know."

"We don't know, Catherine; we don't know," David said gently. "We just have strong suspicions. Unless this wine heist was a well-conceived, long-planned thing with the value of the wine the only goal, he is the only one we can see with an apparent motive."

"Yes, but how would anyone else know we were going to be away for a week in Paris? Grotkopf would know through his son."

"The wine conference Louis was presenting at, a national event, many international participants. I was tempted to go — very interesting the list of participants in the marketing I received."

"I guess you're right, many in the wine industry would know."

When they drove into the courtyard, they were greeted by the gendarme playing groundsman in blue coveralls. "Have you read the news, heard on the radio?"

"No, what is it?"

"Grattien — Lieutenant Grattien wants you to call as soon as you arrive. This is his home number."

"Good evening Madame Ducroix, Monsieur Michaels. How was the service in Louhans?" Grattien's voice sounded over the phone's speaker.

"It was fine; we drove to the Alps after the service to share a last outing with Murielle. But that's not why you wanted us to call. What is it?"

"Two bodies have been found in Bois de Boulogne in Paris."

"Oh, no!" Catherine burst. "You wouldn't be telling us this unless it's..."

"We are not sure yet, Madam. They are still examining the remains, but..." There was a long pause. "But the body profiles match Francine Grotkopf and Pierre Ducroix. Some of the radio and télé stations are reporting it is them, now the newspapers. We need to be sure, and we are waiting for the autopsy reports."

"What about Philippe?"

"Still no trace of him."

"Where were they found?" David asked. "I want to see a wider picture here."

"A man walking his dog off the trails looking for mushrooms. He told Préfecture inspectors his dog began digging in a pile of leaves and branches when it uncovered some cloths..."

"Burlap, like in the canal?" Catherine interrupted.

"No, bed linens. We can look at more details tomorrow, would it be okay if I came in the late morning?"

"Yes, we'll be here," Catherine said, looking at David.

"Good, I would like to continue, but my wife is standing in front of me waving an empty dinner plate."

David and Catherine stood beside the desk in silence, looking at each other after she had clicked off the phone. Then she began, "What is happening? Why is this happening to me? What have I done? Were the nuns right? I am guilty. I will suffer and be punished unless I confess. But I have nothing to confess..."

"Come," David interrupted her torrent. "Come lie against me on the couch, I'll rub your head, and we can talk. We're safe, we're strong, we can move through this. Come."

They settled in on the couch, and for several minutes made no sound except their quiet breathing and her gentle sighs as his hand cupped the back of her head and softly moved with the rhythm of her heart, which he could feel with his chest.

She had calmed quickly and was completely relaxed when David started speaking quietly. "A priest abused me when I was an altar boy. He approached me in the dressing room below the sanctuary. Do you touch yourself down here? he asked, reaching into my underwear and grasping my penis. You're very big for your age. I grabbed my cassock for cover and ran up the stairs to the sanctuary, shocked, embarrassed and confused. I was fourteen."

Catherine had stiffened when he started, but was relaxed when she said, "Confused and embarrassed. That's what I had felt also when that nun began rubbing my breasts, commenting on their development. Then she told me I was too proud and slapped me. I told Mamère, but she scolded me, telling me nuns don't behave that way. She told me I was imaging things."

"Imagining things. That must surely have added to your confusion... It certainly added to mine."

"And to my embarrassment. I started slouching my shoulders, then binding myself. I became ashamed of my body and what it was doing, and I moved even further away from the others."

"Do you remember her name, the nun's?"

"I knew it then and for a time after that; I had to endure ten more weeks of school with her. I remember counting down the weeks as I tried to avoid her, but I forgot her name many years ago."

"It's so strange, I can remember the names of all the other priests, but I cannot remember his. That's lost in the files of my mind, covered over, but I'm sure it's still in there somewhere. I haven't thrown it out. I felt so confused after that priest. Grandmother called it my imagination. She told me to tell no one, or she'd have to wash out my mouth with soap. I didn't tell my parents, thinking they'd not believe me either. I began not believing it myself."

"That's what Mamère said. That it was my imagination. She warned me not to tell Papa; he would beat me again... Oh, my God!" She started to tremble, to shudder, to convulse in deep sobs. A long growing torrent of them.

David held her and the back of her head and gently rocked.

It was a long time, nearly an hour, before she woke. She was relaxed, and after she had composed herself a bit she asked, "You knew the nun molested me, didn't you?"

"Your story about her slapping you and saying you were too proud re-minded me of my abuse by the priest. I suspected there must be a similar story behind your reactions, behind your fear of her and your fear of examining the cause."

Catherine gazed into David's eyes and nodded. "Thank you for probing. I've buried so much of my past. We need to keep digging — but later." She shook her head and blew out a loud breath. "What would you like for dinner? The view won't be as fine as it was at lunch, but the wine and the food will certainly be better."

"The view across at my companion up there was superb. I'm sure it will be as superb down here. You attack the fridge; I'll raid the cellar."

Thursday 17 April 1986

The undercover in blues had finished every last bit of grounds work and had taken the initiative to begin the snail's pace task to one of removing the moss from the masonry of the north façade of the château. He quiet-ly nodded a greeting to Grattien as he drove into the courtyard.

"It is confirmed. The identities are as we had feared," Grattien said as he walked across the gravel from his car.

David and Catherine had been enjoying coffee after their brunch in the sun at the table on the flagstones by the kitchen door. "Sit here, while I pull you an espresso. Ours are just fresh."

David came back with the cup, and Catherine said, "He was telling me that since Philippe is still missing, I'm the closest family. It's left to me to make the funeral arrangements."

"Surely there are others, uncles, aunts?"

"This was their home, yes, but they had no other family left. So many deaths in the war. They knew nobody here that I'm aware of. All their friends I think are in Paris. Louis told me they stayed there after their studies. He didn't even know their friends and associates. Pierre was still single, but he had just begun seeing a woman. We met her when we all dined with Francine and Philippe before all of this. Estelle. We can contact her."

David asked Grattien, "Could we be let into their homes? Look for address books, clues to the friends they had."

"We can arrange that with Paris. The two homes are sealed and under surveillance."

"The remains, when…?"

"They are still doing analysis trying to determine the cause of death. There are no obvious marks, no wounds, no signs of strangulation, it doesn't immediately appear violent. Their bodies had been on the ground for a long time, a lot happens on a forest floor in three weeks — but to answer your question, it could still be several days. When could you go to Paris?"

Catherine looked at David and said, "The barge is still over at Aiserey. We should move it first. Does it still make sense to move it to the basin in Dijon? How long will that take us?"

"It's most of a day from Saint-Jean-de-Losne, thirty kilometres and twenty-two locks, we've done ten kilometres and," looking over his shoulder toward the canal, "one, two, three, four, five, six locks, so sixteen more to go and twenty kilometres. That's four hours for the locks and two-and-a-half to do the pounds, six-and-a-half hours total. There isn't time to do it today."

"But we could easily do it tomorrow?"

"Yes, it's an easy three or four hours in the morning and the same in the afternoon."

Michael Walsh

"What day is tomorrow?" Catherine asked, "I'm totally lost these days without routine."

"Friday," David and Grattien said in harmony. They all smiled.

Chapter Twenty-Nine

Friday 18 April 1986

"I smell that wine again," said Catherine as David helped her out of the car. "Stronger now."

"So do I. Don't look around. Act normally. Your wine is in that péniche. Let's go talk with l'éclusier... He's new," David said in staccato succession with a controlled voice.

"That's why those wine smells the other day were so familiar. It smells like our ageing cellar — like it used to."

"Just follow my lead in the conversation, let's pretend everything is normal and chat with him for a while, you'll soon see."

They stood in friendly conversation with the new lock keeper, learning among other things he was filling in for a few days while the regular keeper was away. David concluded by saying they had just come to make sure the barge was secure.

He led Catherine across the walkway on the gates and then along to the barge. As they checked the lines, she tilted her head and looked at him. "He's part of this, isn't he? He doesn't know the area, he doesn't sound like an éclusier."

"Exactly! Let's finish here and head to a safe phone."

As they walked past the lock keeper, David told him, "That should be safe for another few days. We need some work done. Office de la navigation said it's okay to leave it here until then."

"Tres bien, Monsieur. I will watch."

They headed back to the car, got in and slowly drove off, trying to appear normal as they went back across the bridge, back past the wine. "Look at the elevator and silo. They appear long since abandoned, almost derelict." He drove north to Longecourt and watched to see if they were being followed. It looked good in the mirrors as he drove the three kilometres and then took a right turn at the light to head around the edge of the village, following signs to Château Longecourt.

The only car behind them continued straight at the lights. "Phone booth, we need a phone booth," he said as they slowly drove past the château. At its end, the road teed, and he could see the rise to the bridge across the canal to the right. "We'll use the phone at the lock house. Most of the bridges along here are at the locks. There should be a lock here."

His senses were right, and he pulled onto the towpath, coming to a stop in front of the squat stone structure. A woman stepped out, responding to the sound of the crunching gravel. After the compulsory French greetings, he said. "There is a problem at Écluse Aiserey. You may have heard of the body there last week." Seeing her nod and her hand go to her mouth, he continued, "It's our barge that found her. Now there is more. I need to use your phone to call the Gendarmerie."

He was quickly transferred to Lieutenant Grattien's line, and he briefly outlined what he perceived. The laden péniche still sitting alongside the quai after three weeks, the smell of wine, the strangeness of the lock keeper.

Grattien was immediately decisive. "We will assemble a team, get some support from Dijon and Beaune. Can you come to my office in Gevrey? We can examine what you know about the péniche and other things when you get here. Keep your mind running."

"What's the fastest route?"

"From Longecourt, head toward Dijon, through Thorey then, maybe two kilometres to D-31. This is not a straight road, it takes many lines with other routes, but follow the D-31 signs and then the Gevrey-Chambertin ones. Twenty minutes or less. I should have some of the team assembled when you arrive."

The briefing room gradually filled as more arrived, singles, pairs, small groups, most in uniform, but some in street clothes. Grattien played a slow, repeating tape off the top of his head, splicing pieces into it as they appeared in his mind and as the group grew. He laid out the sequence of events, beginning with the trip to Paris as he seemed to be refreshing his own memory, pulling details out of crevices there. He wasn't presenting his voice to anyone, more thinking aloud, talking to himself.

The sound of "I think most are here now, Sir," coming from LeBlanc effectively pushed his stop button, and he focused on the room.

He reran the sequence of events, now in a logically ordered timeline, finishing with, "There is a major development," and turning to David, he continued, "Now, Monsieur Michaels will tell you what he has told me."

He introduced Catherine and David to the group with a précis of their relationship to the case. "Start with where you first saw the péniche."

David ran his own timeline for the group, starting with pausing at the lock at Aiserey on their way to the broker's in Saint-Jean-de-Losne and seeing the laden péniche moored alongside the quai. "That was Easter Saturday, 29 March," he said, looking down at the notes he had over the past few minutes jotted on a sheet at the back of his Day-Timer.

He finished with their smelling wine, the familiar smell of an ageing cellar and the strangeness of the lock keeper. Then he turned to Catherine and asked, "Have I missed anything?"

Seeing her head slowly shake a negative, Grattien turned to the group. "Questions? Have you any questions for Monsieur Michaels or Madam Ducroix?"

"The registration number on the péniche? We can start there and identify its owner, they are all recorded," said an old adjudant-chef in the front row.

"There were two fours together. LY something four four or four four something. Lyon registered, though, I remember that and thinking the Chinese wouldn't want this barge. Four is unlucky for them. I looked for the number last week when we approached but couldn't see it. The engine stall and what followed took all my focus from there."

"There must be some views of the péniche from our photographers at the scene," added another officer. "There may be some that show the number."

The simple thing would be to send a force to the péniche and recover the wine, but that would almost certainly get nothing but wine, and possibly one or two people who were there, and the pseudo éclusier. But everyone present knew they need to find who's behind this. So the discussion went on, with trained and experienced investigators slowly pulling together ideas on how to proceed.

David interrupted one developing thought on having an officer as a dog walker pass by to observe and report the number. "I may have seen that péniche earlier. A week earlier. It may be the one in the basin at Saint-Usage that my broker had just sold. I didn't see the number from our angle, but the drab paint now in my mind…"

"What's your broker's phone number?" a gendarme at the back interrupted.

"I have it already," Grattien replied.

Officers were assigned tasks: Contact Office national de la navigation to get a confirmation or otherwise on the replacement of the lock keeper; follow the hunch on the péniche with the broker; get sales details if there was a four four in a Lyon number. Gendarmes dressed as a dog walker and a couple on bicycles with a picnic basket were assigned to go past to observe. An officer was instructed to ask trusted people in Aiserey about trucks at the quai, and the list continued to grow.

David offered the use of *Vrouwe Catharina* as an observation post. "I have already told the man at the lock that we need some work done. You can bring in some gendarmes dressed as marine mechanics, a diver also, maybe. Make it look as though we are working on damage to the propeller or rudder."

"Great idea! — LeBlanc, you get this one going," and with a crooked smile, Grattien added, "But show me your plans this time before you do anything. Confer with Monsieur Michaels about the barge." And turning to David, he added, "This is okay with you? You have no other plans for the barge?"

"Our Dijon trip today is certainly cancelled." He looked at Catherine, then back to Grattien. "I'll play broken-down barge with your officers this afternoon."

"True about the cancelled trip," Grattien said with a smile. "But I do not think it would be safe for you to be aboard. Too much possibility of violence, we still have three missing people…"

"Three?" Catherine interrupted, looking with raised eyebrows at Grattien.

"Yes, l'éclusier, the real one will probably now need to be added to the list."

"It might look strange to the new lock keeper if the mechanics arrive without me…"

"*Us*, David — *us*. You're not leaving me behind."

Chapter Thirty

"This smells like a blend," David said. "Doesn't have the clear-cut nose of any individual one of Louis' wines. It could be just the harmony of all the wines breathing through the oak, but it seems stronger than simply that."

"I'm surprised how strong at this distance, but there's a breeze coming up the canal and carrying it," Catherine added as they stood in the wheelhouse watching two men in black coveralls leaning over the stern counter and talking with the diver in the water. "Some high-backed stools would be wonderful in here."

"There could also be leaking staves in some of the pièces. Moving them in a rush, as they must have done, is not kind to them. But whatever the source, it is certainly from Pinot Noir, and of high quality. I'd thought also of a tall pub table here."

"Why else could there be wine here in a péniche? For so long? Why hasn't the péniche left? That would be great for dining."

"It's many years since wine was shipped by péniche here. I haven't seen or heard of it since my first visit in 1966. Maybe they were still, and I simply missed it. So many changes. I remember seeing a horse drawing a barge along the canal near Dijon when I headed back north to Marville. I learned later that was one of the last of the horses. Great place for sunset dinners."

"But why leave the wine here? Why not in more stable storage? Fluctuating temperatures are not good for..."

"That's it. That's why the aroma's so strong. The temperature in the hold is fluctuating. Fortunately, the grain silos block the afternoon sun, but the morning through early afternoon sun hits the dark hull and decks through the trees. That quickly warms the barge hold. The wine expands from the cool of the night, the wine pushes out harder through the oak and likely through some popped bungs."

"The wine is spoiling, then?"

"As powerful and concentrated as your wine is, this is not good for it. You're insured, of course."

"Yes, but based on historical prices, and those have been low because of Grotkopf."

"It's worth a lot more than that. When you've recovered the wine, you can negotiate with the insurers. Settle for lost value. Whatever, it's such a crime to think of decreasing its superb quality."

"But why is the péniche still here? You haven't answered that."

"They could have mechanical problems like we do." He nodded toward the mechanics at the stern rail and laughed.

Over the next hour and a half, the mechanics had David occasionally run the engine. They went back to their peering over the stern and talking with the diver, who was in and out of the water. The scene looked normal. A man searching for mushrooms slowly made his way along the towpath; a couple went down along the canal walking a dog and came back; a cyclist pedalled by, then two more from the opposite direction.

How many of these were plants, David couldn't tell, so he and Catherine began a game, analysing the passers-by and guessing which were real. They named very few as plants, but couldn't articulate why. "I feel it, that's all. Maybe this one's a bit too normal."

The plan had been to close-up the barge at fifteen hundred and head back to the Côtes. The diver left a while earlier, and the two mechanics were loading toolboxes into their van as David locked *Vrouwe Catharina's* wheelhouse and checked the mooring lines, tightening the fore spring.

As they drove across the bridge, David said, "Catherine, look, that van down there on the quai."

"What about it?"

Michael Walsh

"The sign reads *Atelier Fluvial*. That van's from the boatyard, the dry dock and repair facility in Saint-Usage. The péniche has mechanical problems."

Saturday 19 April 1986

"The PTT clerk found a toll call to Atelier Fluvial charged to Laurent Grotkopf's office," was the first thing Grattien said into the phone when Catherine answered it just into their breakfast.

"Wonderful! So he ordered the service vehicle. I think we all knew he is behind this." Catherine smiled at David.

Then Grattien said, "I must go. The examining magistrate has given clearance, we have plans to move in on the lock house, the barge and elsewhere a little later this morning. Stay at home."

Sunday 20 April 1986

On Saturday afternoon, the insurance adjuster had begun organising trucks and drivers, two small cranes and a work crew. A very tough task at short notice for a Sunday morning in France. *For any day at short notice in France,* David thought, *for any Sunday regardless of notice. This is going to cost them a lot, but they're cutting losses.*

On Sunday morning, David parked the car on the quai next to the péniche in Aiserey. Workers lifted the hold shutters back, and the adjuster accompanied Catherine and David on a quick inspection, roughly counting the pièces and checking on their condition. There were many popped bungs in the top layer, they counted fourteen completely blown out and missing. David replaced them from the bag of new ones he had brought. Other bungs were sitting askew in their holes and some just lifted a bit. These were all reset. The adjuster made notes and shot photos, pausing several times to say, "Wonderful bouquet. Reminds me of our cellars at home."

Catherine had brought a score sheet she had drawn up, a grid with the names of the wines down the first column and the number of pièces produced of each in the next. She sat with it in her lap on the quai in the deck chair which David had brought over from *Vrouwe*

Catharina. As the pièces were slung from the hold, David and the adjuster read aloud the chalked names on their ends, and she put a mark in the appropriate line.

They broke for lunch, and while the others scattered to restaurants in town, Catherine pulled from the car's trunk the picnic hamper she had packed, while David went off to *Vrouwe Catharina* for another folding teak deck chair and matching small table.

At thirteen thirty they were all back at their posts and continuing the slow routine. Five minutes after the last of the pièces had been loaded into the trucks, Catherine looked up from her sheet. "We're one short. I've totalled the marks in each line twice now, and added the column three. There should be three hundred and eighty-nine, I show only three eighty-eight."

"The broken one in the cellar," David said. "Check your Bourgogne Rouge line."

"Got it! That's it. So three hundred and eighty-eight."

"An excellent total. Very lucky. Eight is the luckiest Chinese number, it means prosperity and wealth. Double eights add joy and happiness to that. We have a large Chinese population in Vancouver, and their house numbers and phone numbers are loaded with eights. They avoid fours like the plague, it sounds similar to their word for *death*. Speaking of four, I wonder how the investigation is going on the registration number."

"It looks like it's been painted over, you can see a fresh patch back there on the hull, that's where my uncle had his number." She pointed.

"I'll ask Grattien when we talk. He said he would meet us at the domaine."

The convoy of trucks and the two cranes followed David and Catherine as they drove across the flat plain to the Côtes. The adjuster said he had another call to make, but would be at the domaine when he was finished with it.

The unloading down through the shaft moved smoothly, with one crane on each side and the gantry working the middle. Six men with hand-barrows rolled each pièce to the place that Catherine directed from her cellar plan and placed it straddling the lettered and numbered notches in the pairs of concrete rails running across the cellar floor. She had drawn up the plan for Louis so he could keep track of the pièces after he had filled them from the fermenting vats. It was still in its folder with the other data on the '85 vintage.

They were a few lifts into the last truck when Grattien drove into the courtyard and parked by the sliding doors. "Madame Ducroix, Monsieur Michaels — the Gendarmes are here for you," came Grattien's voice from the top of the shaft.

"You go up, David, we're nearly finished." Then turning her head sharply up, she called, "Bonjour Lieutenant," at Grattien's backlit face peering down at her. "David will be right up, I'll stay here as the slave in the pit until we've finished. We're very close now. You boys go play."

"She is a very strong woman," Grattien commented as he shook hands with David at the top of the cellar steps.

"And getting stronger by the minute, she amazes me. So tell me about the raid, about the latest developments. Can I get you a glass of wine? You're off duty."

"Normally, I would accept, but I still have much to do this evening, maybe another time. Besides," he added with a smile, "wine on my breath would not be good for when I get home with a story of working late again on a Sunday."

"Coffee, then?"

"Perfect, I'll follow you, and we can talk as you pull it. The péniche was indeed the one you had seen in Saint-Usage. The broker gave us copies of all the documents. It was bought through a company in Martinique, and we traced it to a group in Marseille. We are just beginning to put together a dossier on them, they are in the bulk wine and forwarding business in the port...."

David had slowly nodded as he followed the stream of information, but at the mention of Marseille and bulk wine, he interrupted, "Grotkopf. He brought tank trucks of bulk wine up from the Midi. Check if there's a connection."

"Grotkopf, I was just going to tell you — Laurent Grotkopf was found dead when we entered his home. It appears to have been suicide, but maybe too much."

Chapter Thirty-One

"The coward. What a fucking horrible coward he was," Catherine said after David rejoined her in the cellar to help see the last few pièces into place. "What else did the Lieutenant have to say?"

David started telling her the story, but Catherine kept interrupting as the pièces continued to come down. "Let's put the story on hold until I can concentrate on it, enjoy it more." She turned her focus back to finishing her task.

There were only a couple dozen pièces left to come down and the men on the barrows were having a much easier time finding the places to put them. It was now a matter of simply filling in the last few gaps in the rows.

"I feel grubby," she said, after the last pièce was in place, after they had thanked the workers and had seen the last of them out of the courtyard. "You lock-up here. I'm going to take a quick shower and change into something clean."

"Take a long one, here comes the adjuster." David nodded to the car driving in. "I'll handle him," and then gently squeezing her hand, he added, "I have some good winespeak to use to argue for value of loss."

It was a good meeting. The adjuster understood quality wine, understood market, having grown up in a wine family in Gevrey. He had documented and photographed the puddles of wine which had overflowed from popped bungs into the bilges of the péniche.

David got a pipette and two glasses from the rack in the pantry and pointed out the door. "Let's go down and look at the wine."

The adjuster paused frequently to shoot photographs as he was led through the pièces. David stopped in front of the ones marked *aux Combottes*. While the adjuster continued looking around and shooting, David thought of the write-up he used to describe this wine in his catalogue. *This Premier Cru is often confused for a Grand Cru in blind tastings, and for good reason. It is completely surrounded by them: Latricières-Chambertin to its east, Mazoyères-Chambertin to its south and Clos-de-la-Roche on its west and north.*

He had been disappointed with it a few weeks ago during his tasting with Louis, who had talked about the runaway fermentation. Louis had been unable for a long while to keep the temperature from climbing, and the wine had a slightly cooked taste. David turned to the broker and pointed to the chalk script on end of the pièce. "Do you know this wine?"

"I certainly do, this is one of my father's favourite vineyards. He has rows of it against Latricières, and his plot continues across the line. Some years his Premier is better than his Grand Cru."

David thumped out the bung and pulled a taste into the glasses. There was a long silence but for the sniffing and gurgling, then the adjuster pulled his nose away from his glass. "It suffers badly from heat."

"A dark steel hull in the sun gets hot inside."

Catherine called down the cellar steps, "Are you boys finished playing yet?"

"I'm done here," the adjuster said. "My report is already written in my head. I can do the calculations later."

After a brief conversation at the top of the stairs, David locked the door, and they walked the adjuster to his car, waved him off and headed inside.

"I didn't have to use my winespeak on him, I let the wine speak for itself." He told the story as they walked into the kitchen.

"You're a rascal, you are. A very fast thinking rascal. Go get some wine, I'll pull out some cheese and baguette, then we can sit in front of a fire, and you can tell me a longer story."

"If you put a slab of persillé on the board, I'll join you."

"Persillé is a given here. Pick a big wine, the bigger, the older, the better."

David exchanged the ageing cellar key for the one to the house cellar and headed down. He spent a long time searching through the bins for an appropriate bottle, not knowing the cellar as intimately as Louis, who himself was still learning his way around more than four years since he had taken it over. He finally emerged, locked the door, returned the key and walked into the long salon, cradling a bottle in a pannier in his arm.

The fire was already turning from yellows, and the low table was set with glasses and a board of cheese, ham and baguette when he arrived. She looked up from the couch and asked, "What have you found for us down there?"

"I thought the '61 Bonnes-Mares would be an appropriate celebratory drink."

They sat nosing the wine, losing themselves in it for a long while. Finally, she said, "So tell me."

David slowly began, "Grattien apologised to us for not giving us details on the raid on the péniche. Said he was busy all day with the team, gathering evidence aboard and around the area, wanting to have it completed so we could start moving the wine off this morning.

"Eleven thirty was the start time. Laurent Grotkopf was found dead of apparent suicide when his home was entered and searched. Two bicyclists on the canal towpath arrested the lock keeper as a large team moved in on the péniche. There was nobody there.

"The péniche was indeed the one Jean-Luc had sold just before my viewings. Gendarmes obtained the documents and all the information Jean-Luc had on the deal. The purchase had been poorly disguised in offshore money in an easily unravelled chain that led to a bulk wine and shipping company in Marseille…"

"Bulk wine shipping?" Catherine looked up from her glass. "What about the plonk Grotkopf brought up from the south to stretch his Bourgogne? Louis always said he was selling Midi with fancier labels."

David nodded. "I told Grattien of the bulk wine shipments from the south, and I suggested he search through the files. He told me they have now seized all the Grotkopf files and are nearly ready to move in on the Marseille group."

After a long pause looking blankly into the fire, Catherine said, "We have our wine back — but not the people. There are still three missing people: Louis, Philippe and l'éclusier."

"Yes, but…"

"Tell me a nicer story, a happier story, I want to enjoy this wine, this moment. Try to forget the bad stuff for a while."

"Why don't you tell me a story?" David softly asked. "Share with me some things from your past, some happy things from your childhood."

"I still have trouble looking at that. Let's do something easy tonight. It's so easy listening to you."

"Pick a topic then. Do you want something from my childhood? Coins? Air Force? Navy? Climbing? Wine?…"

"Talk about climbing — Mont Blanc this week, that was amazing." She tilted her head and peered into his eyes. "Tell me why you climb."

"I don't know. Something inside. A drive. I've never really asked myself. I was simply drawn to the mountains the first time I saw them, and I had to go stand on one. I don't know why. Maybe it was to get a broader view. More than that, though. The view of the mountains from below is often as fine as the view from tops of them." David paused to gather his thoughts.

"I had a student one summer, part of a group of naval Officer Cadets, officers in training. I was conducting leadership training using mountaineering and wilderness survival as teaching vehicles. On the first day of a week-long exercise, we had paused at the crest of the ridge, up out of the treeline and into the alpine. We sat on the heather slope by a tarn, quenching our thirsts, resting and looking at the view. Most were in awe of it, most had never been up into the mountains before. They talked excitedly about the spectacular view and of how they had never seen anything to compare.

"Then one of them commented with a puzzled look on her face, *I can't see much view, the mountains are all in the way of it.* We didn't understand what she meant, until she added, *Out in the wheat fields there's nothing in the way of the view.*" He shrugged and smiled.

"View — point of view is so different in each of us. Some see things invisible to others while looking at the same scene. Our minds are our eyes, they interpret the messages that come in. Each mind has a slightly different interpretation, though most are nearly identical. Some, a few, like that young Officer Cadet from the flatness of Saskatchewan, see some things *very* differently."

He paused to take another sip of wine and bite of cheese. "I'm not boring you with this, am I?... Your eyes just went strange."

She reached across and laid her hand on his arm and gently squeezed. "Oh my goodness, no. Not in the least. I'm fascinated with your thought that our minds are our eyes. That makes so much sense. Everybody sees things differently. Please continue."

He smiled and took another sip of wine. "But the view wasn't why I climbed. When I arrived in Comox on Vancouver Island to serve with Search and Rescue, my first view was of the peaks around Comox Glacier. That sight compelled me to go stand on top, up there at the end of the view which dominated the valley.

"My first few weeks on base, I asked nearly everyone I met how to get up there. Nobody seemed at all interested in it, satisfied with simply looking at the view, some not even interested in that.

"During breaks in the hangar, I started going upstairs to the search coordination office and looking at the quilts of topographical maps mounted on the walls. I quickly found the map area showing the end of my view, the peaks around Comox Glacier: Mount Harmston, Mount Argus, the Red Pillar, they had names now. I stood there studying the contours, pulling the lines into three-dimensional images in my mind, until my breaks were over." He made a grasping and pulling motion with his hands.

"On one of these frequent trips, a young flight lieutenant asked me what I was looking for. He said he had seen me there often, and his curiosity finally overcame him. I told him I was looking for the best way to get up onto Comox Glacier and the peaks around it. He told me to wait a minute, then came back with a large sheet of paper, about a yard square, the sheet of topographical map I had been poring over. I still remember the sheet number, 92F/11. *Take this back to the barracks, study it there,* he had said, then he folded it on the counter, explaining how to accordion it with the printing outward. He gave it to me, asking, *Why do you want to go up there?* I told him I didn't know, all I knew is that I had to.

"He told me about a sporting goods store in Courtenay that had some hiking and camping equipment. That Saturday I hitched a ride into town and made my first visit to Happy's. I explained to the sad old man behind the counter what I wanted to do. I asked him what equipment I would need. He asked, *Why do you want to go up there?* I told him I didn't know, except that something inside is pulling me there." David shrugged and took a sip of wine.

"A few weeks later, after work on Friday afternoon with a clear weekend weather forecast, I headed out. On a rugged, second-hand bike I had bought, I pedalled through Comox and Courtenay and then on the logging roads around Comox Lake, up the Cruickshank Canyon and then along southward to a branch heading toward my goal. Thirteen miles on pavement and a very rough fifteen on gravel. I very quickly lost sight of my goal, lost behind the ridges growing in the foreground, but I could still feel its pull, it was not lost inside... It was stronger.

"The pedal took me almost four hours balancing a large pack on my back, and it was nearly dark when I reached the end of the last spur of logging road. I watched Saturday morning's sunrise from a rock outcrop a third of the way up the side of the ridge. An hour earlier I had struck my camp into my new pack and headed up through the forest. I had awakened well before dawn and couldn't get back to sleep, so I got up and headed up the ridge, pulled by an unknown force." He saw Catherine was still interested, so he took a sip of wine and continued.

"Late morning I was sitting on the summit at the far side of the glacier. An hour and a half later I was down off that peak, back across the glacier, along a ridge, down into a col and up onto the top of Mount Argus, about a hundred feet higher. The Comox airbase was below me, off to the east, beside the Straits of Georgia.

"It's the same line of sight between the mountains and Comox, but I felt no compulsion to go there, unlike the pull I had felt in the opposite direction. I still don't know what that pull was — or is. I don't know why I climb.

"I see all of this so clearly still, as though it has just happened. The details become more vivid as I relive them. I suppose the more intense the experience, the more deeply the records are engraved into our memory."

Catherine added, "Maybe sometimes so deeply, they get buried. They get lost in the folds of pain, of shame, of guilt…"

He reached over and put his hand on the back of her head as she continued, "I have so many dark patches of memory from my past, but there are some happy ones, which are still so clear."

She leaned against his chest and started pouring out a story, rambling through adventures from her joyous summer on the péniche and then gradually and more haltingly, to her return home afterwards.

Catherine stopped. Shook herself. Sat up, and turning a slow no with her head as she slowly said, "I am not — I am not the guilty one — He had turned around from the wheel to hit me when he veered the car off the road. The crash wasn't my fault." She shook her head. "All these years, I've…"

She stared wide-eyed into David's eyes. "He had turned to hit me for saying I didn't want to go back to school."

Chapter Thirty-Two

Monday 21 April 1986

"The lab is still working on the cause of death," Grattien's voice said over the speaker. "There were no wounds or trauma, there was no apparent struggle, the lungs don't show signs of suffocation, they have tested the common poisons and now…"

"What about chloroform?" Catherine asked.

"That is only in the cheap crime novels, it is a very complex thing to administer, even for a trained anaesthesiologist. But to continue, he is a chemist, with access…"

"He? Who's he?" David asked, shrugging a shoulder.

"Sorry — Francine's husband, Philippe, I see I haven't told you. We think he is involved in this. The circumstances are too strong to ignore. We still have no trace of him, have his house under close watch. The pharmacy where he worked part time is going through a thorough audit of their drugs and records under the direction of the médecin légiste, I think you say, coroner."

"So this isn't a good time for us to go to Paris to begin making arrangements." She looked at David then back at the phone.

"No, and highly unsafe until we find Philippe Grotkopf. The autopsy on Laurent showed his death was not from hanging. He was dead before he was strung up. Philippe is also the only suspect with this."

"Is it okay for us to move *Vrouwe Catharina*, our barge now?" David asked.

"I see no problem with that, I don't think anybody would have connected it to the wine. It's not likely any of the ones we missed at the péniche would have stayed in the area, anyway."

"We've been planning to continue into Dijon, it's still nearly three weeks before Atelier Fluvial can take us in their dock."

"When will you do that? I can drive you over just to be sure."

"That would be very convenient. We were going to take the bike and put it aboard so we can drive back down here from Dijon. We can take a taxi instead." He looked at Catherine and nodded.

"That is not necessary, we can have you picked up when you get there. We want to keep a close eye on you."

"This rain is supposed to end tonight with the passing of the front, and the forecasts for tomorrow appears good. The lock keepers begin at nine, how's eight thirty from here?"

"I can do that on my way to the office."

Grattien gave an update on Marseille and on the Grotkopf files, saying there was very little of interest yet. They had drawn samples of wine from the bulk wine tanks at Grotkopf's chais in Nuits and sent them to the lab for analysis of origin. Then interrupting his "à demain" closing, he added, "Of course, we will keep the guards at your place while you're away. We don't want a repeat."

"Analysis of origin? You can do that with a wine?" Catherine asked after she had clicked off the phone.

"Yes, it's done increasingly now to keep wine fraud in check. Through spectrographic analysis and increasingly, through other laboratory methods, grape varieties and regional characteristics can be quite accurately determined." Quickly assessing that he could mention him now, David asked, "You remember I referred to the Cruse scandal when Louis and I were talking a few weeks ago?"

"Yes, but I didn't follow. You boys lost me in that one, as you often do when you get into some of the technical stuff. Tell me about the scandal."

"The short version, or the long one?"

"The long one, of course. We have the rest of the day. Go find a nice wine, I'll lay out a board."

She looked up from the couch as David came in. "And the sommelier recommends this afternoon?"

"I thought the '78 aux Combottes would be appropriate. Its youngest brother did a great job with the adjuster last evening." David removed the foil and began drawing the cork.

"I have often thought the owner of this plot at the time the vineyards were officially rated in 1861, had refused to pay the fee to be included in the Grand Cru classification. Probably no validity to this, but..."

"You were going to tell me about Cruse."

He chuckled. "I was getting there... It started in June 1973 when inspectors found Cruse to have passed off simple table wine as genuine Bordeaux. At the time, Bordeaux prices were at historic highs. Lionel Cruse was the head of one of the oldest and most prestigious of the Bordeaux wine shippers, and they owned several great wine châteaux. He tried to cover-up, but the investigations dug deeper and implicated half a dozen others. Some two million bottles of wine were involved at Cruse alone.

"The trial began at the end of October 1974. The indictment stating that the quantities involved indicated not a small, temporary lapse, but it appeared the uncovered fraud was regular company practice. They further implied it must have been going on for a long time before being uncovered..."

"That sounds a lot like Grotkopf," Catherine said, curling her lip.

"Very much so. Grotkopf was quite likely doing his long before Cruse was caught. I'm sure he tiptoed around for a long while in 1973 and through the trial and its aftermath. He probably used the court proceedings to learn ways to better sidestep detection." David shook his head in disgust.

"The scandal, the findings of the investigation and the court case destroyed Cruse. That was good and deserved. What was undeserved, was the crash in the price of Bordeaux wine. Prices continued steadily down, then languished through the rest of the decade." He paused for a sip of wine.

"The whole Bordeaux market collapsed. Large, long-established exporting companies went bankrupt, great châteaux were sold for well below value. Distributors and retailers in Britain and northern Europe watched helplessly as their investments in futures of the mediocre '71s and the poor '72s collapsed in value. They cancelled their orders for the '73s.

"The expanding, but still unsophisticated market for French wine around the world, particularly in the United States, painted all French wines with the same dirty brush they used on Bordeaux. The entire French wine market went into a long slump."

"So sad." Catherine shook her head. "All because of greed."

"Yes, greed. Not satisfied to work hard and honestly for a fair return. Not working harder and smarter if they wanted a bigger return. There was a severe and quick tightening of regulations between the time of the scandal and the trial, in an attempt to close loopholes and slow wine fraud. Still, the purchases of Bordeaux declined. Half a billion bottles a year were being produced at the start of the scandal, and the lake of unsold wine rapidly increased with each successive vintage."

"That must have been hard for your wine business."

"No, I did extremely well." He looked at her and smiled.

"Well? How?" She tilted her head and wrinkled her brow.

"In June 1975 I started a sabbatical from the Navy to go on a...."

"This is where I always get confused. Sometimes you talk about being in the Air Force, sometimes in the Navy," she looked at him with a sly grin.

"Both, I joined the Air Force when I quit school. Trained as an aero-engine technician, was posted to Vancouver Island, started climbing, and in the winter, ski-mountaineering. I was seconded to the National Ski Team and trained in biathlon and cross-country toward the Grenoble Olympics. After two seasons there in Kananaskis, near Banff, I didn't make the cut to continue and was posted back to Comox and soon after that I was posted with NATO to northern France, north of Metz, up near Luxembourg."

He lifted his glass, looked into it and smiled. "It was from there I met Louis' father and discovered wine. President de Gaulle kicked us out of France in early 1967 when he left NATO. Our Squadron moved to Lahr in the Black Forest area of Germany. During a personnel review after we had settled in at the new base, the Squadron Administration Officer asked me why I was working on planes rather than flying them. He started paperwork to send me to Victoria, at the southern end of Vancouver Island to finish my high school in a new program the Navy had started, and on completion, to enter Officer Candidate School and then train as a pilot..."

"That seems a complex way to get to the Navy."

"I'm not there yet. There was..." He was interrupted by the telephone ring.

They both got up and briskly walked across to the small salon. "Oui, allo," Catherine said toward the phone after she had pushed the button.

"Madame Ducroix — I have some very sad news for you," Grattien's voice sounded into the room.

"Louis?"

"Yes, I am so sorry."

Chapter Thirty-Three

"We knew that, didn't we? We were prepared for it," Catherine said quietly and dry-eyed, as they sat back on the couch, then she leaned onto David's chest and started to sob.

David held her, and he stroked the back of her head as they gently rocked. Her sobs were subdued, without the intense heaving of recent outpourings. They slowly faded, and she lay quiet for many minutes as he continued to hold her. Catherine started to speak very softly, her voice muffled against David's chest. She rolled back a bit to look up to his eyes and repeated, "You won't leave me now, will you?"

Straightening more, she continued, "I still have a little piece of Louis in here," she looked down and patted the bulge of her belly. "But I have a growing piece of you here." With her hand, she cupped her left breast over her heart.

"I said I would stay until Louis came back. He's not back yet. No, I won't leave." He gently pulled her into his chest again, placed his hand on the back her head and stroked.

Tuesday 22 April 1986

Lieutenant Grattien arrived promptly at eight thirty, the appointed hour, but David and Catherine knew his coming wasn't to drive them to the barge. They sat around the kitchen table sharing coffees and talking about arrangements to receive the remains. The autopsy had been completed, and there was no longer any need to hold the body. Grattien gave Catherine a page with names and phone numbers of funeral services she could use, and he gave his personal recommendation. It was a controlled, measured process. He had been through it often.

Then Catherine asked bluntly, with no visible emotion, "How did Grotkopf kill him?"

"One of the tall stainless steel wine vats. A blending vat. The lab found blood and... and other non-wine substances in its analysis of the sample."

"He was dumped into a vat of wine?"

"No, there is no large access at the top, only the stainless filling pipe and breathing vent. The inspection and cleaning access hatch at the bottom was used. He was — I am sorry, please tell me to stop, if you wish, Madame."

"No, please continue, I need to know it all. I think I have the strength." She looked across and into David's eyes.

"The conclusion is he had been beaten and was bleeding when he was stuffed into the vat. The hatch was then closed, and wine was pumped into it, filling the bottom two metres on the sight gauge. His death was from drowning."

She closed her eyes and nodded, then blew out a deep breath. "Do we know when this happened?"

"From the autopsy report, there was little beard growth, they concluded it happened within a day of his last shave. We are assuming it was shortly after he went over to encounter Laurent Grotkopf on 27 March."

Saturday 26 April 1986

Louis' memorial was a very large gathering, the people filling the courtyard of the château and overflowing onto the lawns. The announcement had quickly been sent out by the regional federation to all its members, the Burgundy wine producers and the wine merchants. RSVPs had flooded in, and two additional marquees had to be ordered from the catering company, plus six more three-metre draped tables and ten more flats of glasses. Catherine tripled the order for the buffet spread and David ordered three additional portable toilets.

Michael Walsh

Louis sat on a draped pedestal in the middle of a marquee, overlooking the vines. His ashes had been placed in a magnum which was dressed with a label Catherine had drawn. It read:

Louis Marc Ducroix
Grand Cru
1954

The invitation asked Louis' friends and associates to bring a bottle of their own wine to share in a celebration of his life. It said there will be no church service, this will be a friendly gathering without structure. The invitation concluded with a caution to leave the mourning and expressions of grief behind. This will be a joyous event.

The positive response to the RSVP totalled two hundred and seventy-three, but David's approximations as he tried several times to count the mingling people, always reached over three hundred. The tables under the marquees were crowded with open bottles. Many had brought two or more of their finest wines to share.

The growers, the producers and the merchants had all been following the events of the past month with intense interest. This whole affair was too close to them to ignore. The tone of the afternoon floated on the strong underpinnings of their relief, their release from the tensions of the past weeks. This fed the lively spirit, and the seemingly limitless bottles of Grands and Premiers Crus certainly added to it.

Catherine had invited others, such as the boulanger down the street where Louis walked most mornings for croissants or a baguette; the boucher a little farther along, who always saved the best pieces of tenderloin for him; the little cheese merchant in Nuits who always cut a sample for him of a newly arrived cheese. The list included the branch manager who always had time to deal personally with his banking; his two favourite school teachers, the ones who had inspired him; his professors from the University of Bordeaux; his mentor at the oenological station; and Father Lefroy, the pastor of the church, where Louis was baptised and where he and Catherine were married.

Of the nearly two dozen on this personal list, all had accepted the invitation, except the priest. He admonished Catherine for not having a proper

Catholic funeral and for organising a pagan ritual. He warned her that Louis' soul would not be released and he would suffer long in Purgatory.

The celebration ran into the evening before the gathering visibly thinned. When the security lights came on at dusk, there were still large groups engaging in lively conversation. The lights caused a near universal looking at watches, almost as a choreographed move.

The last to leave was Father Lefroy, who had stopped in on his way by mid-afternoon, drawn by the size and the spirit of the gathering. He very obviously enjoyed the energy and joined in with the celebration of Louis' life. Catherine and David stood for a short while talking with him at the gate as he left. His parting comment was, "I must rethink my ideas on such things."

"I think Louis enjoyed his farewell," Catherine added as they wished the pastor adieu.

She and David stood for a long while back in the middle of the courtyard. Then picking up the magnum of Louis from the pedestal, she said as they headed inside, "Tomorrow we can take Louis for a walk through the rows. We can scatter him among his vines so he can continue giving them his energy."

Chapter Thirty-Four

Monday 28 April 1986

Grattien had been surprised, as many had, by the mood of the celebration on Saturday. He quickly settled in and became part of the crowd, and he frequently had information being offered by the wine people who knew him. The information was often tempered by, *But that is only my suspicion* or *This is what I heard*, or *This is the common opinion.* He learned there was a broad concern about some of the operations at Grotkopf. Rather than spoiling his enjoyment, he responded with requests to come to his office early next week when concentration is easier, then he asked for recommendations on which wine he and his wife should taste next.

He had several times sought-out Catherine in the crowd to confirm she still wanted to move the barge on Monday. On one of these occasions, David had said, "I've been running this through my mind. It now makes more sense to head back down canal to the basin in Saint-Usage. It's nearly the end of April, and we were going to head down in early May, anyway. I saw a winding hole just below the lock in Longecourt when I phoned last week — I guess it's more than that now." He shrugged.

"There may be a place to turn before that. We'll head up, wind around and head back down. The eight thirty ride to Aiserey on Monday is still good timing. Maybe you can have someone from the Saint-Jean-de-Losne brigade drive us back. We can call them from the Atelier office."

So at eight thirty on Monday, Grattien arrived and drove them across the plain. On the way, he told them the audit of the pharmacy in Paris had found a discrepancy in a new drug, he couldn't remember its name, but one used by veterinarians to put down large animals, very large dogs, even horses. Four vials were missing. "The lab confirmed on Saturday afternoon this drug was the cause of the deaths of both Francine and Pierre."

"So their bodies are now released?" Catherine asked.

"Yes, but Paris is still unsafe — we have no trace of Philippe. He is now suspect in all the deaths. Tissue samples from Laurent Grotkopf are being sent to the Paris lab."

Grattien dropped them at the entrance to the towpath. "Our brigade in Saint-Jean-de-Losne is expecting your call."

"With no traffic, we'll arrive around fourteen thirty. We'll have to wait above the last lock for l'éclusier to have lunch," David replied.

Grattien watched them aboard and then backed out and left.

David unlocked the wheelhouse, put the picnic hamper inside and started the engine. "I'll get the springs, you go forward and take the turns off the bow line and flip it off the bollard. I'll meet you up there and give the bow a push off."

The bow swung slowly out from his push as he walked aft to the stern bollard, lifted the line off and flipped it aboard and stepped up onto the deck. They motored away from the bank, and he had settled into centre canal with the engine up to 1200 rpm when Catherine had finished coiling the lines on the foredeck and returned to the wheelhouse.

"The surveyor missed this." David held up a broken door latch and pointed to the starboard door. "Fell apart in my hands."

"That looks easily replaced." Catherine started down the steps with the hamper. "Do you want another coffee?"

"A nice long one would be good."

"Daaa..!" came the loud truncated scream from below, then there was the sound of scuffling and banging.

"Are you okay? What is it?" He pulled the lever into neutral and then quickly astern and revved the engine to its limit. "I'll be right down."

"No, you won't," came a male voice from below. "Put the shift lever back where it was or your delicious little slut will get hurt. Very badly hurt."

"He has a gun, Daa…" Then there was the crack of a hard slap.

"Shut-up, bitch."

David pushed the lever back through neutral and wound the engine back up to 1200 as his mind wound up faster.

"That's it. Keep it there. Like your slut said, I have a gun — no, that's wrong — I have guns."

David's mind was spinning. He had to slow it. This wasn't the time to be thinking. *I need feeling, sensing, understanding, not chasing mental rabbits and tangents.*

He saw a pair of cyclists approaching on the towpath, and as they pedalled by, he did his best pantomimes to signal for help. The cyclists laughed, waved back and continued.

"It's about a kilometre and a half to the next lock," David said loudly toward the saloon. "I'll need help with the lines."

"We're not going that far. Stop before the bridge. Do you see my car just before it?"

"Yes."

"Stop beside the car. I will be up shortly to make sure you don't try anything crazy, as soon as I get her taped-up."

So, David thought, *that's the ripping sound. Duct tape to bind her.*

"I'm beginning to slow for your car." He called down the companionway as he slowly pulled the lever back.

The man stepped up into the wheelhouse, holding a gun toward David and taking a quick look around, then another slower all-around search. "Nothing stupid, now. Everything is normal."

The man looked like a slimmer version of the Laurent Grotkopf David remembered. *Must be Philippe. Maybe a brother if he has one.*

"I parked beside a big stone. You can tie the barge to it."

As they approached, David saw the PK 231 bourne, and chuckled almost to himself, then said, "Another kilometre closer to Dijon."

"You find something amusing?"

"It's the bourne there. We stopped on one only two weeks ago. This is becoming a habit."

David slowed *Vrouwe Catharina* gracefully to the bank, using the walk of her left-handed screw to kick in her stern as she stopped.

"I'll stay here with the gun on you as you tie the lines. Remember, stupid is dead. Both of you dead."

David left the wheelhouse and started forward. "Don't go away, I'll be right back."

"You find a strange time for humour."

He took the breast line, hopped ashore with it and did a walk around the bourne while thinking, *I'm getting good at this.* He hopped back aboard and placed a wrap on the cleat, then he paused and turned to look at Philippe, who was motioning him back to the wheelhouse.

"Down. Get down there, it's your turn for bandaging."

David arrived below in the saloon to see Catherine crumpled on the sole with her face against the wing of the galley counter and her hands taped behind her with her ankles bound and linked to them. *Surgical adhesive tape,* he thought, *and more rolls of it on the counter.*

"Hi Catherine, taking a nap?"

"Yes, I was feeling a bit tired," she replied softly.

"You two are sick — that or stupid. Come here, let me bandage you also."

When he finished, he climbed to the wheelhouse for a quick look around, then came quickly down, muttering, "Damned cyclists!"

Half a minute later he poked his head up again and paused to scan before he climbed the rest of the way into the wheelhouse. He quickly came down and cut the tape from Catherine's ankles and helped her to her feet. "Remember, I have guns."

He put the rolls of tape into his shoulder bag, cut David's feet free, and kicking at his ribs with his pointed shoe, said, "Get up."

"Thank you for the kick-start, but I can manage quite well on my own."

"This is not funny. I am deadly serious."

David decided not to continue with that lead. He manoeuvred to his feet, and he watched as the man went up and did another look around from the wheelhouse.

"Come up. You first Katy, then your stud."

David was surprised to hear him use that name. *That's what Louis calls her intimately and among close friends.* But then he remembered, as strange as it now seemed, *Philippe is a friend, he's family. She and Louis had dined with him in Paris recently. And now this?*

"Come on, bitch," Philippe called from the top of the stair. "We haven't all day."

"I was checking that my lipstick is on straight."

"Enough of this fucking humour. I'm serious here."

He tumbled Catherine into the car trunk, then told David to join her. "Be good in there," he said as he closed the lid. "You're a widow in mourning, don't screw around." He choked a snicker and added, "See I can be funny too. But now I'm serious again."

There was the stench of oily rags in the trunk and something with the gagging smell of rotting potatoes. *Has to be potatoes. The car must be stolen, Philippe wouldn't risk driving in his own. Surely he's aware the Gendarmes are after him.*

David counted the seconds to himself and kept track of the minutes with his fingers each time he reached sixty. While his mind was counting, another part of him was sensing the turns and stops the car made, noting and recording them.

It was forty-six minutes when at a stop he heard the car door open. He listened to sliding metal on metal, then after the door closed, the car moved again. He had arrived at twenty-six seconds when the car stopped, and the door opened again.

There was squeal of grating metal and a low rumble, then it stopped, the car door slammed, and they moved again. This time for only a few seconds before it stopped. From the other direction he heard the rattle and low rumble again, a thud and grating, squealing metal. He heard a door close, *a shed door, maybe a house door.* Then there was silence.

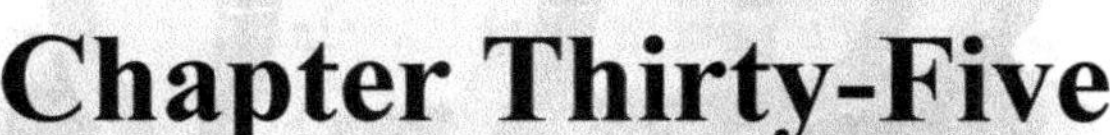

Chapter Thirty-Five

David and Catherine remained quiet, listening for sounds. Any sound at all as clues to where they might be. In the background, a low whining hum had started, or maybe was already there, and he was just attuning to it. *A steady hum.* "The low steady whining hum," David said quietly, "I can't think what it might be, does it sound familiar to you?"

"I've been trying to think what it is myself."

"Do you hear anything else?"

"No, do you?"

"No."

They remained quiet and still, saving their energy, thinking it might be a long wait. David sensed they had been stopped there about an hour and a half, maybe a bit less, when Catherine quietly said, "Good thing I peed after breakfast before we left the house, but I need to pee again."

"Try not to think about it. It'll be noon shortly and whatever is going on out there should stop then. We haven't left France, so everything will stop, and the workers will go for lunch."

"How do you know it's almost noon?"

"I was just calculating it to myself. I remembered making a mental note for the deck log that it was zero nine thirteen when I finished mooring *Vrouwe Catharina* to the bourne."

"You did that? Even under threat of imminent death, you did that?"

He chuckled softly and continued, "It was for *Vrouwe Catharina's* logbook. *Your watch isn't over until you have completed the logbook,* were the stern words of my training officer when I was beginning my bridge watch-keeping training. Lieutenant Summers would be pleased to know I still comply."

"Okay, but how did you remember the time, zero nine-whatever?" She sighed. "I can't even remember it after less than a minute."

"I remembered the time because for decades I've used the dates of coins as tags in my mind. Memory tags to use later. Canadian coins are a natural for this, most of the dates from their beginning in 1858 had scarce or rare varieties or were the beginnings or ends of a series or a design change. Decades ago, I assembled a tag for every number from one to a hundred, I had to throw in a few rare US and foreign coins. I had finished mooring *Vrouwe Catharina* at Thirteen Broad Leaf, the scarce variety of the 1913 ten cents piece, and I tagged that to my brain.

"So, from the time of our mooring, it was only ten or twelve minutes until we were locked in the car trunk. The drive took us Design in Six minutes —"

"Design in six minutes?"

"The 1946 Fifty Cents piece had a chip in one of the dies in the loop of the six. It slowly enlarged until it filled the entire loop, then the die cracked and was discarded. The coins struck from the last stages of that deteriorating die are quite scarce and very rare uncirculated."

"Okay, so forty-six minutes for the drive, how'd you know that?"

"I counted the seconds. So it was nine thirteen plus ten or twelve plus forty-six; that takes it to between ten oh nine and ten eleven when we arrived outside here, when we stopped in front of what I imagine as a gate and then a roll-up door. I sense we are in a garage or shed, and by my count, we've been here now an hour and a half, now a bit more."

They were quiet for another quarter hour or so, then, "There!" David said with a start. "The pitch is decreasing, quickly running down. The pump has been turned off. It's lunch time."

"That's it, a pump," Catherine said. "When it wound down, it reminded me of the transfer pump we use to move wine from the cuves to the pièces."

"This one has been running steadily since we got here. It's connected to a very large tank. Wine is already in pièces from the last harvest, so this is much simpler wine than yours. Could be white, could be a Village red, they could be blending tanks. We're probably in a winery, one with large tanks. If it weren't for that horrid stench in here, we'd probably smell the wine."

"My bet is Philippe will move us to a more hidden place."

Then they waited in silence. Waited another ten, maybe twelve minutes before there was the click of a door latch and the sound of footsteps approaching the car.

"Time to stretch your legs." Philippe's voice came from the other side of the trunk lid. "Remember, only one of us has guns here, don't try anything stupid."

He opened the lid, and both Catherine and David took deep breaths as the fresh air filled into the trunk. They smelt wine. "Slowly, move slowly," he prodded David's ribs with the gun muzzle. "Climb out of there."

"My right leg is asleep, I can't even move slowly until I can get it working again, and then I'll have to get some of these kinks out of my joints."

"Move!" He prodded the gun forcefully into at David's back.

"I'm trying." He couldn't sit up, his head was under the back of the trunk. He strained to unfold his left leg and roll himself onto his front. Slowly, using moves he had never used before, not even in snaking and grovelling up chimneys too narrow on mountain faces, he levered with a shoulder and an elbow and then with his head, his neck muscles screaming as he lifted to draw his left knee up under his chest.

He managed to swing his still partially numb leg over the lip of the trunk and hop it along while he coaxed his other knee sideways with a press of his neck, his head mashed into the burlap bag of rotting potatoes.

"I said get out of there! Don't just squirm around." Philip laughed with obvious joy. He grabbed David's taped arms and flipped him out and let him fall to the concrete floor.

David looked at the tires of several trucks. *I was right. We're in a garage, a large truck garage.* Then he thought, *That means so little right now, so...* He winced in pain as Philippe hauled Catherine roughly out of the trunk and dumped her on top of him, cushioning her fall.

"Get up, you wimps." Philippe prodded David's ribs with his pointed toe. "Grovelling at my feet won't win either of you any favours from me."

He directed them ahead with his pointed gun, up two steps and in through a doorway to a hall. Then following them in, he closed the door and locked it behind him.

"I really need to pee," Catherine said. "Can't hold it much longer."

"Women! Your plumbing is always such a problem." He pointed the gun toward an open door. "Over there, leave the door open. Remember I have a gun on your stud."

"My hands are tied, I can't get my pants down."

He mumbled and cursed unintelligibly, then dug a pair of scissors out of his bag. "Remember, there are many other things I can cut with these — maybe neuter your stud." He laughed as he turned to poke the scissors into David's crotch.

Philippe turned back to Catherine, grabbing an arm to turn her. "Stupid me — why cut you free?" He ripped her slacks open and hauled them down over her hips. "Let's see Louis' little playground." He snipped her panties at both hips and yanked them away. "Now your pants are down." He spun her and shoved her toward the doorway. "Keep the door open, we'll try not to watch."

After she had finished, he directed them to another doorway. She moved slowly, hobbled by her slacks now at her ankles. Inside he ordered them to sit on straight-back chairs, then taped David's ankles to his chair's legs. He then did the same with hers. Next, he taped their arms at the elbows to the spindles, cut the tape from their wrists and re-taped them to the bottoms of the spindles.

"Stay here folks, be good, I'll be back in a while." After a cackling laugh, he added, "So you really are a redhead."

"At least we can see each other now," Catherine said after Philippe had left.

"And it's certainly less cramped in here, though there's still the stench of rotting potato."

"That's probably what's caked on your forehead and plastered in your hair."

"Remind me not to do a face press again, it's not a good climbing move."

After a short pause, David quietly spoke. "I've been running my tapes, trying to sense where we are. Did you feel the hill?"

"We went up for a long while, not steadily, but definitely up. Rolling against you wasn't just trying to be close, I was being pulled toward the back of the boot."

"The obvious hills around here are the Côtes. The driving was quite flat for much of the first half hour, so he could have headed across the river and into the hills in the Jura. There's wine there, but that's more than a forty-six-minute drive. I feel we're in the Hautes Côtes."

"Yes, but not the Nuits, though, those are too close. The Hautes Côtes de Beaune are the right distance."

"Up the valley from Meursault, through Auxey-Duresses. We could be in the Saint-Romain area. I've bought wines from Alain Gras there, and there's the tonnellerie…"

"We buy our pièces from them, François Frères. I love watching the coopers."

"There's been a lot of new development up in this area, assuming that's where we are. New plantings, new wineries, modern installations; the land is much more affordable than down on the Côtes."

"This place seems quite new."

They continued the light conversation, not burdening themselves by thoughts of the desperate situation they were in, but talking of things peripheral to that and then rambling into stories from their past. Catherine began talking about her time in Ireland, some images from her early days there. She talked of walks along the seashore with her two cousins and their friends. "It was down the slope in front of the house, but was so different from my experience of the seashore in Brittany. There the sea broke onto the rocks in great white crashes, here it was mostly a calm sea, ripples, sometimes small waves, except in strong west winds, or when there was a big storm offshore."

She smiled at her thoughts. "The house sat at the edge of Kenmare, a small town at the head of a long bay, more than thirty miles in from the open sea, from the North Atlantic. I thought if the storms out there at the mouth of the bay were strong enough to push waves this far in, I wanted to go see them."

"I don't know Kenmare, I can't picture it on the maps in my head."

"It's about a twenty-mile drive from Killarney, do you know Killarney?"

David nodded. "Yes, south-west corner of Ireland."

"Can you picture the deep inlets, the jagged coast down in that corner?"

"I see four or five sharp headlands reaching out to sea."

"There are five. It's in the centre of those, the middle inlet, the deepest one." She continued to reminisce about hiking in the hills above the inlet and out at the ends of the peninsulas. Of drives into Killarney through the national park and around the shores of Lough Leane. Of pausing to watch rowers out on the lake. "We would often picnic on grass in the park there. It was..."

"Enough of your fucking talking!" Philippe's angry voice surprised them. He strode across to the table, grabbed a roll of tape. "This will shut you up."

He wrapped the broad adhesive across Catherine's open mouth and tightly around her head.

"Aay meed thoo feeeee," Catherine mumbled through the tape.

"What are you mumbling for? Speak up, woman." He laughed as he headed across the room to tape David's mouth.

"She said she needs to pee."

"What again? She went only a couple of hours ago."

"She's pregnant, remember, she nmmm…" and the tape stopped the rest of David's sentence.

"I can fix both those problems." He laughed as he finished the taping, then strode back across the room and slammed his fist into her abdomen. And again. And again. And then harder.

David watched in horror from the opposite corner, straining at his lashings as the yellow puddle grew and dribbled to the floor.

"Stay here." Philippe looked at them, then laughed. "I'm going to get some medicine for you. Something to ease your pain, all of your pains." As he walked through the doorway, he paused and said, "With you gone, I own Domaine Ducroix. That's another forty million added to my rapidly growing empire." He closed the door and locked it behind him.

Catherine was convulsing, writhing in her seat, her face drained of colour, and David sat straining at his bindings, unable to do anything to help her.

Then there was a gunshot, then three more. Then silence, a long silence. Then two more shots. Through the wall was the squeal of grating metal and a low rumble. David pictured the garage door being rolled up. Then the car started, roared, squealed tires, and its sounds faded into the distance.

Then there was silence again.

Chapter Thirty-Six

David's mouth had been closed when Philippe taped it. His mumble was nearly unintelligible to his own ears, but Catherine seemed to understand what he was saying. *Maybe she's sensing my meaning through the vowel patterns.* He wasn't able to force out anything even remotely approximating a consonant.

He was able to understand her more easily, her mouth had been taped open, so she had the use of a few consonants, "Ayyy hink aahmm affortheeng."

As sobs shook her body, David sat watching, unable to help, unable to comfort her but with his mumbles. He hummed soothing thoughts hoping to ease her with the sound of his voice.

She looked down in horror as her water broke, then her sobs turned to abdominal convulsions. Tears streamed down her face as the contractions increased in frequency and intensity.

He stared across the room, unable to do anything but mumble as he watched her agony increase. *God... Hasn't she been through enough already?* He looked down at the tapes around his wrists to see what progress he had made in his struggle to get free. *Done nothing but bloody them from torn skin.*

David's bladder let go as he watched the baby slowly emerge and slide off the chair to the floor then lie shaking at Catherine's feet. It made a few cries, then it gradually stilled.

Catherine leaned forward and watched helplessly as the baby's movements decreased then stopped. She was unable to do anything but mumble, "Mnoo, mnoo Oh mny Hod! Mnooo."

David looked up to Catherine's face and cried with her. After a long while, she shook her head and closed her eyes, then slumped her head forward.

He watched her. *I wish I could do something. Hold her head, rub it.* Seeing her breathing gradually slow, her body relax, he felt his own tensions also begin easing toward sleep.

They were both awakened by the activity outside, the loud, assertive voices. They heard the sound of doors crashed open, then heavy boots in the hall. Then another pair of boots and another. There was a sharp crash close by, and they watched the frame splinter as the door was smashed open. The muzzle of a gun appeared, followed instantly by a helmeted head, its face behind a plexi visor.

They relaxed as they watched the body-armoured gendarme follow his head into the room and bark out orders over his shoulder.

Three hours later David was sitting quietly on Catherine's bed, holding her hand and stroking it, when a nurse came in and asked if she felt strong enough to see Lieutenant Grattien.

Grattien sat in silence with them for a long while as they looked at each other blankly. Then Catherine said, "The baby's gone. They said there's no apparent other damage, besides the heavy bruises."

The three sat quietly again, looking at each other.

"Two of our brigade are dead, one seriously wounded, still in the operating room," Grattien said finally. "This is a very sad day for all of us." They were again quiet for a long while.

Grattien again cut the silence. "Our brigade in Saint-Jean-de-Losne was contacted to investigate a collision on the canal near Aiserey. A passing péniche had pulled your barge off the bank as it approached and there was no way to keep from hitting it."

Grattien continued slowly. "By the time the skipper was able to stop, he was nearly at the Aiserey lock, so he headed in to moor and report the incident. The lock keeper from the next lock, Pontangey I think it is, pedalled down to your barge to check for injuries and found it unlocked and abandoned."

"Great," David said. "I had simply placed the line around the cleat, one turn, hoping that might happen. I had seen a péniche coming down in the next lock." Catherine squeezed his hand.

"One of the gendarmes sent to investigate had been at the barge on that Sunday when you…" Grattien looked at Catherine and paused.

"When we found Murielle," she completed for him. "You don't need to tiptoe around, I can handle anything — after all this."

"He contacted our office. I had arrived only ten minutes before from dropping you off. I drove back to the canal and went directly to l'éclusier. He didn't see you leave, you were gone when he stepped out to prepare the lock for a péniche coming down from Longecourt, and was back inside when he heard the collision.

"L'éclusier at the next lock had seen your barge stop and moor at the bridge. He told me it was an unusual place to stop to wait for a down-bound barge. But he dismissed it, saying things are getting stranger with the new boat rental companies and all the inexperienced boaters." Grattien shook his head.

"He had seen a dark yellow or dirty gold car by the barge, an old Peugeot, he thought, but it was gone when the collision happened."

"So how did you trace us to the tank farm up in the Hautes Côtes?" Catherine asked.

"We didn't."

"So how did you find us, then?"

"Our investigations on the group in Marseille and through Grotkopf's files led us to a new warehouse up there. Three of our gendarmes were sent to investigate. Two were shot dead immediately. The third was seriously wounded while calling the brigade for backup. We added the events together."

"How is he?" David asked.

"She. I spoke with the doctors before I came here. Abdominal wounds, a lot of blood loss, but nothing critical they hope. They think she should fully recover. It was the backup squad, sent in response to her call, that found you."

"And Philippe?"

"No trace."

Again a long silence.

"Not too safe out there for us at the moment," Catherine said in a low voice.

"We have authorization to add more guards, we're looking at moving you to a safer location."

After another pause, Grattien continued, "We have a psychiatrist and a psychologist on their way to interview you. We need a better picture of Philippe's mental profile, his possible motivations. He has just killed your baby and two gendarmes. Most likely he killed his wife, his brother-in-law and his father. Probably your husband and your maid, possibly l'éclusier and his wife at Aiserey..."

"And his wife?"

"Yes, both are missing... And from what you told the gendarmes on your way here, he was about to kill you. He is obviously not stable — I didn't think you would mind their visit."

"I think we can both..." Catherine paused to look for David's agreement, then continued, "We can both add a lot on this."

"This is so ironic." David pointed to the name on the information sheet which was sitting on the overbed table. "*Centre hospitalier Philippe-le-Bon*... Here we are in Philippe-the-Good Hospital, looking for ways to stop a maniacal Philippe-the-Evil."

Michael Walsh

Chapter Thirty-Seven

Grattien remained in the room when the psychiatrist and psychologist arrived, first to give them an overview of the case, then to focus them on what they were trying to understand. When he was satisfied they were ready to begin, he said he would remain to gain additional insights for the investigation.

They began by examining Catherine's description of Philippe and when she had first met him and where. "The first time I met him was at Louis' father's funeral in 1982. He died on the first day of Spring, the day of new life, I had thought. The funeral was the following Tuesday. I had been engaged to Louis only a short while then…"

"Do you remember noting anything unusual about Philippe at that time?" the psychiatrist asked.

"No — no, I don't, but that's likely because I was much more focused on Louis, and on his feelings at the passing of his father, to notice much else around me. I had met Philippe's wife, Francine, several times before that when she had come to visit her dying father."

"Did Louis say anything about him? Had he discussed Philippe with you then or before?"

"Louis talked very little about him at any time." After a searching pause, she added, "And thinking of it now — I haven't thought of this before, but I'm sensing that he might not have liked Philippe."

She stared unfocused across the room for a while, then continued. "The next time was at my wedding with Louis four years ago, on 5 May 1982 — our fourth anniversary will be next…" Catherine pressed her hands to her mouth and closed her eyes tightly as she shuddered. She shook her head and reached for some tissue.

David gently squeezed her arm, then turned to look at the doctors and said quietly, "Maybe we can do this later. She's been through a few hells." He moved his hand to her back.

She shook her head. "No, I'll be fine, just give me a few moments." A short while later, she looked up and continued, "Where was I? — I'm remembering now Louis had been

194

saddened that Philippe hadn't visited when his father, when Philippe's wife's own father was dying."

"And after your first two meetings, did you see him often?"

"Only twice. They lived in Paris, and we went there rarely. Louis was always too busy, and he was reluctant to leave his vines and his wine for more than a day. Last month was only our second visit."

"What about his visits with you down here?"

"Francine came down occasionally with her brother, Pierre. She would tell us Philippe was too busy with chemistry projects."

"Chemistry?"

"Yes, he's a chemist. Francine told us he was always away, travelling on projects."

"He worked for a company?"

"Other than for the pharmacy, I don't think so. Francine never mentioned it anyway. He filled in sometimes at a pharmacy, mostly for holidays or to cover other chemist's absences. To me it didn't look like it was for money, they appeared to be very comfortable..."

"Most likely as a source of controlled chemicals," Lieutenant Grattien interrupted.

"And other chemicals... This now starts to make more sense to me," David added. "His chemistry projects were likely blending wines. Taking big complex wines, like yours." He looked at Catherine. "He probably added your wines to cheap, characterless wines, then balanced the resulting soup as necessary with acids, fruit syrups, tannins — but this is heading off on a tangent."

"I love tangents," Grattien said.

"Yes, so do I — okay, I think I can now see why Grotkopf wanted most of Louis' big wines. He could ameliorate them, bastardise them and still have sufficient character remaining to allow them to sell under their Appellation labels without much concern of detection. They'd have the paperwork, the harvest declarations, invoices and so on from Louis, in case there were..."

"We haven't gotten very far into Philippe's head yet," the psychiatrist interrupted impatiently.

"We're far beyond that," Catherine snapped back at him, then in a more controlled voice, she continued, "But we now see his motivation — very clearly see it. Philippe had probably depended on Louis' wines since he married Francine. The wines are likely *why* he married her, and likely why he was able to kill her."

The conversation continued now with Catherine and David alternating as they recounted their experiences from their first encounter with Philippe in the barge. What emerged was the image of a very focused man with calculated moves. A cruel, sadistic man who will let nothing and nobody stand in the way of his dreams.

Catherine concluded with, "The last words we heard him say were, *With you gone, I own Domaine Ducroix. That's another forty million added to my rapidly growing empire.*"

The psychiatrist and the psychologist conferred in hushed voices for a short while with various noddings and shakings of heads, then the psychiatrist said, "We have no more questions. Unless you have more to add, it seems we are done." He turned to Grattien. "My colleague and I will submit independent reports to you on our findings." They thanked David and Catherine, then left.

After several minutes of rapid back-and-forth, further analysing what they knew about Philippe, Grattien said, "I must go check on the wounded gendarme. I will be back shortly, then we can discuss getting you out of here safely. We have two gendarmes posted outside your door." Twirling a finger around his temple and contorting his face, he added, "You can never predict the crazies."

David and Catherine sat quietly after he left. Then with a start, Catherine said, "I wonder if the laundry has finished with our clothes, we're still here in hospital gowns, at least you've got a bathrobe. Where's that call button?"

David was still in the bathroom getting dressed as he heard a male voice through the door. He froze. Listened. Relaxed. He recognised it to be Grattien. "Looks like you are ready to go, where's Monsieur Michaels?"

"Here," David said as he opened the door and finished buckling his belt. "How is she?"

"She was very lucky. Both bullets missed hitting vital organs. She took one in her upper arm, the other through her lower abdomen, piercing her colon, the bullet lodged in her pelvis. She is out of the operating room, still in intensive care, but now off the critical list."

"Please let us know when we can visit, we'd love to thank her." Catherine blew out a deep breath, then added, "She got us out of there. What are your plans to get us out of here?"

Half an hour later, a two-car convoy drove north out of Beaune, Catherine and David in an unmarked car driven by LeBlanc in street clothes. Grattien followed behind in his car with three gendarmes. As they drove through Nuits and passed under the Grotkopf banner, Catherine said, almost to herself, "I wonder how *Vrouwe Catharina* had fared with the collision."

"She's a tough lady, she'll be okay. She's another Lady Catherine." With a glance at his watch, David added, "Do you realise we'll be arriving home — back at the château…"

"*Home,* David, it's *home.*"

"Arriving home not much later than we would have had we gone to Saint-Jean-de-Losne?"

"From the opposite direction, but still driven by the Gendarmes."

LeBlanc stopped the car on the street a hundred metres short of the château. "Lieutenant Grattien wants to take the men in and do a search to make sure the place is safe for you."

Finally inside, they stood in the kitchen talking with Grattien. "I will relieve your cleaning ladies and the grounds keepers from their shifts," he said with a smile. "I have arranged two uniformed guards at the gate to the courtyard, and a third one on a roof down the street with a clear view of the approaches to the château. This is a big house. How many rooms?"

"I'm not sure, we don't use the top floor. There are six bedrooms and four bathrooms upstairs on the first floor, and down here on the ground floor, there are the kitchen, the pantry, the three rooms of the servants quarters, the laundry room and a pair of guest washrooms. Then there are the dining room, the lounge and the reception room. Downstairs over there is the wine cellar, and there's the boiler room down at the side from the courtyard."

"We checked them all except the wine cellar and the boiler room. They were locked. We have many things yet this evening. Two dead gendarmes, one wounded seriously, families to contact, paperwork, lots and lots of paperwork. And we still have to track down Philippe." Grattien and LeBlanc said good night and left.

"The answering machine's light is flashing," Catherine said. "You check it, I've got to go again, my bladder's still a bit funny."

The message was a pause and a click. There was a second similar message and a third. "I would love to know when these calls were made and by whom," David said as Catherine came back. "Three blanks, three empty messages."

"It's amazing how loud silence can be." She looked at him for a long while silently, then added, "I'm still bloated from that hospital food." Seeing him play blowfish with his cheeks, she continued, "Come lie with me tonight. Just lie with me and hold me."

Chapter Thirty-Eight

Tuesday 29 April 1986

While the gendarme went down the street to fetch croissants for their breakfast, David phoned Jean-Luc to ask about moving *Vrouwe Catharina*.

"She's on the bottom, she has sunk. Where are you? What has happened? I tried to call yesterday many times."

"That's not good — how did…"

"Office de la navigation want it moved immediately. You must do something."

"Have you seen in the papers about the two killed gendarmes?"

"Yes, terrible... No! You're not involved in that too, are you?"

"Sadly, yes, and we can't leave here, we're under a protective security guard. Philippe is still out there, not very stable and most likely looking for us... So, on to much brighter things, our sunken barge, how did it happen?"

Jean-Luc gave a quick synopsis. He had gone up to the site and talked with the lock keeper to get the story from him. The péniche skipper had reported the collision as a glancing one, a prolonged grating of metal on metal, but no damage apparent other than a burst fender and a large area of paint scrubbed to bare metal. After the confusion and after the gendarmes had left, the two éclusiers had hauled her along the short distance to the bollards above the lock, and they had secured her there.

When the lock keeper came out after lunch to prepare for an up-bound, he noticed the barge was very low in the water. Her deck disappeared less than an hour later. Her wheelhouse and the curve of the top of her forward house were all that showed a short while later. Jean-Luc ended with, "It looks to be a slow leak, probably a ruptured weld somewhere." Then he added, "I contacted your insurer. Have they contacted you yet?"

"No, we were away on an involuntary tour of the Hautes Côtes, and we weren't here to answer the phone. Probably some of the blank messages. I'm sure they'll try again this morning."

The sunken barge took their minds off Philippe for a short while, but they soon ran into a reminder of him again as the gendarme returned with a paper wrap of croissants. They couldn't safely leave the château. "We're trapped here," Catherine said as she unwrapped the croissants. "We can't even get our own food."

"We can do a lot from here. The situation doesn't control us. We can find ways to make it work."

"What can we do from here?"

"We don't need to be anywhere near *Vrouwe Catharina* for a long while. The insurers will figure out how to re-float her, how to get her to dry dock. Those are their responsibilities and their expenses, not mine. Expenses will be covered quickly, then the insurers will have to sort out later between them, the péniche's insurers and mine. Sort which will cover the loss or what portion of it each will take." He started pulling the espressos.

"They'll have to repair the hull damage that caused the leak. A damage survey will be commissioned, and it is extremely remote the thin plating has eroded much in three years and it will almost certainly still measure above three point five millimetres, well above the French limit. The cause of the sinking, as Jean-Luc hinted, was likely a cracked weld. It could also have been from tearing on sharp rocks along the canal bank. Rubble and riprap are frequently used to strengthen the banks. Except near the locks or in regular mooring places, the canal banks are risky to approach without a careful watch and at anything above dead slow."

Michael Walsh

He set the two coffees on the table, sat down and began unwrapping the point from a croissant as he continued. "Her interior will most likely be condemned by any surveyor, and the insurer will have to replace it. Probably no great damage to the engine and machinery, but it will all need to be cleaned, overhauled and made operational. Our survey report will clearly show her condition before the accident. When I negotiated the insurance coverage with AXA, I had opted for replacement value, which is restored to the condition at purchase."

"Axa?" Catherine interrupted, "What's axa?"

"That's the new name for Mutuelles Unies/Drouot, the insurer I use for my wine. The AXA name surprised me as well. Last year the financial group changed names, wanting something simpler, a name easier to pronounce in any language. They're expanding rapidly internationally. A decade ago, when I started with them, their name was Mutuelles Unies."

"I've seen the AXA signs appearing, but hadn't stopped to think what they were about. At least the choice is better than MUD."

"Mud?"

"M-U-D, Mutuelles Unies Dru-whatever. What's A-X-A stand for?"

"Probably nothing, probably just an easily pronounced name from a think tank. Marketing is changing at a fast pace these days."

"So what do we do now about *Vrouwe Catharina*?"

"The same as we would if we could go over to Aiserey to watch the process, except it's drier here out of the rain." He laughed, nodding to the rain-splattered window.

"And it's much more comfortable — so what shall we do as we wait?"

"We could go sit comfortably while you tell me more stories from your past."

"No, you tell me some. You have so many wonderful stories, I have so few."

"You have as many as I do, you just need to find where you've hidden them. Your whole life, every moment is recorded somewhere in your mind, in your soul. They are part of your being. But they are all right there in that pretty little head. I wish I could look in."

Catherine started by talking about the monthly fair days in Kenmare. "We would go into town to watch. The farmers from around the area would bring their animals into the centre of town and stand with them along the streets for display. We would pretend we were some of the visiting stock dealers who came to buy. We would walk along carefully examining the cattle, the sheep, the horses, I really liked the horses…"

The ringing interrupted her, and they both headed to the phone. "Oui, allo," she said, after pushing the button.

"Hello, this is Michel Poirier, insurance adjuster for AXA, I was told that I could find Monsieur David Michaels at this number."

"You were told correctly, this is David," he said into the speakerphone.

"Good morning Monsieur Michaels…"

"Please call me David."

"You are very difficult to track down. We must discuss your barge. You must come to the canal with me and decide on how to proceed. Office de la navigation wants the barge removed immediately. We were contacted by a Monsieur Delong about your insurance coverage through us."

"We can't leave here at the moment. We're under protective guard by the Gendarmes. Have you seen the reports in the papers about the dead gendarmes up on the Hautes Côtes yesterday, the…"

"Oh, my God! You're that Monsieur Michaels, the one I've been reading about."

"Yes, I guess we're famous now. Anyway, do whatever you need to do to raise her and get her to Saint-Usage. We have a scheduled dry docking with Atelier Fluvial the end of next week, possibly they can shuffle us in earlier."

"You must be very stressed with all of that and now with this — this barge seems so trivial by comparison. Maybe we can continue this conversation later, after you've had a chance to get over the stress, to…"

"Stress gives energy," David interrupted, "Its force moves us along. Mishandling stress, fighting against it is what gives the pain, the confusion. I'm not in distress, though I understand *Vrouwe Catharina* is. Let's see if we can relieve her of that."

"Okay..." Then there was a long pause. "I'll need your most recent survey to use as a base in assessing damage."

"There was one done a few weeks ago, the report is aboard... Probably a bit wet. Your head office should have the copy that was with my insurance application. You could likely get a copy of it faster from the surveyor, Georges Augin in Saint-Jean-de-Losne. Contact Jean-Luc Delong at Bourgogne Bateaux along the quai on the river, he's my broker. He'll help sort things out with you. You can probably hire him to oversee the re-floating if you need, he's an experienced professional, and he knows barges."

After David concluded the conversation and clicked off, Catherine said, "I like that, what you said about stress. It makes so much sense to me. Fighting the current is so much more difficult than simply flowing with it."

She continued the thought as they walked back to their seat on the couch. "We would play in the current up the Roughty, the river that flows down the valley into the bay at Kenmare. Trying to swim upstream was so difficult, especially at low tide, so we would get out and walk up the path to jump back in and ride the current down. Across the bridge toward Ashgrove, River Keene comes more quickly down from the hills and was even more fun, a stronger current and small cataracts to play with."

She paused and sat staring silently at the strange flatness of her abdomen. Then she looked up at David and asked, "What was that yesterday in the hospital? About Philippe-le-Bon?"

"He was one of the Dukes of Burgundy. He had inherited the title from his father in the early fifteenth century, around 1420 or so. His father had been stabbed to death by order of Charles, the heir to the French throne."

"So why is he called the Good?"

"It's a long story..."

"Great!"

"Okay... Where do I start? The Dukes had built the Burgundy into the wealthiest and the most cultured region in Europe, and its influence was steadily growing, its territory expanding. The future King Charles VII of France felt threatened.

"The Duke's family had for generations married very well, linking noble families through much of western Europe. Philippe used family ties and the great wealth from generations of prosperity to expand the Burgundian reach. A decade into his reign he purchased Namur in the southern Netherlands from one of his relatives. A few years later through war settlement, he acquired Holland, Friesland and Zeeland on the lowlands at the mouths of the Rhine and Meuse Rivers. He inherited the Duchies of Brabant and Limberg and region around Antwerp on the death of a cousin. In the 1440s he purchased Luxembourg..."

"It sounds like he assembled Europe like Burgundy families here now assemble vineyards into domains."

"I like that." He gave her a wide smile. "Can I use it?"

"Sure, I thought you'd like it... But back to the story..."

"Yes... Anyway, by the time of his death in 1467, he was the most influential ruler in Europe. His court was seen as the most splendid, the Burgundy was Europe's centre of music, and it became the accepted leader of taste and of fashion. This fed the Burgundian economy as Burgundian luxury products were sought by the elites throughout the continent. Many of the luxury products were from Flanders where oil painting and other fine arts were flourishing. The Burgundy was the centre of art and culture long before the cobwebs began being disturbed in Florence and Venice with the Italian Renaissance. Oil paints were introduced to Italy from the Burgundian Netherlands in the 1460s."

Catherine looked up into his eyes and said, "The history I was taught in school missed these things. We were told the Italian Renaissance was the beginning of European culture."

"That's the Church — the popes much later began manipulating history to add to their power. The papacy had left Rome for what is now France in the early 1300s... Then there was the struggle of the schism until the early 1400s. The Roman popes began to emphasise all things Italian and diminish any French influence."

He smiled as he looked down at her laying across his lap. "The Italian Renaissance thing is what I was taught by the nuns. But, back to the story of Philippe-le-Bon. During his reign the Hospices de Beaune was built, a huge charitable hospital for the people. That was in 1443, the year he had bought Luxembourg. He was a benevolent ruler, thus the name, Philippe-the-Good."

"And after his death in the 1460s... What happened to the Burgundy? Was there still good?"

"His son, Charles the Bold succeeded in 1467, consolidating the family holdings and expanding them, acquiring the Alsace among other territories. Burgundy's size then rivalled France to its west and the Habsburg Empire to its east, and it exceeded them in most other ways. He began a campaign to acquire the Lorraine to link his Duchy to the Burgundian territories in the north: Luxembourg, Flanders and the Netherlands. Louis, the King of France, felt threatened and negotiated with the Duke of Lorraine, some of the Habsburg dukes, Swiss free towns and others to band together against Charles. He was killed in battle in the Lorraine, at Nancy in 1477."

"And after he was killed? What happened to the Burgundy?"

"Immediately after his death, King Louis sent troops to Dijon in a ploy to protect Charles' daughter Mary, now the new Duchess of Burgundy. She was just nineteen and unmarried. The King was trying to get her to marry his son and finally bring the Burgundy and its vast holdings into the Kingdom of France. Mary fled north, and several months later, she married Archduke Maximilian of Austria, to whom she had much earlier been betrothed. The Burgundy lands, which had become the buffering boundary between France and the Germanic Habsburg Empire, fell to the Habsburg side.

"France seized the Duchy of Burgundy. Huge numbers of its most skilled, talented and wealthy people fled northward to Flanders and the Netherlands, and in the following century, they helped build that region into the richest and most influential in Europe. Alsace, Lorraine and southern Flanders continued for centuries as disputed territories, and the struggle for their possession sparked many wars, including the two World Wars this century."

Catherine squeezed his arm lightly, "So, Philippe was called the Good, Charles was the Bold, what was Mary called?"

"Mary the Rich."

"You love history, don't you? I see your eyes alive, your face full of energy as you tell me things like this."

"I couldn't stand history in school... My teachers, their teaching methods made it so boring."

Chapter Thirty-Nine

Wednesday 30 April 1986

David spent most of Wednesday morning answering and sending faxes. He had phoned two weeks ago telling his office his return to Vancouver would be delayed. He was now a week overdue. His six-week buying trip was stretching to seven, and it appeared it would stretch much further. Overnight a long scroll of paper had arrived in response to the fax he sent to Vancouver before he had gone to bed.

He figured that if he could handle the sunken barge from afar, then he could also run the wine importing business that way. He had a very efficient woman, Lynn, who handled all the paperwork and administration for him, and she needed little direction.

The reply he began drafting was to resolve questions Lynn couldn't answer, such as: *The order from Giacomo Bologna didn't make it in time for the container consolidation. Do you want to wait for the next container, or move it more quickly?* and *Mas de Daumas Gassac has sent a price for the '84 and '85, what do I do with this?* and *The Brand's Laira, Lake's Folly and Plantagenet shipments are stuck in a labour dispute in Melbourne*; and *Should I get in contact with Empson on the short ship on Poggio Antico, or go directly to them?* and a dozen and a half similar things which she had put on hold until his return.

The phone call from the adjuster interrupted him part way through, and he delightedly took a break from the process.

"Your barge is afloat again," were the first words he heard as he answered. "It was a long process, but it is now floating. Good morning, you are well?"

"I'm fine, thank you, and you?" David replied to complete the greeting which almost invariably precedes anything else in France. "Great news, how was it accomplished?"

"With Monsieur Dulong's assistance, we brought in a crane and two large pumps. The crane lifted until her scuppers were all above water and we started pumping her out. She holds a lot of water, and of course, she still has a leak. We have one pump still running to keep ahead of the inflow and the other pump is standing by in case the rupture increases."

"She is still at Écluse Aiserey?"

"Yes, but we have a small *remorqueur*, a yard tug coming later this morning from Saint-Usage to tow her down."

"And the dry dock? Can we get in?"

"Yes, they often push aside schedules for more urgent needs. She will go directly in when she arrives. They have already begun their preparations."

David finished the conversation with Michel and returned to his draft of a reply. A gentle hand on each shoulder a few minutes later stopped him mid-sentence. He looked up from the stack of paper, let his arms fall to his sides and relaxed as Catherine gently kneaded the knots from his concentration.

"I miss you," she said. "You've been away in another world."

"I'm almost finished now... No! I'm finished now." He hung his head and let it roll to the rhythm of her massage.

"I've interrupted your work," she said softly a few minutes later, as she continued the gentle massage.

"Not really. I'd been sitting here trying to figure out what to do with the new warehousing agreement, and I've gotten nowhere. You've allowed me to relax and stop thinking about it, and I'm beginning to see it more clearly. I'll let it sit for a while longer, give it time to further untie. Let's go check the pièces, the lees will have settled by now from their move. They need to be racked off."

"Also, some of the lighter '84 Premiers Crus need bottling soon. We have the flowchart Louis maintained. It shows his planned workflow for the next few months. He always plotted a schedule, adding as he went, projecting it out several months."

Catherine searched for the flowchart while David gathered his papers and placed them in a folder and into his bag. They sat looking at the chart for a while and allowed it to sink in, then David said, "We missed the scheduled stirring of lees on the first of April, but the thieves did that for us. We missed the racking on the 15th and the lees were stirred again on that Sunday when we moved the pièces back here, what date was that?"

Catherine looked at the calendar for a long while, running her finger up and down its squares, then said, "I've lost track of time, that seems so long ago now — I know it isn't, but so much has happened since then. I don't even know what day it is now."

"I'm quite confused myself. I had to look for the date on Le Figaro last night when I wrote the letter to Lynn. Today's 30 April, Wednesday," and he put his finger on that square. "We brought the wine back on the 20th so the lees have had ten days to settle, but Louis scheduled racking two weeks after bâtonnage. We should follow that."

"That's 4 May." She wrote *Racking* in the square.

"Nothing else in the cellar coming up, but there's a lot of work needed in the vineyards. Look at all his entries here with long lines from mid-April to mid-May: *Débuttage, Bouéchage, Griffage*, and here, here's a note to remind him re-set stakes and to re-tension loose wires as he checked the bud break. Do you have…"

"Bud break! — Louis was talking about checking the bud break when we got home from Paris. He expected it to start happening the following week. I think we need to hire someone, a good viticulturist to care for the vineyards."

"I was always surprised Louis still hadn't hired any help."

"He said if his father and grandfather could do it alone, so could he. He was so tired some days when he came in. I told him so often he needed help."

"He had added so many things to the workload to improve the quality, no wonder he was tired. We can check with FIVB to see if there are any good vineyard workers looking for employment. Get started there and then search for a viticulturist to hire."

"But the money for this? We have a tight budget. Louis always said we couldn't afford to hire help."

"That's not the case anymore. You're no longer selling to Grosskopf at half price. You'll be getting real prices for all your wine now. There should also be a substantial payment coming from your insurers as compensation for loss of value from damage to the wine."

"Funny — I hadn't thought of those. We've been too busy with other things."

Chapter Forty

Michel phoned late Wednesday afternoon to tell David that *Vrouwe Catharina* was safely in the dock. During the draining of the dock chamber, he had seen a small stream of water coming from the end of a long crease in the round of her starboard bilge. "It looks as though it scraped along a sharp rock, and when it got to the frame, the metal there was pierced. The frame is bent, and likely we'll find associated weld fractures there as well. She will be dry inside when we go back on Monday."

"Monday?"

"Tomorrow is the first of May."

David then scrolled the first of May across his mind. *All of France shuts down for Labour Day. On Friday nearly everyone will fait le pont, make the bridge to the weekend, another French tradition. Labourers don't labour on Saturdays and Sundays are sacred, a day when labourers take another break to practice for the slowness of Monday.*

Sunday 4 May 1986

Yet here David and Catherine were on a Sunday, down in the ageing cellar racking wine. They had discussed the procedure. He had helped Louis' father with it on some of his visits, and Catherine had regularly assisted Louis.

It was a long process. Gently pump the wine off its sediment and into a clean pièce, then filter the last bit from the barrel bottom, before moving the emptied pièce out and trundling it along to the water wand, washing its interior and setting it bung down to drain. The next barrel along is broached to continue topping up the pièce while the washed and drained pièce is trundled into the newly vacated slot. When the barrel has been filled, it is bunged, and the pumping continues into the fresh empty pièce. The old chalk is washed from the butt end, and the new vineyard name and vintage are chalked there. Repeat.

At the final pièce of each vineyard lot, if there is sufficient extra in the collection of feuillettes, quartauts and bidons, the pièce is topped up and bunged. If its contents are insufficient, they are pumped off their sediment into the appropriate combination of feuillette, quartaut and bidons, which are then chalked and wheeled to the remainders storage. Repeat with each vineyard lot.

They paused just before noon for a baguette and some cheese after they had finished the Clos de Bèze. "Four and three-quarter hours, fourteen pièces, that's just over twenty minutes per pièce. We're speeding up as we refine the technique."

"Louis and I would aim for three per hour, forty per day."

"So with three hundred and eighty-eight pièces down there, we'll be done in ten days."

"No, well before that. The '84s are bung-on-side. They were closed a couple of months ago, finished their racking before Grotkopf came to take his purchase. They all looked good when they came back down here, whenever that was, I've lost track."

"With them eliminated from our list, how many need racking?"

"We don't have to do the Village wines either. We'll be racking those straight into the bottling tank in a few weeks when we get to that."

"That leaves us with how many, now?"

"From my look at the list a couple of days ago, two hundred and thirty-nine pièces need to be racked. It should take us six days."

"That's far better than ten,." David looked in the pantry and fridge for more cheese. "We'll need lots more fuel to keep us running, we're down to the last of the cheese and persillé."

"We're out of nearly everything. There are still things in the freezer, but we're out of nearly everything fresh. I feel like we're in prison here. Maybe we'll have to resign ourselves to bread and water."

"We'll talk with Grattien tomorrow. Arrange to go shopping."

They ate and returned to the cellar to continue racking, completing the Clos-de-la-Roche, and they were well past the midway point with the Bonnes-Mares, when Catherine stopped suddenly. She looked up at David from the pump switch and asked, "How did Philippe know we would be on the barge?"

"Stupid, isn't it?" He twisted his face. "I hadn't thought of that at all."

They remained fixed in their postures, staring at each other while thoughts and images reeled through their minds. Then David said sharply, "Merde! Switch off the pump." He watched wine roil up from the bunghole and flow down the sides of the barrel.

He leaned against the barrel, licking the wine off his wet hand, and chuckling, "Not the ideal way to taste Bonnes-Mares, but I'm disturbed with thoughts of Philippe — how he knew."

After she had switched off the pump, Catherine rose to join him, and they continued their glazed look as their brains spun.

"We have five, no four pièces left of the Bonnes-Mares," Catherine said after the long silence. "Then we're finished the Grands Crus. Do you want to stop now?"

"No, let's complete what we set for ourselves, the forty-one pièces. We can focus on that and slow our minds from churning. The answer will come when we stop thinking about it."

Two pièces later, Catherine switched off the pump and looked up at David. "Someone at our celebration of Louis was part of the Grotkopf operation."

"Possibly from the tank farm on the Hautes Côtes."

"Or from his chais in Nuits."

"Maybe the Marseille connection."

"The only person I talked with about *Vrouwe Catharina* is Grattien.

Nobody else there even knows about the barge."

"We could have been overheard."

"Most likely the answer. Too late to call Grattien now. We'll call him in the morning. Let's finish this then go clean up. Long hot showers. Those steaks will be well thawed. I could eat a horse right now."

"You'll have to settle for a steer tonight," she laughed, "I took out Charolais tenderloin."

Later, as they walked up the stairs toward their rooms to clean before preparing dinner, Catherine paused. She turned and took his hand and softly said, "We could save water, David. I'm too stiff to do my own back — some help would be welcome."

"I'm beginning to get rather stiff myself. Your shower or mine?"

They had a very late dinner.

Chapter Forty-One

Monday 5 May 1986

David and Catherine were back in the cellar shortly past seven on Monday morning, and after moving eight pièces along the row of Genavrières, they took a break for breakfast. Catherine had gone up a short while before with some change and asked one of the gendarmes to go get half a dozen croissants. He had come down into the cellar with the paper bundle.

They sat with their coffees and croissants at the mahogany table in the small salon, talking to Grattien on the phone. He too had thought someone must have overheard their conversation about moving *Vrouwe Catharina*. "We had two officers in street clothes mingling with the crowd and observing you and those who approached. One of the officers was new to our brigade, the other from Dole, outside the Burgundy, both unlikely to be recognised."

"I didn't see them," David said, "and I was very alert and careful with our surroundings that entire afternoon and evening. Your men are good."

"We don't only stand roadside stopping cars." Grattien laughed. "We are skilled in other areas too. One of them was playing photographer — you must have seen the press photographer who kept coming by to shoot pictures of Madame Ducroix with all the wine producers. There were so many high-profile wine people there."

"Yes, we were delighted to see all the names on the guest list as it grew. The big houses like Drouhin, Jadot, Latour, Faiveley, the individuals like Jean-Claude Boisset, Bernard Repolte, Lalou Bize-Leroy. They all wanted to talk and offer their sympathies. The photographer blended in very well. Did he report anything unusual?"

"When the photographs were analysed, one face appears far too often for coincidence in shots when I was talking with you. The photos of the woman are being enlarged to see if we can identify her. All photos are now being re-examined, looking for the unusual, looking for something else to pop out."

"A woman?"

"Yes, evil doesn't discriminate, it comes in all sexes, colours and religions. I haven't seen the photos yet, we're still waiting for the package from Dole."

"This is getting weird again," Catherine said. "And speaking of women, how is the wounded gendarme doing?"

"She is recovering well. The doctors were able to repair the gut wound without a colostomy. Amazing what they do now. She is still on a liquid diet until her gut heals, but she should be out in a few days to continue mending at home."

"That's a relief. We still need to thank her for saving our lives."

"She is fully aware of you now. She has the full story on what they, she and the other two gendarmes had run into up there."

"That's another thing we wanted to talk with you about. We're nearly on a liquid diet ourselves here. We're out of almost everything but wine, and we need to do some shopping."

"It is not safe for you outside... We'll have to organise shopping for you. Put together a shopping list and I'll have it taken care of." He laughed, then continued, "Remember, we do more than stop cars on the road."

After they had clicked off the phone, Catherine went to pull two more coffees while David dialled Michel to get an update on *Vrouwe Catharina*.

As she returned with the refreshed cups, she heard the adjuster's voice, "… isn't pretty inside, almost everything will have to be removed and discarded, everything but the engine and generator and some pumps, likely. The surveyor hasn't started on damage assessment yet, but he did give me a report of his drilling and measuring around the rip in the hull. The steel was between four point three and four point six millimetres thick. He couldn't get at the inside to examine the frames involved or to see any related damage. Workers are tearing away the interior as we speak to give him access."

"Is that the same surveyor we had last month?" Catherine asked. "What was his name?"

"Georges Augin," David replied.

"No, in our process we must use an independent surveyor, one with no links to any of the parties involved, and not influenced by previous surveys. He is looking first for the cause of the sinking and the damage related to it. Then he will begin examining the related subsequent damage."

Catherine had started compiling a shopping list, listening to the conversation with a corner of her mind as Michel and David discussed the next steps. As soon as the phone was clicked off, she asked, "Do you mind bottled Béarnaise? We're out of shallots and fresh tarragon…"

"I use the Mailly in Vancouver, it's very good. I discovered it in their boutique in Dijon a few years ago. Besides, we're too busy to make our own sauces at the moment." He gazed into Catherine's eyes for a short pause, then continued, "You need to hire two experienced cellar workers."

Catherine stopped her writing and looked up. "I've told Louis for so long that he needed help, not only in the cellar, but also in the vineyards. He always said we can't afford them. He worked ten to twelve hours every day, between the vineyards and the cellar, seventy or eighty hours each week, some weeks longer, like during harvest, during fermentation, with the racking, with the pruning, the bottling…"

"I'm calling FIVB right now to start looking for a viticulturist and two skilled cellar workers, all of them to start immediately." He stared at the beige box on the desk. "Could you look up FIVB on the Minitel for me? I still haven't learned how to use that keyboard layout, it's so different from qwerty."

Catherine clicked away at the keyboard and came up blank. "What does FIVB stand for again? I always forget."

"It's Fédération Interprofessionnelle des vins de Bourgogne," David replied.

She clicked the long name in, and they watched the entry come up on the monitor screen. After David had dialled the number into the telephone, he shook his head. "You would think they'd add their acronym to the listing... But this is France."

It was an easy phone call. He was quickly transferred to the right office and was soon talking with woman who told him there were two viticulturists on their list and over two dozen cavistes looking for work. David told her two dozen was too many to interview and asked if she had any information on their length of experience.

She replied, "Most of them ticked the more than five years box on the form."

"Do you show their ages on the form?"

"Yes, we do."

"Good, can you please give me the phone numbers of the five youngest who have more than five years experience, and also the contact numbers for the two viticulturists."

After he had hung up, Catherine asked, "The youngest? Why do you want the youngest?"

"It's probably more likely the younger ones will have more energy, and will be more open-minded, rather than have fixed ideas and broken spirits."

"But the older ones would have more experience, be wiser, wouldn't they?"

"This is basic labour, so long experience is not necessarily good. Doing things ineffectively or the wrong way repeatedly also results in long experience. At home, the unions protect that type and clog the workplace with them. I think what you need is someone who can catch the spirit of the wine here and move with it. What you don't want is someone who will try to mould the wine into something from staid concepts or misguided practice." He paused and looked at the sheet of paper in front of her and asked, "How's the shopping list coming along?"

"I stopped at Mailly Béarnaise."

"If you keep adding to it, I'll phone these people and see if we can set-up interviews with them."

After he had completed the sixth call and was well into redrafting his scribbled notes into a more easily read format, the phone rang. It was Michel again.

"The surveyor found one badly bent frame with some fractured welds along it and two frames with slight bending. Beyond that, he sees no further structural damage. Sighting along the topsides shows no distortion to the lines, except at the tear."

"That's a relief."

"He has written-off the entire interior and is now back in the engine room assessing the damage there. I'll call you after he tells me his findings." Catherine returned to the shopping list while David continued with, and then concluded the phone conversation.

After he had clicked the phone, he organised the interview schedule to make it more readable. "We still have to hear from two of the cellar workers and one of the vineyard men, but we have interviews beginning at 1500." He looked at his watch. "I'll go continue with the racking, see if I can finish the Genavrières before the first interview. You stay here finishing the shopping list and if the others phone, add them into the schedule."

She stood and picked up his hand. "Come here, you — you're not getting away without a hug."

Chapter Forty-Two

The decision on the two cellar workers had been easy. When David contacted Gerrard, he had said, "We can each work half time if my wife can work with me. We're a good team in the cellar." He was delighted when David told him they needed two workers.

Catherine and David interviewed the couple together. They were deeply tanned and bright-eyed, having recently returned from a wild adventure. In the early summer of '84, after the cellar work had wound down before harvest, they left their jobs at Faiveley and bought a small sailboat in La Rochelle. After repairing and outfitting it, they sailed south in the autumn.

A year and a half into the voyage, halfway around, they ran short of money and sold the boat in Auckland. They then enjoyed the rest of southern summer travelling and exploring wine in New Zealand and Australia. They had returned with an eagerness to get back to work and start building another kitty.

After the quick interview, Catherine amused herself with some of the strange interpretations from her shopping list as she unpacked and stowed items from the three cartons which had been delivered. David took Gerrard and Sophie to the cellar to show them around, and then continued racking the Genavrières with them, hiring them before they finished the first pièce.

David and Catherine sat on the couch in the early evening sharing their separate notes from the afternoon's interviews. They had liked both viticulturists equally and were trying to decide between them.

"Both have solid credentials, good experience with Pinot Noir," David said. "Each spoke from an obvious enjoyment of their work, from an appreciation of natural cycles. Both chose *shepherd* as their role with the vines, not the other options we gave, not *master*, not *tamer*, not *slave*."

"Jean-Paul had been seven years with Jacob until the family reorganisation earlier this year." Catherine ran her finger across her notes. "Straight out of Montpellier. Loic has slightly shorter experience, four years here with Drouhin, then two and a half years in California with Chandon, until he came back to care for his mother. But he has experience in both the old and the new world methods."

"They both seem full of energy, eager... It's a tough choice... What if you hire both?... For six months, until after the harvest. There's so much catching-up to do in the vineyards, anyway. You can make a decision later." David paused and put his finger up to hold his position. "That might be difficult for one or both of them, the uncertainty, the lack of commitment."

After another pause, Catherine said, "We can assure them they'll be free to continue seeking a position elsewhere, looking for a commitment elsewhere."

"You can give them time to pursue other openings. It's an unusual proposal, but you can start by seeing if they are interested in it. Otherwise, you'll have to decide between them now."

As David got up from the couch to go phone Jean-Paul and Loic with the unusual employment proposal, Catherine said, "We finally have some fresh food in the house, I'll go start preparing dinner."

"Still a bit early for dinner, isn't it?"

"We can go to bed early," She replied softly.

Tuesday 6 May 1986

"Employment law is changing in France in the use of fixed-term contracts. With changes of governments, they were liberalised in 1979, pulled back and restricted in 1982, and the movement now is back toward a more widespread use." These were the comments of the lawyer as David and Catherine sat with him trying to sort out the terms of the employment contracts for Loic and Jean-Paul.

Both had accepted the proposal that was offered, and they were coming at fourteen hundred to meet each other and to examine their terms of employment. On Monday afternoon, after they had decided to hire the young couple, Catherine had phoned their lawyer, the one Louis and his father used for many years. He said he would shuffle his next day's appointments and be there before noon. The gendarmes screened him in at ten forty.

The contracts for Gerrard and Sophie were easy, standard formatted things, but trying to find a way to handle the six months for the viticulturists was more complex. The lawyer thought it best to offer a six month fixed-term in a standard format, but add that besides mutual agreement, serious breech or act of God, termination could also be by reason of being offered a permanent job. This would allow not only a worker to cut the term short, but also allow Catherine to offer permanent employment to the other worker, thereby cutting his fixed contract.

The four contracts, each typed in triplicate, were delivered by a young man shortly before thirteen thirty, after he had been accosted by the gendarme at the arched gate.

"The new vignerons need to be shown the estate, but I don't know where all the vineyards are, even though I've visited all of them over the years," David said after they had reviewed the contracts and waited for their meeting. "Have you a plot, a map that shows them all?"

"There's a collection of drawings and plans in the files, some old documents, surveys from early in the century, pages from generations of estate settlements, a court order and some arbitration agreements, a lot of other papers, sketches, scribbled notes. I've tried to get Louis to draw up a proper plan since his father died." She looked up and did a good rendition of Louis' Gallic shrug. "He said he knew where all his vines are, where his rows begin and where they end. He contended that all his neighbours also know these details for their vines."

"There must be a legal registry of the titles, details of the ownership of the land. That should include precise surveys. This land is far too valuable to be imprecise."

"We can talk with Jean-Paul and Loic about this. They must know about the land registry or whatever it's called here, and how to put together a vineyard plot from the commune records. That can be a job for one of them as we begin to reorganise."

"The prices of Grand Cru vineyards have moved above five million Francs per hectare in the last few years, and they're continuing to rise. Two square metres of Grand Cru are worth a thousand Francs, a twenty-metre row of vines sits on more than ten thousand Francs worth of land. Centimetres and millimetres count here..."

His thought was interrupted by a gendarme at the door. With him were Loic and Jean-Paul, and minutes later, sitting at the mahogany table in the small salon, they both signed the contracts after a brief read-through. Jean-Paul and Loic had studied viticulture together at Montpellier and had been friends there. They were delighted to be working together.

With the formalities over, they started looking through the sketches, plot plans, maps and folders of papers that Catherine had laid out on the table. Loic said the *cadastres* at the *mairie* will have all the plots in their records. "Since shortly after the Revolution, 1791 I remember from my studies, the communes have held central records of all property. Napoleon later tightened the system to use for tax purposes."

Jean-Paul added, "The vineyards are in three communes, so we'll have to go to all three of the mairies, Chambolle-Musigny, Morey-Saint-Denis and Gevrey-Chambertin. I can do the one in Gevrey-Chambertin, I know the person who runs the cadastre office in *l'hôtel de ville* there."

"I won't be able to start until tomorrow morning," Loic said. "There are things this afternoon I promised my mother I..."

"Yes, both of you must have loose ends to tie-up," Catherine interrupted. "When can you start? We hadn't discussed that."

"I can start first thing tomorrow morning," Loic replied. "I'll go to the mairie in Chambolle on the way here."

"Tomorrow is also good for me," Jean-Paul added. "I'll stop in Gevrey-Chambertin on my way here. Whichever of us arrives here first can go down the street to the Morey mairie. Then we can take a tour and assess what needs doing and get at it."

Wednesday 7 May 1986

David was in the cellar, having finished organising Gerrard and Sophie with the continuation of the racking and now helping them along with it, when Lieutenant Grattien came down.

"We are now certain the woman in the photos is involved in this." He nodded to the door. "Can you come outside to talk?"

Confident the new cellar hands knew what they were doing, David motioned Grattien toward the stone stairs and followed him up.

"We've run profiles on the four you've hired," Grattien continued when they reached the courtyard. "They all check out fine, but thank you for thinking to let us know. It saves the possibility of surprises later."

"That was Catherine's idea... Coffee?"

They sat around the kitchen table with their espressos while Grattien showed them a folder of photos. A woman in a dark blue dress was in every picture, many with clear images of her face, some recognisable only by her dress or her brunette hair pulled into a large bun. "She is in so many of the pictures, I have selected only the best twenty or so." He opened another folder. "And here are some blow-ups of her face."

"I don't recognise her," said Catherine. "I don't remember talking with her, but there were so many there that day."

"She is clever. She stayed near me, not you. Look here, here and here." Grattien shuffled through the photos. "She is shown closest to me in every shot where I'm talking with you, but she is in no shots of you when I'm not around."

"She knows you even out of uniform," David added. "Do you recognise her?"

"Not at all, but she is unremarkable, attractive, but not overly, no unusual features, easily forgettable. The profile of an ideal spy, plainly dressed, conservative hair, nothing to attract attention. We've sent out packets to the surrounding brigades, and also to Marseille — frontal and profile blow-ups of her face plus two good body shots."

David updated Grattien on the situation with *Vrouwe Catharina*, and after the Lieutenant had left, David phoned Michel to get an update on the survey. He left a message with his secretary, then phoned Jean-Luc and left a message on the answering machine there. He phoned Atelier Fluvial and asked if Michel Poirier, the insurance adjuster for AXA was in the yard. They said he had left half an hour ago.

They were leaving the salon when the phone rang. "I've now completed my assessment on *Vrouwe Catharina*," said Michel's voice on the speaker, after the usual formalities. "I'm back in my office in Dijon and about to start writing my report, but thought I'd contact you first."

"Ignore the message I left with your office, it was just that I was sensing you had something for me."

"The barge is a write-off, worth salvage, scrap metal and a few thousand for the machinery. I'm recommending the claim be settled at your purchase price."

"Can I take the salvage rights?"

"I was going to suggest you might want to do that, she's a very beautiful lady."

Chapter Forty-Three

Loic arrived with photocopies of all the Domaine Ducroix holdings in Chambolle-Musigny, and then he went off to the Morey mairie to get copies, returning with them before Jean-Paul had arrived from Gevrey.

He was studying maps of scattered parcels with Catherine and David when Jean-Paul came in and said, "The woman I know in the cadastre office has been away from her desk for a week. The office is in a lot of confusion from the unexpected absence, the fill-in staff is trying to catch-up with a backlog and to sort things out. After my long wait, they told me to come back Friday."

"Well, that can wait, there's no rush." Catherine shrugged. "We have the Chambolle and the Morey plots. You can start working at that end and by the time you're ready to move into the Chambertin parcels, they should have given us those plans."

Jean-Paul and Loic seemed excited to be working together as they tumbled ideas around on where to start and with what. Catherine gave them the flowchart Louis had compiled, and they decided to begin with an assessment walk-through at the southern end of the Chambolle vineyards.

Toward the end of the afternoon, when they had returned, they both expressed how surprised they were to see that Louis had put as much care into the Premiers Crus vines as he had with those of the Grands Crus. They were even more amazed to find the vineyards for the Village wines received the same care.

David and Catherine took them down to the cellars to show them the results of the care. They introduced them to Gerrard and Sophie and then took the four of them on a tasting tour to introduce them to the wines.

"Louis copied his father's opinion. Treat the vines well, they will do the same for you," David said. "This Chambolle-Musigny is nearly as good as the Bonnes-Mares from some producers."

"This is better than the stuff I had last month that was labelled Bonnes-Mares." Loic laughed. "A friend brought a bottle from Grotkopf to a..." He paused and looked up at Catherine and David, "Not the best time or place to mention that name, is it?"

Catherine put up her hand. "No, that's okay. I think we can talk about that. His game is over now, we're just waiting for the last pieces of his little empire to fall."

They continued the tasting, ending with the Clos de Bèze. As they nosed their glasses, David raised his arm and swept it around the cellar. "This is what Madame Ducroix is working to maintain."

Catherine looked at David and said, "What *we* — what all of us are working to maintain." Then turning to Jean-Paul and Loic, "Have you two finished your stroll through the Chambolle and Morey vineyards?"

"Almost, just some up at the tops here, Clos-de-la-Roche and above, we should be only two more hours three at the most." Jean-Paul looked at Loic and added, "We'll finish it on Friday."

"Friday?" Catherine asked. "Have I missed a day again?"

"Tomorrow is 8 May, Victoire 1945, the commemorative of the end of the war," Jean-Paul replied, "It's a national holiday."

"But that was cancelled by de Gaulle in 1959, the year I started school. I remember my brother complaining he would miss a school holiday. He wrote a letter to the President telling him to think of all the sad school kids." She chuckled. "So innocent."

"Mitterrand restored it three or four years ago," David said.

"Guess I've been too busy to notice. Louis rarely took a day off."

Thursday 8 May 1986

David and Catherine spent a very quiet holiday, which began by relaxing in bed and telling each other stories from their pasts until they got hungry around mid-morning.

After breakfast they continued with the stories, cuddled in the corner of the couch. "You still haven't finished telling me about your change from the Air Force to the Navy."

"Where was I with that?"

"You were in Germany, heading back to finish school."

"Okay... So in mid-June, I was told my application had been accepted, and I was to start school the beginning of September in Esquimalt, the Navy base in Victoria. That was still ten weeks away, so I reorganised and changed my plans for annual leave. We got thirty days per year then, and I still had my full thirty days accumulated from when I was on the National Ski Team..."

"Skiing and playing in the mountains for a living, getting paid for it and still getting leave." She laughed. "How does one get a job like that?"

"Application, apply yourself to whatever is in front of you." He winked and laughed. "Anyway, I had sixty days plus a week's leave for packing and moving. The last week of June I crammed my climbing gear into the small trunk of the Healey and headed to the..."

"A Healey — Martha, one of my cousins in Kenmare, had a boyfriend with an Austin-Healey. He called it a *frog eye*. It had no boot lid, he had to flop the seats forward and stuff the bags into the space from there. Cute little car."

"They were called frog eyes because of the bulging headlights. In Canada they were called *bugeyes*. Mine wasn't a bugeye, though. It was a 3000, a 1961 Mark II, named for its three-litre engine, more than three times the size of the one in the bugeye. The sound of its exhaust from the six-cylinder was very distinctive. Its low rumble was so unlike the sound of any other car at the time. It was always so easy to identify one approaching.

"So, I packed up the car and drove south to the Burgundy to spend a few days helping Louis in the vineyards, then I drove up into the mountains through Chamonix, over the col and down through Martigny and up the upper Rhône Valley. I left the car at Saint-Niklaus; no cars were allowed beyond there in those days, and I took the train to Zermatt.

"The hikers and climbers thought I was strange, pitching my tent and camping. Everyone else then, and most now, stay in the alpine huts, which aren't anything like huts. Many are two or three level stone buildings, closer to hotels than huts.

"I camped the second night at the base of the Hörnli Ridge of the Matterhorn. The next day was Canada's one-hundredth birthday, one hundred years since Confederation, and the big thing for most Canadians in the months leading to 1 July was to have a Centennial project. Mine had been to stand on the summit of the Matterhorn."

"You certainly don't do things small, do you? Who were you climbing with?"

"My spirit. I frequently climbed alone, in the beginning, back on the Island, I couldn't find anyone else interested. I joined the local mountaineering club — they were more like hikers. Then I met a few climbers from another club and we did some ascents together, but I felt held back, restrained. I climbed solo a lot."

"But weren't you afraid?"

"Certainly, I was. Fear is natural and a wonderful tool, an essential one. Fear is the body's message to be careful. Respond to it, hear its message, it guides us. React to it and it becomes dangerous. Ignore fear and the consequences are severe. Fear is essential. So the short answer is yes. Thankfully, I was afraid.

"One of the things I used to tell my climbing students was that *Beginning climbers are afraid of falling, but experienced climbers are afraid of things falling on them…*"

"That was the thing which bothered me the most." Catherine said. "When we scrambled up the sea cliffs, the biggest danger was always from the falling rocks loosened by those climbing above us."

"Was that out on the headlands or closer to Kenmare?"

"No, long before that, when we lived on the Brittany coast along from Saint-Brieuc before we moved to Rennes."

"My favourite scallops in France come from Saint-Brieuc."

"Papa fished them when I was young, but he didn't like the new restrictions on fishing. Closing his areas, restricting his days, limiting his hours when he could go out. He said he was being bossed around. Papa sold his boat, and we moved inland to Rennes.

"He was never happy after that, always a fast temper, threw things around — at us..." There was a long pause as she sat trembling, then slowly she steadied herself and sat staring at nothing. Very quietly she croaked, "Hold me, David. Rub my head."

Much later, as they sat at the table after dinner savouring the last bit of their wine, they heard sharp cracks, gunshots outside in the distance. They both tensed.

"Sounds like we're in the States." David twisted his face. "So much violence there, so many weapons."

They sat still and listened intently, then Catherine relaxed and laughed. "No, not gunshots, those are the sounds of fireworks, celebrating victory in 1945. Let's go watch."

From the north windows, they saw the fireworks above Gevrey, across the Chambertin vineyards. "There's a better view of them from upstairs in our bedroom." Catherine took his hand and softly squeezed it. "And after we've finished watching them, we can play with setting off more of our own fireworks."

Friday 9 May 1986

They lay in bed relaxing Friday morning, pleased to have nothing pressing to do. Then Catherine leaned up on an elbow and with a quizzical look, she asked, "So, do I have this right? You were on the Matterhorn on your way to the Navy. That seems a strange way to get there."

"I've never chosen the beaten path." A wide grin spread across his face. "That climb was the first of many I did through July and August. I climbed there around Zermatt, then above Grindelwald, down in the Italian Dolomites, back across to the Chamonix Aiguilles and Mont Blanc. I also spent some time working with Louis. Such a glorious summer."

"And you did all this alone?"

"Much easier that way, no one to worry about, nobody to slow me. I knew going back to school was going to be a grind, a very tough slog. I wanted to have a last great fling, to experience my freedom before being bound. I love my independence."

She reached down under the duvet and gently cupped her hand around him and felt him expand. Half an hour later, she said, still lightly panting, "It's not always good to be alone. Some things are much better with company. But, I've interrupted your story. Please continue, please tell me of your return to school."

"You can interrupt me this way as often as you wish," he said as they lay still connected. "Where was I? Arriving in Victoria the last day of August... I started school the following week, and a week later I turned twenty-three. There I was still in high school at the age of twenty-three. It was much better than I had feared. They weren't like the teachers from my bad memories, they were skilled adult-educators, aware their students had experiential education. They knew how to build on our knowledge, and there was much less cramming-in.

"It was a five-day schedule of classes, overlaid with Navy routine and discipline, but my weekends were free. I drove up Island most Friday afternoons, into the mountains with my gear, and I climbed.

"I found a small apartment to rent, so I didn't have to live in barracks. I was deeply disappointed with the wine selection on the liquor store shelves. The alcohol distribution was a tightly controlled government monopoly. The only wine from the Côte d'Or was a Village wine from Chambolle-Musigny, bottled by Joseph Drouhin. It was okay, but it lacked the quality I had become accustomed to. I began looking into importing wine from Louis so I would have something decent to drink.

"There were many government hurdles as I tried to find out how to do this. I had to go through an importing agent, but none of them had any interest in all the paperwork involved in bringing in a special order of only six cases. They all said it was too much work for so little money. In frustration, I set-up a company and got my own liquor importing licence..."

"You were still the young entrepreneur."

"Often it's necessary to do things on your own, often it turns out better — much better. In our communications course in Prep School, we had to prepare and present half-hour demonstrations on topics of interest to us. The first one I did was a slide show on exploring in the mountains. The second one was on the origin of wine quality. My head was still so fresh from all the things I had learned and experienced with Louis — Louis' father.

"I talked about how wine quality begins in the vineyards, explaining how care there can coax the vines to grow finer fruit. I described the careful shepherding of the natural fermentation process, described how the work in the cellar contributes to making great wine. My presentation finished with a demonstration on tasting, explaining the techniques which enable us to best appreciate the quality of the wine. They didn't allow me to use wine, so I used tea.

"The course instructor, a naval officer, was impressed, and he immediately asked me if I would do the presentation at the Wardroom, the Officers' Mess, though this time with wine. I told him I had some bottles of Burgundy left from those I had brought back from Europe. He told me they could charge a small fee to compensate.

"There was a large group, I forget how many now, but during the questions afterwards, I spoke of my importing venture. The interest evolved into the beginning of my wine importing club and the initiation of my trademark, *Taste-Before-You-Buy*. We started with sixty-six cases of Louis' wines…"

"Hold that thought, I've got to pee," she said as she unplugged from him and rolled out of bed, holding herself.

She was soon back looking much more relaxed, "The thought of all that wine had me almost going." She giggled as she crawled back into bed and reached down to him beneath the duvet.

As they were into their third espresso of their late breakfast, Jean-Paul knocked at the kitchen door and opened it. He looked quite panicked as he came in, saw them at the table and started talking excitedly. "There are no records of property in the name of Domaine Ducroix on the cadastre. They searched through twice. I pulled out…"

"But that is impossible," Catherine interrupted. "We have a large piece of Clos de Bèze there, aux Combottes, Petite Chapelle, aux Echézeaux, others."

"I had the man look up Clos de Bèze, show me the map. Your rows are listed as belonging to Philippe Grotkopf."

"Bastard! That fucking bastard — pardon my language."

"Don't worry Madame, I speak that one fluently myself... We checked aux Combottes, the same thing."

"Fuck, fuck, fuuuu…"

David interrupted her eloquence with, "The woman you knew in the mairie, what did she look like?"

"About my height, a metre-seventy or so tall, brown hair, can't remember her face, nothing particular, just another woman behind a counter. I would recognise her easily enough, but I can't describe her."

Catherine had dashed to the phone and was dialling Grattien's number while Jean-Paul was finishing. She told the lieutenant, "We've identified the woman."

Chapter Forty-Four

Grattien arrived within fifteen minutes of the phone click, and he was opening his dossier as he walked across to the kitchen table.

"That's definitely her," said Jean-Paul as he stared at the photos. No doubt at all.

"Her name is Eva Malpas. We've already sent two gendarmes to the office to get their files on her. How do you know Eva?"

"Only from across the counter in the cadastre office. I was there many times earlier this year getting files and maps for Monsieur Jacob. He sent me for more things every few days for a couple of weeks, wanting to know who all his neighbours were around his rows and patches. There was a dispute with his brothers and a sister, he didn't talk much of it, but what he did say didn't sound pretty. He finally had to let me go — but that's not the story here…"

"No, not precisely, but it matters — everything matters. The broader the view, the more we see," David said. "I don't think Lieutenant Grattien minds additional peripheral information. It makes our minds step out of bounds, to look beyond and to see much more."

"Monsieur Michaels is right. Following thought tangents, splinters and weird ideas is how many riddles are solved, riddles that have stumped the most brilliant analytical thinking. I think — why did I say that? — No, I feel there is much to be said for slowing the brain and letting the senses take over. Let's all do that. You have my phone number, please interrupt my weekend. We need to resolve this."

Michael Walsh

Saturday 10 May 1986

David and Catherine lay in bed cuddling on Saturday morning with blank minds, knowing they had nothing to do through the weekend ahead. The cellar and the vineyards were finally in good hands again, so they were free to do whatever pleased them. But they couldn't go anywhere, still being captives in the château.

The thought of watching television repulsed both of them, so they had decided to tell each other stories. "So Katy, tell me about your bike. That's not a standard Triumph."

"It's a '69 Triumph Tiger Daytona, a 490cc parallel twin. Neat engine, low torque at the bottom end, but wind it to 3500 and above, it screams with power. You have to know where its sweet spots are and how to use them."

"It sounds like you competed."

"Never side-by-side, only time trials and hill climbs. I had fun, and I did very well. I rode to the events and stripped the bike there, didn't have the money for the fancy carbs, the porting and polishing, the other things those who trailered their bikes did. But I had another advantage, I was light, more than forty pounds lighter than most of the fellows I competed with, fifty, sixty and more pounds lighter than some of them. I usually finished at or near the top of my class.

"I won my class several times at Shelsley Walsh, the oldest motorsport competition in the world. It's a wonderful hill climb, steep with sharp curves followed by a really fast push to the finish.

"I loved Baitings Dam in Yorkshire. A wonderful course up the access road to the dam. Very narrow road, steep to the first hairpin then quickly the second and the third hairpin, all off camber, then a lengthy straight to a square right-hander and a bumpy run to the finish. That is definitely a riders hill, and the power boys couldn't compete with skill. I always did well there. Almost always won."

"I love this passion you have, this energy you bring as you speak. It's as if you're back there on your bike competing. You're still living the adventure, it's a part of you. When was that?"

"That was a few years after I had left my studies in Killarney. Aunt Elizabeth, Mamère's sister, had encouraged me to learn a trade, and I settled

234

on drafting. I loved drawing and painting, but she said there is no money in those, so the closest we could find was mechanical drafting. I got bored with it and moved to architectural drafting. Same thing with that, so I left and headed out on my own in 1971 when I turned eighteen."

"What did you do to support yourself?"

"I started with the usual thing girls did at the time to make money, I worked as a waitress. I ended up in Cork in a fancy place, I can't remember its name at the moment, I've probably buried it too deeply. The owner was a sleazy fellow who also ran the strip house down the street. He kept leering at me, then suddenly one day he groped me and told me I could make a lot more working down the street, he only wanted to check if my tits were real, he said."

She winced and squirmed at the memory. "I moved on to better things, moved to London and lived in a cheap place in Earl's Court for a while until I could afford something better as I worked my way up in the restaurant service. I had realised the value of my assets. I knew I was very attractive, and I was fluent in both French and English. Then I could afford the bike. By 1976 I was serving in an upscale restaurant in Knightsbridge, the Capital..."

"I dined several times at the Capital in 1976, a Michelin star in Basil Street, just along from Harrod's."

"That's the place. My God, maybe I served you. What were you doing in London in 1976?"

"I don't remember any ravishing redhead. I must have always been there on your days off... You were probably out racing."

"So what were you doing there?"

"Do you remember I started telling you about taking a sabbatical from the Navy in 1975?"

"You mentioned it, but we drifted off to something else, or we were interrupted. We've been interrupted by a lot of things."

"Well in late 1974 , I was driving a desk at headquarters in Ottawa, editing a Secret NATO naval warfare experimental tactics manual, among other boring admin duties. I had applied for special leave to go on a two-month mountaineering expedition to the Hindu Kush in the summer of '75. My request was denied so I requested permission to resign my commission. They countered with an offer of a sabbatical. I asked how long and they said up to two years.

"I started the sabbatical the spring of '75. In June I flew to Hanover to the Volkswagen factory and picked up the duty-free empty window van the group had ordered. From there, I drove it to the Air Base in Lahr, where, in a friend's garage, I converted it into a simple camper before going to Calais to pick up the members of the group arriving on the Hover-Lloyd from England. They had flown from Vancouver to London. Then we drove to Afghanistan..."

"You drove to Afghanistan? You say that like driving across town. But how does that put you dining at the Capital in London in 1976?"

"It was an amazing drive, both ways. Remind me to tell you about it some-time. We were in Afghanistan four and a half years before the Russians invaded. After some first ascents in the Hindu Kush, we drove back. One of the party, Joe stopped in Yugoslavia on the way back to visit family. He later joined me in the Alps, and we climbed there for a while, got weathered off the Eiger a few times, so we went to Chamonix before he had to go back.

"We dropped the van off in Emden to be put on the Volkswagen Transporter to Halifax, then we took the ferry across from Hoek van Holland and the train into London. Joe flew back to Canada, and I took rooms in Earl's Court, probably just down the street from..."

"That doesn't sound like the normal route from Canada to London. I would think the travel agents would have trouble selling that itinerary." She laughed. "But why had you come to London? What were you doing in my restaurant?"

"Simpson's, the Ritz and other London standards were boring me, so I start-ed looking for more adventurous dining. I also found le Gavroche in Sloan Street. I had come to London in September '75 for the wine auctions. The fallout from the Cruse scandal was winding its way through the auction rooms. Retailers, merchants, châteaux were dumping wine to try to save their skins as the French market collapsed. I figured prices would be weak, so I was prepared to buy and hold. I was wrong; prices were abysmal, so I bought heavily."

He looked to see if her eyes had glazed over. *She really does appear in-terested.* Relieved, he continued with the story. "I attended the pre-auction tastings at Christie's, Southeby's and Bonhams. Even Phillips was getting into the wine sale game. I tasted so many wonderful old wines, some of them more than double my age at the time. I loved the tastings Broadbent led at Christie's.

"There were many amazing wines being dumped. Most in very large quantities, divided into a few one-case lots, then some twos, a few fives and then ten and twenty-case lots. Prices for the small lots were weak, but a few lots along in the catalogue, as the five, ten and twenty-case lots came under the hammer, prices per case were down to less than half those of the small lots.

"I bought many large lots at thirty-five to fifty percent of the very low price others were willing to pay for small lots only a few minutes earlier. I figured my wine club would be delighted. Things such as 1961 Château Cos d'Estournel and..."

"So let me get this right," Catherine interrupted. "The European wine market is collapsing, everybody is panicking and dumping wine which nobody seems to want, and you start buying heavily." She stroked his cheek. "You certainly *are* a strange businessman. Were others also buying heavily?"

"No, not in the beginning, I was one of a very few commercial buyers. I soon realised the auction houses want to sell. They make no money, in fact, they lose money from their cataloguing and house expenses on unsold lots. After each sale, I negotiated with the auction houses for unsold lots, buying a magnificent selection at their reserves without the tension of the bidding floor.

"I bought mainly large lots that were in bond, non-duty-paid, and had them transferred to Saint Olaf's warehouse in bond. I immediately re-consigned about a third of my purchases to the next available sales, requesting they be catalogued as single case lots. I doubled-up on most of the lots, and after the auction house commissions and warehouse expenses, I was still ahead well over eighty percent.

"There were some magnificent old ports at a Bonhams pre-sale tasting in Hyde Park, unrelated to the Cruse thing. A hotel chain had decided to thin its port cellars. Taylor's, Fonseca, Croft, Graham's Warre's, Quinta do Noval, most of the big houses — 1955s. '48s, '47s, '35s, '34s, '27s, '12s. '08s. I was in heaven. It was in the Officers Mess of one of those horsey Army regiments, the Cavalry or Horse Artillery, I can't remember. All I remember of the place is that it was a bleak rainy late autumn day outside and absolutely sublime inside."

He ran his fingers across her lips and looked deeply into her eyes. "But that's a very long way from your motorcycle racing and your waiting at the Capital. How long did you work there?"

"For a bit over two years, then I finally felt the confidence to head back to France. I hadn't been there in over ten years, since I was fourteen. I had no desire to go to Brittany. Instead, I came south to the Burgundy, to Seurre and stayed a while with my aunt and uncle, Papa's brother and his wife. They had a small house just out of town, on the banks of the Saône. They had moved there the previous year, after they had sold the péniche... Remind me we need to visit them. I've ignored them, forgotten about them since shortly after Louis and I married... We were always too busy.

"I liked the Burgundy, so I decided to stay and find a job. I started at the two star Côte d'Or in Nuits a few weeks later, and that's where I met Louis in the spring of 1981. He started dining there several days a week, we chatted increasingly, and finally after three weeks, he asked me out."

"That's where I first saw you. I sat in the corner watching you, enjoying your beauty, your graceful movement. I dined at Côte d'Or on many of the nights I was in the Burgundy, every trip, 1978, '79, '80, certainly for Jean Crotet's wonderful cooking, but also to watch you. You wouldn't remember me, but..."

"Oh, I remember you very well. The mysterious, handsome man in the corner. You always appeared to be so content, satisfied and confident, but you were always alone. I began fantasising about you — sexual fantasies. Why didn't you ever say hello? Start a conversation?"

He shook his head and blew out a deep breath. "It takes a lot of courage to approach a stunningly beautiful woman."

"What do you mean?"

"Men will often — possibly it's only me — but I've always found it difficult to approach a beautiful woman, any woman, for that matter, thinking her beyond reach." He tilted his head and gave her a sheepish grin. "This may sound crazy, but to satisfy my cravings, I'd spend time watching the most beautiful I could find, but I never dared approach any. You've been my favourite unapproachable fantasy for a long time."

She felt his increased throbbing on her belly as they lay cuddling. She unwrapped from him and flipped the duvet aside as she rose and settled astride him, pretending to be riding her old Triumph Tiger Daytona. She growled an engine sound, maybe it was a tiger sound as she used his arms for handlebars while she bounced up the climb.

"No, I guess it's not a normal Triumph…"

Chapter Forty-Five

David and Catherine eventually got up for brunch, and they spent the afternoon lounging on the couch and telling more stories. She could now talk about her childhood in Saint-Brieuc and of warmer, friendlier times with her father, before he sold the boat and they moved inland.

"Even after the move to Rennes, he was often quite gentle and fun, but he had a terrible temper, so easily triggered. We all learned to tiptoe around anything that might set him off. It became more difficult — it was impossible to predict what would send him into a rampage." She paused and thought for a short while.

"It was a very strange spring. I was confused with the blood in my underwear; Mamère had told me nothing. The evil nun who molested me made me even more confused about my body, made me ashamed of my development. Never knowing when Papa would hit me or with what, made me ache with tension. I was so relieved to spend the summer on the péniche. That was such a wonderful escape. I felt free for the first time in a very long while."

David nodded. "We should all feel free, all the time. I wonder why some people find power in making others suffer. Don't they realise they make themselves unhappy? All they need to do is accept the situation, change their *own* attitude, not spread their discontent, not try to change others. One of my favourite thoughts is, *Give me the peace to accept the things I cannot change, the strength to change the things I can and the wisdom to know the difference.* This sort of says it all, doesn't it?"

Sunday 11 May 1986

On Sunday morning, David and Catherine cuddled in bed and continued relating things from their pasts. "So there's a gap in your story, David. I last saw you setting up a wine business and a wine club and importing wine. But yesterday, you jumped to driving to Afghanistan, climbing and then doing the auctions in London. What happened between setting up the wine importing thing and London?"

"I finished school, then went through Venture, the officer candidate school in Esquimalt. I ended up as the Class Captain and then became the Cadet Commander of the school, came second in the class and was sent to Camp Borden to begin pilot training. We called it Camp Boredom, in the sands a hundred kilometres or so north of Toronto.

"I had done some club racing with the Healey on the west coast — I had shipped it back from Germany. But by this time it was seven years old, so I bought a new Triumph GT6 to be more competitive..."

"So you raced also?" She ran a finger across his lips.

"Yes, more for variety earlier, but now the mountains were too far away to play in, so I poured more of my energy into the racing."

"You were in the Navy then?"

"No, still in the Air Force, the Navy came later. Anyway, the Triumph was a very peppy and lively car with a 1998cc six-cylinder engine. It did well in the one point eight to two-litre class, but I didn't like its rear suspension. It had swing axles, and it humped horribly in the corners, the ass-end lifted, hopped then let go with little notice. I added torsion bars, and they helped but not enough.

"I traded it for a new E-Type Jag. It was a powerful beast, but it ploughed. It had a horrible understeer, and often when I tried to correct, it popped to oversteer with little warning. I soon traded it for a new Lotus Europa. It tracked the corners as if on rails..."

"You spent a lot on cars." She trailed a finger across his chest.

"I had a lot to spend, and I was looking for something that worked, that fit my needs. I quickly came to appreciate what Colin Chapman was doing with his little cars. I loved the Lotus."

He winced. "Then everything changed — I broke my neck..."

"That wasn't a smart thing to do." She sat up and looked at his neck, fingering it lightly. "It seems to have healed." She giggled. "Your head is still attached ... Was that racing?"

"No, rugger. I was never one to play at chasing balls around or to watch others do it, but on one of the sports afternoons during training, rugger was the exercise. I barely understood the concept, except that the aim was to grab the ball and run to the end with it, so I dived into the first scrum and got a boot in the back of my neck."

"Somebody kicked you?" She cuddled back into him.

"What I didn't understand was that the ball is normally kicked out and then grabbed. I was taken by ambulance unconscious to the base hospital late on a Friday afternoon. They put on a neck collar and kept in for observation overnight. The doctor on Saturday morning rounds didn't like the swelling, so he kept me in again. The same on Sunday.

"On Monday they walked me up to x-ray, then quickly wheeled me down to surgery. I had a broken fifth and some other vertebra damage. They told me I should be a quadriplegic, so I apologised for disappointing them. The doctors surmised my strong musculature from years of slinging newspaper bags over my shoulders, and from the climbing, had held things in place. After I had sufficiently recovered, I was thoroughly tested at IAM in Downsview..."

"Eyayem, what's that?"

"Institute of Aviation Medicine, on the airbase on the north side of Toronto. I had some loss of sensation in my little fingers and the next ones and down the outsides of my arms. I had lost a range of mobility with my neck, had lost fine motor control of my hands, but fortunately, that was all. Well, not all — I also lost my flying qualification."

"You must have been devastated." She reached below the duvet.

"No, I was alive and very healthy otherwise. I transferred to the Navy and began training as Bridge Watchkeeper."

"So, we finally get to the Navy. That was a rather complex approach. How about some breakfast?"

"Great idea. How about an appetiser here first?"

"Another great idea." She giggled. "I thought you'd never ask."

242

After a late brunch, they settled in on the couch and continued reminiscing. "So the change from the Air Force to the Navy, that must have been strange. Why didn't you stay in the Air Force and do something else there?"

"I wanted to be active, out there doing things, not sitting at a desk, so I looked at all the options, and the Navy seemed to offer the most promise of adventure. I had a small sailboat when I was in Comox and had done some sailing, first as a break from climbing, then to get to mountains I could see across the Straits. On the rough passages back, I dreamed of sailing Cape Horn. Told myself I would do that one day. I still may."

"Where's Cape Horn?"

"The south tip of South America, one of the most treacherous and challenging pieces of water on the planet. Fewer people sail their boats around Cape Horn than climb Mount Everest. It's the Everest for adventuresome sailors."

"Why would you want to go there?"

"For the same reasons I climb. I don't know."

"Your broken neck, surely that must have stopped your climbing, didn't it?"

"Only for a short while. After I got out of hospital, after IAM and the decision on transferring to the Navy, I drove across to the west coast to continue my recovery and my sick leave. I went hiking up Vancouver Island to relax. Some of my finest first ascents were done while I was recovering. I wanted to learn how to use my new arms, the limited feeling and control in four fingers. Over the following decade and a half, I made hundreds of climbs, racked up more than six dozen first ascents on four continents. So no, I guess the broken neck didn't stop my climbing, maybe just slowed it."

"So after your sick leave, you had to start your training all over again, wouldn't you? Air Force and Navy are so different."

"They were integrating, merging into a single force, administratively easier. The business end of things was the same, but the pointy ends, ground pounders, the fliers, the sailors were the main differences. I had to take weather again, but from a different perspective, and I had to learn navigation in a new way, adding astro to it..."

"Astro? What's that?"

"Astronomical navigation, celestial navigation, navigating by the stars, the sun, the moon and the planets. I still remember the first day of astro. At the end of his lecture, the instructor said, *If you can create a solvable problem including three stars a planet and the moon, I'll give you a pass.*

"I signed-out some books of tables from the school library and took them along with my new textbooks back to the wardroom. I finally got the assignment done a little past midnight. When I handed the problem to the instructor the next morning, he asked, *What's this?* I told him it was our assignment.

"He said, *I haven't given any assignments yet, those start later in the week.* I told him I understood we had to write a problem if we wanted to pass the course and said this is my problem. He said he was being facetious, then he asked me where I got it, he seemed doubtful.

I told him I had written it last night, using the HO214, the star charts, the tables and the Almanac I had taken back to my room. I worked backwards to calculated where everything would be. Then I told him it had taken a long time to teach myself how, but I could do it much more quickly now.

"The instructor shook his head and said, *This is a very complex subject. You can't learn it in a few hours. Some never grasp it. You'll have to write me another problem. This time, I'll give you the position and time, and you tell me where everything is.* I gave him the prepared problem less than half an hour later...."

"I don't understand this — this problem thing." Catherine looked at him with a strange expression.

"In astral navigation, the navigator uses a sextant to measure angles between..."

"A sextant?"

"A precision instrument with mirrors and lenses and scales used to measure the angle between one distant object and another from the viewer's position." He looked to see her eyes still sparkling.

"For astro, the angle is the height above the horizon of a star, a planet, the sun or the moon. The altitude above the horizon is measured precisely, and the time is noted to the exact second at that instant. This is then reduced to a line of position on the surface of the earth by using information from the Nautical Almanac, a book of tables which track the earth's rotation in relation to the positions of the heavenly bodies..."

He paused and eyed her up and down, "Heavenly body."

"Back to the navigation," she said with a giggle and a delighted smile.

"The observer with the sextant is somewhere along the line of position. There are books of tables that serve as a short-cut to having to use spherical trig to calculate the line of position, which is then drawn on the chart. Another star or planet is shot and calculated, its line added to the chart, then a third, fourth, sometimes more are added. The lines are adjusted in time according to the ship's movement along its course during shooting of the bodies. Where the lines of position cross on the chart is where the navigator was with the sextant when the angles were shot.

"So to write a solvable problem, I had to first wrap my head around this and then run it backwards to calculate what stars and planets I would then see from that spot, and exactly where they and the moon would be at the instant of observation."

"And you failed math in school?"

"Miserably."

Chapter Forty-Six

Monday 12 May 1986

"Unfortunately, I had a very quiet weekend," Grattien said as he sat with David and Catherine at the kitchen table. "But that is also good. I finally had a Sunday lunch with my mother."

He had brought a half dozen croissants and had invited himself to breakfast, arriving just as David stepped into the courtyard, intending to send a gendarme to the boulangerie.

"Not much yet on Eva Malpas, other than she lives, or she lived in a house in Fixin. Our men were there late Friday afternoon. It showed signs of having been quickly vacated. Mail in the box, rotting vegetables in the fridge, and many other indications. From the newspaper collection, it looks like she left on the Monday you were abducted, two weeks ago."

"Have you anything new on the Marseille connection?"

"From the cadastre in Fixin, records indicate the house is registered to a company in Martinique. After yesterday's lunch with my mother, I stopped in at my office and confirmed from our files that it is the same company which had bought the péniche.

"We are now hoping this information, added to their financial interest in the tank warehouse on the Hautes Côtes, and the records of the wine shipments there and to Grotkopf in Nuits, will convince the investigative magistrate. They had wanted more evidence and information before they give us authorisation to act. Maybe this will do it — our social system seems to protect the bad guys."

"Unfortunately, we're also moving that way in Canada. The civil liberties movement appears stuffed with the desire to protect criminal activity. In the States, the police simply shoot everybody then ask questions. There must be a middle ground."

"We have been watching the buildings up in the Côtes, near Baubigny. None of the people in the area know anything about the operation, other than talking about the tank trucks regularly coming and going. None knew any of the people who worked there, and they say they rarely saw them. No local people seem to be involved."

"What about the wine in the tanks?" David asked. "We smelled wine when we were let out of the car trunk."

"We are still waiting for test results to come from the lab. They must be back by now — I haven't checked for a few days, I've been busy with so many other things, funerals, hospital visits…" He faded off, then said, "You must need groceries again — put together another list, I'll have one of our gendarmes come by this afternoon for it... A woman this time," he added with a chuckle as he looked at Catherine.

After Grattien had left, Catherine and David went to the cellar to check on the progress with the racking. Gerrard and Sophie were nearing half way and estimated another six days to complete the job. This surprised Catherine, and she was about to speak, but stopped herself.

After a pause, she said, "The Village wines need bottling when this is finished, then the '84 Premiers."

"What about the '84 Grands Crus?" Gerrard asked.

"Louis' notes show waiting until the beginning of summer."

"We should tap a few. Start with some Premiers to see how they are," David said. "Check how they were affected by the heat in the barge."

"Good idea, I'll go get the glasses, you get the drill and pry."

"Do you know where he keeps them?"

"There's a box over by the bidons."

They walked along the row of '84 pièces trying to decide where to start. "Here! Finally!" David pointed. "Les Chabiots is the most delicate of the Premiers. If any had suffered, this would show the most."

He drilled a hole in the butt end, placed a glass beneath it and pushed the end of the small curved pry into the croze and levered it to squeeze a small stream of wine into the glass. "I've often watched this, but I've never done it." David used the pry to pound a small oak taper into the hole, then looked up and smiled.

Catherine decanted from the full glass into the three others, then they all nosed, sipped, gurgled and chewed. After a long pause, Catherine said, "Wonderful wine. There's no reason to bottle early."

"I fully agree," David added. "A bit diminished, but still great."

"I keep hearing the '84 was a bad year." Sophie put her nose back into the glass. Looking up, she continued, "This is a superb wine."

"There's no need to broach another barrel, this is the lightest one. The others can be tasted in a few weeks, when they're closer to bottling." David lifted his glass. "But since we have glasses in hand, let's go taste the lot you're working on now, the '85 les Chaffots."

As David and Catherine walked back across the courtyard, she said, "I almost asked down there, *Why do you still have six days left? It's only a six-day job,* but I caught myself."

"I noticed that, and I had to choke back a laugh. Our twelve, thirteen, fourteen-hour days are far different from the standard pace."

They were just settling into the couch when the phone rang.

After all the usual introductory things, Michel's voice said, "Paris has come back with a decision on my report. Since it is a total loss, except scrap salvage, and the policy is only a few weeks old, they were reluctant to settle…"

"So, where does that leave us?" David interrupted.

"I was saying they *were* reluctant, but that was before one of the members of the review board pointed to the fact that you are a long-time client, with a policy on your wine shipments across the world for many years without claim. They are offering you 221,500 Francs and the salvage of *Vrouwe Catharina.*"

"That sounds about right, thirteen five for the scrap. Seems to be a fair calculation."

"I can come by with the settlement offer for you to sign. Where are you? What time is convenient for you?"

"The Beaux-Arts château, the north edge of Morey-Saint-Denis. The one with the gendarmes at the gate. We're still a captive audience here, and we're not going anywhere."

"That's a beautiful place. It's always been one of my favourites. I can leave now, and see you in twenty, twenty-five minutes."

"I'll tell the gendarmes to expect you around ten fifteen or ten twenty. That'll make it easier for you at the gate."

Chapter Forty-Seven

After a brief meeting, and David's acceptance signature, Michel told him that the cheque should arrive in a week or ten days.

Back inside from waving Michel off, Catherine leaned against the kitchen door and said slowly, "So, the 235,000 had cost you a bunch of coins — the coins cost you far less than the assessed scrap value of *Vrouwe Catharina*. Now they give you back most of the money — and you still have the barge. Let me check your ears, you must have four-leaf clovers growing in there."

As they walked through to the long room, she continued, "My cousins taught me an old Irish rhyme about their symbol for good luck:

> *One leaf is for fame,*
> *And one leaf is for wealth,*
> *And one is for a faithful lover,*
> *And one to bring you glorious health,*
> *Are all in the four-leaved clover*

"They said four-leaf clovers are far luckier than shamrocks."

"That may be. Many people see someone else's success as luck, but what they don't see is the huge effort, the picking up and starting over repeatedly, the incessant push that finally leads to success." With a huge grin distorting his face, he continued, "But I must admit, this outcome with *Vrouwe Catharina* is nothing but dumb luck — maybe you *should* check my ears."

As they walked through toward the kitchen with their dinner dishes in the late evening, Catherine pointed to a short curl of fax paper from the machine. She tore it off, and noting it was from Lynn, she handed it to David.

He paused to read it through while she carried on into the kitchen. Then he sat silently, spinning things through his mind, before reading it again.

"What is it, David, something wrong?" she asked as she came back.

"No, it's just something that has set my mind spinning. So many things all over the place. Confusing, conflicting thoughts."

"What's it about?"

"Lynn says Corgram have proposed buying my importing company and merging it with theirs. They also want to engage me as their purchasing consultant."

"That's wonderful. I think more ear checking is needed, they're probably full of four-leaf clovers."

"The company was not just dumb luck like the barge. This one's the result of long, hard work. It took me a long time to build it, to invent ways to do things, to push government regulations, to max out on multiple credit cards while waiting for the next chunk of money to come in. No luck involved there."

"No, I mean for me. This is good luck for me."

"For you? I don't follow."

"Accept the offer, sell, stay here with me... Maxing-out on credit cards, that doesn't sound like your normally wise financial management. Why didn't you get bank financing for the company?"

"I had no credit rating. I had never borrowed, I never had any need to. When I applied, I was denied as an unknown risk. We have a strange banking system. Now with the company prosperous and financially healthy, with no need of their money, the banks keep badgering me to borrow from them, to set-up lines of credit."

David read the fax through again and stared blankly as his mind whirled. They sat at the mahogany table and Catherine's eyes seemed to be boring into his head, trying to see what was going on in there.

"They want to buy me, and I see why. For a long while I've known my growth is diminishing their sales — and those of others."

"Does it say how much they're offering?"

"No, they want to meet with me and discuss the details, negotiate. But, that's not what's winding around in my head the most noisily at this moment."

"Something else in the letter?"

"No, not that — it's what you said a short while ago about staying here with you. That has put a lot more things spinning."

"Don't you want to stay?"

"I began a few minutes ago realising that I've never thought about staying, I've stayed simply through circumstance. Stayed to offer you my support. Now, trying to think of anything but staying is proving rather difficult."

"Well, that's easy then." She picked up his arm and pulled him toward her. "Stop your mind spinning. Stay."

"I need to set this aside. I need to let my head clear. The dinner dishes can wait. Let's go to bed and do something to distract me."

Tuesday 13 May 1986

David had spent until mid-morning on Monday lying in bed with Catherine, exercising, cuddling and dream-storming. Then he got up and started drafting a reply to Lynn, with punchy sentences to outline what he needed done: *Tell Corgram I'm looking favourably at the offer and will be back in Vancouver next week with an open schedule. Phone Edith at CP and book the first available seats from the 17th onward out of Amsterdam; the other passenger is Catherine Ducroix. Call Estella to have her take the dust covers off and give the loft a good cleaning. Tell her to put double the standard things in the fridge the day of our arrival. Buy a two-week pass to Expo or a couple of one week passes or whatever, I already hold a season pass.*

He read the draft twice, the second time aloud to Catherine, then he typed it out and put it through the fax machine.

"Passport? I hadn't thought of your passport. Have you a valid one?"

"No, I don't have one." Catherine paused and gave David an impish grin. "I have two, my Irish and my French, and both recently renewed. I did them a few months ago when I was hoping to convince Louis to take a break and go travelling."

"I love travelling. Let's phone Grattien and ask him the best way to get out of here safely and on our way to Amsterdam."

"I don't understand why we're flying from Amsterdam, Paris is much closer, Geneva is even closer than Paris."

"Canadian Pacific Airlines doesn't fly to France or Switzerland. Air Canada has that monopoly from Canada."

"Why don't we fly Air Canada, then?"

"I will always go far out of my way to avoid flying Air Canada. They're the national airline, a subsidiary of the government. Their service and attitude are horrid, condescending, privileged, like many other things related to un-ionised government employees. The Civil Service is uncivil."

"Worth a detour, as Michelin says, but a detour away from." Catherine chuckled. "What's this expo thing? Passes?"

"Vancouver's hosting a huge fair this year, celebrating its hundredth birthday. A five-month party along the shores of False Creek, which until the fair was a crumbling, polluted industrial backwater in the heart of the expanding city. The idea for the party started half a dozen years ago as a local celebration, and it has dramatically grown into a World's Fair. Last time I looked, there were fifty-four countries participating, with over seventy pavilions and exhibits.

"The loft where I live — I've spoken before with you and Louis about it. It's less than two blocks away from the entrance gate, in an old industrial building I bought when the area was dying. I converted half the top floor to my home and office... We've got to phone Grattien."

Grattien was quiet as David outlined their intentions, then he said, "We can take you by plain car to the station in Dijon, swapping cars in our garage in Gevrey on the way in case we're followed from here. We'll have the TGV tickets purchased in advance, and we'll stand with you on the platform until departure. Then have you met at Gare de Lyon, driven to Gare du Nord, and see you aboard the train to Lille and onward to Amsterdam. A simple operation. Good idea to get out of the country for a while. When do you want to go?"

"I've asked for flights from the 17th onward, so we'll leave here from Friday morning onward, depending on what my airline agent can book. There should be a reply from Vancouver overnight."

"On the name changes in the cadastre, we have found deeds of transfer to Philippe Grotkopf, signed by Louis Ducroix, Pierre Ducroix and Francine Grotkopf. They are hand-drawn, not witnessed or notarised, but unless they are challenged, they stand. We have taken photocopies of them and a search of the entire cadastre has been ordered to look for similar documents. We need to compare the signatures to genuine ones."

"I have all the bank records here, Louis' signature is on the cheques with mine. I may have a letter from Francine — no, much better, I have the negotiated cheques in an archive, there'll be endorsements on their annual shareholder cheques. I'll start digging those out."

"Good, I can come by and pick them up tomorrow morning. Croissants again?"

"That would be nice, but we must pay you for them."

"And I must give the money back for all the coffee." He laughed.

The next task on David's list was to organise with the boat yard to continue gutting *Vrouwe Catharina*. He phoned Atelier Fluvial and explained what he wanted. "Repair the bent frames, re-plate her bottom, and when she's ready to safely refloat, put her in the basin and complete gutting her interior to bare ribs. All wiring, all plumbing, everything out."

The yard owner said, "We need a signed work order and we must see your clear title to the barge. The insurance company is involved."

"I accepted their settlement offer yesterday morning and bought the salvage rights. Michel Poirier from AXA said he would be sending you the documents. They'll probably arrive in tomorrow's mail. As for signing the work order, I can't leave here, we're still under the protection of the gendarmes."

"Yes, I have heard from several about your recent adventures... I can draw up a work order and drive over with it. You are near Gevrey? Where exactly?"

"The Beaux-Art château, the first building in Morey-Saint-Denis as you come down the small road from Gevrey."

"I know that château, very pretty, impossible to miss."

"Even more so now with the gendarme guards at the gate. When will you come? I can tell the guards to expect you."

"How is ten tomorrow morning?"

"Perfect."

After he had clicked off, David looked at his list. "Only one big thing left to do." Looking at his watch, he continued, "Staff meeting at seventeen hundred. Let's have lunch and relax until then."

On Friday, David had initiated a daily meeting around the kitchen table at seventeen hundred to discuss the day's work, the progress, the problems, the observations, and to gather a picture of the current situation. He had told Catherine that these were a regular routine in the Navy, where they're called a *sitrep*, a situation report, from which decisions and plans for follow-up action were made.

Later, at the meeting, after each in turn had given a sitrep, David outlined their proposed trip to Vancouver without filling in any detail. Then looking at Loic and across to Jean-Paul, he asked, "Which of you wants to be in charge while we're gone?"

"He's more the manager." Loic nodded across the table to Jean-Paul. "I'm the artist."

"Well, Jean-Paul?" Catherine asked. "What do you think?"

"That's a lot of responsibility for me so early. I barely know my way around the vineyards."

"We're at the other end of the fax machine. You send daily reports, we'll answer. Our Vancouver number is on the dial list, all punched in and ready to go. Are you familiar with the fax?"

"No, I've never used one."

"No problem," Loic said. "I used them a lot when I was with Chandon planting the vineyards in Carneros, I'll show you, you'll quickly learn."

"With support like that, how can I say no?" Jean-Paul shrugged and smiled.

"Great! We want the four of you to continue these daily meetings, to coordinate your efforts." Catherine swept her arm around the kitchen. "Use this table, the coffee machine over there, the fridge to store your lunches. This place has been used for generations as the meeting room."

Chapter Forty-Eight

Wednesday 14 May 1986

David and Catherine saw that the fax had spooled out a short page when they came down in the morning. He tore the page off on the cutter and read; *The flights are all oversold, but the front looks good on the 17th and 19th. It appears all of Holland is coming to Expo. I told Edith to book two seats on each day, and I'd tell her which to cancel. When do you want to fly?*

David turned to Catherine and asked, "How's the seventeenth sound to you?"

"I don't understand. All the flights are oversold, but we can still get seats?"

"In the front. Often there are unsold seats at the much higher First Class fare. Our booking First Class makes two fewer seats for the lower fare passengers to spill over into the front from the oversold rear of the plane."

"So, the ones who are moved to the First Class section, they get all the extra service and comfort but still pay the lower fare?"

"A few do. Some of the airlines have now started frequent client loyalty programs. CP keeps a list of its best customers and treats us well, selecting who to move forward to fill unsold First Class seats. Since I supply the airline with their French, Italian and Australian wine, they treat me extremely well. At check-in, I am almost always moved forward, and I'm given full first class service. Some who are moved forward get only a seat, a larger and more comfortable seat, but the ordinary food and wine from the rear."

"You supply wine to the airlines? You continue to amaze me. How did you manage to arrange that?"

"A few years ago, after I finally got tired enough of the swill they were serving on the flights, I phoned Ian Gray, the airline's President — their headquarters are in Vancouver. He had taken a wine tasting course I was teaching, so this gave me an easy in. I laid out a plan that would provide higher quality wine to customers and cost the airline much less. The idea intrigued him."

"Higher quality for lower cost. That idea intrigues me too. What's the catch?" She started pulling him toward the kitchen.

"No catch. At the time they were buying all their alcohol through the LDB, the government liquor monopoly, at full shelf price. They were excused the import duty and excise taxes for international flights. That was standard practice with the Canadian airlines. I suggested they save shipping costs, import expenses, government markups and buy their Australian wines in Australia, their Italian in Italy and their French wines in France and warehouse them in bond in at the airports in Sydney, Malpensa and Schiphol."

"Sounds like a no-brainer to me."

"That's the thing, isn't it? Everybody was using their brains trying to devise ways to save money, manipulating processes, cutting quality, spinning, spinning... My solution was organic, sensed, not contrived. There was thinking involved, of course in setting up the mechanics, but the inspiration wasn't from conceptualising, wasn't from designing camels."

"Designing camels?"

"Comes from the old joke; *What's a camel? It's a horse that's been designed by a committee.* So back to the question, what do you think of flying on the seventeenth? That's this Saturday, we'd have to leave here on Friday."

"Great! — If that's when you're going — I'll go when you do." She gave him an impish grin.

"Saturday's flight is much better, non-stop, the polar route. Monday is through Toronto with a change."

"Polar route?"

"It heads up over Iceland, the middle of Greenland and Baffin Island well above the Arctic Circle."

"That seems crazy to me. Why does it go so far out of the way?"

"It's a much quicker route, cuts an hour and a half off the trip."

"The plane goes faster near the pole?"

"No, it's a shorter distance. Do you have a globe? I'll show you."

"There's one Louis had as a kid, a bit battered, but he still looked at it some-times to sort geography in his mind. I'll go get it, you get the espresso ma-chine ready, Grattien should be here shortly."

David looked at the two other paragraphs on the fax, pleased to see everything seemed in order or in progress. The cogs were turning in his head as he filled the reservoir with water and poured beans into the hopper. *If I sell the company, I'll be free again to move as I please... But I had set-up the company to allow me to travel and wander freely, so what's the differ-ence? I'll be able to concentrate more fully on...*

Then there was an increasing blur of confusing and conflicting thoughts. *When this whole thing finishes, when Philippe, and whoever else is part of this, when they've been captured, when the craziness ends, then what? Will she thank me for the support and...*

"You're spilling the beans all over the counter." Catherine laughed, inter-rupting his spinning mind. "You seem somewhere else."

He looked up, then down at the beans coned above the top of the hopper, "Good thing the bag's empty." He forced a soft chuckle, then turned and said, "I need a hug."

They were still in the long silent embrace when Grattien knocked on the door and opened it with a cheery, "Bonjour." He paused in the doorway asking, "Am I interrupting something?"

"Not at all." Catherine looked up. "We're just saying good morning. We like to take our time with it."

Grattien had no new developments to report. Catherine gave him several cheques with specimens of the three signatures and a short grocery list to do them until Friday morning.

"Our flight leaves Amsterdam at thirteen forty-five on Saturday," David said. "We'll need to leave here on Friday, stay at my favourite hotel in Aalsmeer near the airport, if they have room. There'll still be tulips in bloom — I must re-member to fax them — I'll give you the money for the tickets." He pulled notes from his wallet. "This should be sufficient to buy First Class for us through to Amsterdam."

Catherine told Grattien that Jean-Paul would be in charge of the domaine while they are away, and David filled him in on the situation with *Vrouwe Catharina*.

"Croissants and coffee again tomorrow?" Grattien asked as he got up from the table half an hour later. "I'll bring the train tickets."

After Grattien had left, Catherine took David's hand and looked questioningly at him. Following a long pause, she asked softly, "The hug? What was that about? You seemed so fragile. So unlike you."

"Just my head churning, grinding out crazy thoughts."

"What kind of thoughts? What was disturbing you?"

"Just thinking about things... My mind's trying to grasp where everything's going, probably getting ready to strike a committee to design a successor to the camel." He laughed unconvincingly.

"More than that, David." She took his hand and lead him across the room. "Let's go sit and talk about it."

They were almost to the couch when there was a knock on the door. They turned and headed back. Both had forgotten about the meeting with the boatyard owner until the knock.

The gendarme at the door said, "Monsieur Doiron at the gate, says he is from Atelier Fluvial. We were expecting Monsieur Cornu."

"It's probably okay, but to be safe, hold him until I phone Saint-Usage and confirm with Cornu." David dialled the number.

The speaker sounded, "Sorry, I didn't even think. I sent Aristide Doiron, my project manager thinking it would be easier..."

"Hold on a moment, please — I have to tell the gendarme to let him in." David looked across to the kitchen doorway and gave Catherine a big thumb and an exaggerated nod. "He's on his way in — you were saying..."

"Christ! You're living in a bunker there. I didn't even think — I thought it would be easier to send my project manager. I'm just the owner here, he does all the organisation. There'll be much less lost in interpretation by dealing directly with him."

"I like that way of thinking. Have the documents arrived yet from AXA?"

"I haven't gone through my morning's stack yet, let me... Let me shuffle through — here's an envelope from AXA." After the sound of ripping and a short pause, he continued. "This is it, I'll read it through later, I'm sure it is correct."

"I'll give my Vancouver fax number to Aristide. If you need to contact me, you can get it from him."

Aristide came in and the three of them sat around the mahogany table filling in the work order to strip *Vrouwe Catharina's* interior to bare hull, repair her damaged ribs, cut away any plate thinner than four point five millimetres and re-plate with six.

Then David put up a finger and paused the process. "Why compromise? — Strip all her frames from the boot-topping down, then re-plate with six, easier than doing it selectively. Give her another six or seven decades of carefree life." He paused and nodded.

"When you get the interior stripped out, make a series of rough sketches with accurate dimensions, a plan view, a longitudinal section and some transverse sections, probably the mid station and fore and aft where the hull starts to taper. Fax these to me and we can start dreaming an interior layout. What have we missed?"

"We can haul her out on the slipway and block her on the hard. It will be easier to work on her there than in the water. Either is less expensive for you than remaining in the dock. This is going to be a long project, six or eight weeks to gut her then repair and re-plate the hull, but five or six months to finish her interior."

"We have time."

After they had fine-tuned the work order, David had signed it, and Aristide had left, Catherine picked up David's hand and said quietly, "We were going to talk about what's spinning in that head. Come! To the couch. Let Doctor Katy examine your troubled mind."

He lay back next to the corner of the couch, and she stretched out, her back across his midriff with her shoulders nestled into the soft cushion. They looked silently at each other.

Finally, Catherine said very softly, as she stroked his chest, "So what is troubling you — what's going on?"

"I'm not sure... I've so much noise in my head... So many conflicting messages, images of climbing, free, alone, unfettered. On a mountain arête, searching, sensing the route that leads onward, higher. Reaching the summit and finding immense pleasure in the moment but then finding no one there but me." He sighed.

"I've climbed solo most of my life, even before I saw my first mountain. I've done things on my own — in my own way. I've always loved my freedom to come and go, to move with my will, with my impulses, to follow my whims. They've always been good to me... Alone, I've always enjoyed my solitude and my self-sufficiency. Maybe I've simply convinced myself I'm happy being free because I've never found anyone to share my life with."

There was a long pause, then he said, "I'm afraid, I'm…" he looked away, then back at her eyes, "I love you," he said, his eyes watering.

"I don't see that as a problem at all," she said, as she sat to lick a tear as it rolled onto his lip. "I've known that for a long time."

"Yes, I suppose you must have — I'm not at all good at hiding my emotions, am I? — I just don't know how to express them in words."

"Often words aren't needed, David. Our spirits speak quite eloquently when we allow them to... Allowing them to is the thing."

"So why is loving you a problem for me? Why do I…?"

The phone rang. They kissed, and Catherine said, "You stay there, I'll get it. Keep that thought, I'll be right back."

Across the speaker came Grattien's voice telling her analysis easily showed the signatures on the transfer papers to be forgeries, crude forgeries. "The cadastral records are now being restored. You'll soon own the vineyards in Chambertin again."

"That's certainly a relief. I'm now back to half ownership of the domaine."

"Half?"

"Yes, Philippe inherits Francine's share as her widower. Pierre had no wife, no children. We don't even know if he had a will — yes he did —

of course, he did. Why didn't I think of this earlier?" She snuggled her bum into David's front as he came up behind and wrapped her in his arms. "Being a lawyer, Pierre had insisted his brother and sister make wills. Both Francine and Pierre had given copies of their wills to Louis, naming him as their executor. They're upstairs in the vault with the other papers."

"You should look at those," Grattien said. "They will assist you in deciding what to do with the ashes. They are still at the crematorium in Paris waiting for your further instructions."

"Another thing I had forgotten about."

"I am being buzzed on the other line. I will see you with croissants and train tickets in the morning."

"I have the combination written down somewhere," Catherine said as she led David up the stairs. "Hidden where nobody would find it, probably not even me."

A few minutes later, as she was bending over and searching the back of a low cedar chest, he nuzzled up behind her, put one hand around her waist and the other across her chest to cup her left breast.

She sat up in bed nearly an hour later. "I know where it is." She hopped up and crossed the room to an armchair in the corner, then rolled it onto its side and read the three numbers off an oak slat on the bottom.

At the back of the small safe was a bundle in black ribbon. They sat on the bed as she untied it. "Which should I look at first?" She looked up at him and giggled. "Put that thing down. Didn't we just finish playing with it."

He looked down. "I guess it's on autopilot. You're such a gorgeous creature, it can't help saluting you."

She broke the seal on the envelope and pulled out Louis' will. "I knew this, he had told me everything of his would be left to me."

"Now Pierre," she said as she opened the next envelope and scanned through the simple testament. "Divided equally between Francine and Louis is the gist of it, a very simple will."

Catherine opened the third envelope and pulled out two separately folded pages, one imprinted *Dernières Volontés*, the other handwritten *Tres Im-*

portant. She looked up and into David's eyes. "This is interesting, I would think she wanted Louis to read this one first."

She unfolded the page and read, her eyes welling with tears, her hand beginning to tremble. "That fucking evil monster, that…"

"What is it?"

There was silence as Catherine sat staring at the page shaking in her hand. She slowly handed it to David then lay back on the bed and wept, the convulsive sobs shaking her whole body.

David read the short handwritten note, then quietly said, "I've heard of suicide notes... This is a murder note."

Francine had calmly explained that Philippe was a violent man, and that he often abused her verbally, emotionally and physically. She completed the note with, *If I am found dead in mysterious circumstance, Philippe will have acted upon his frequent threat. Have my death very closely examined.*

He moved across the bed to Catherine, pulled the duvet over them and they cuddled, his hand cradling the back of her head.

Chapter Forty-Nine

It was almost noon when David awoke, still entwined with Catherine. They had drifted off to sleep, emotionally drained. She was still quietly asleep as he lay there and relaxed, enjoying her presence. *My mind has stopped spinning. I'm amazed how empty it is.*

She began to stir a quarter hour or so later, then she opened her eyes, kissed him gently, lifted her head off the pillow, untangled herself and leaned on an elbow. "He's a very sick man, he doesn't give a fuck about others. He murdered his wife and brother-in-law and we don't know how many others to get half this domaine, and he was about to murder me — to murder us to get the rest of it."

She paused and fixed her gaze on the folded paper still at the foot of the bed. "I don't think Francine would have left him anything in her will."

She pulled the duvet aside, and as she crawled toward the end of the bed, David softly said, "That view isn't good for my relaxed state."

"Later." She giggled. "Give me a moment with this first."

She unfolded Francine's will and skimmed it. "Nothing! The evil fucker gets nothing. Divided equally between Louis and Pierre."

Still on hands and knees, she turned to look over her shoulder with a big grin. With a little shake of her butt, she asked, "Now, what were you saying about un-relaxing?"

Half an hour later, Catherine lifted onto an elbow and gazed into David's eyes. "Stay with me, David. Marry me."

"Are you proposing?"

She smiled and reached her face up to run her tongue across his lips. "I would love you to take the salvage rights on a second Lady Catherine."

Epilogue

David and Catherine arrived safely in Vancouver. Three days later, they took a break from negotiating the sale of his company to be married in a simple ceremony in Stanley Park.

The following day, they received a fax from Grattien informing them Philippe Grotkopf and Eva Malpas were among those apprehended when the bulk wine company in Marseille was raided.